HASHTAG MAGIC
WEB OF TROLLS

# HASHTAG MAGIC SERIES

BLUE SCREEN OF DEATH  
CONTROL ALT DELETE  
WEB OF TROLLS  
OPEN SOURCE (2017)  
SELFIE SACRIFICE (2018)

# HASHTAG MAGIC

# WEB OF TROLLS

by

## J. STEVEN YOUNG

Chapter 1 .......................................................... 1
Chapter 2 .......................................................... 7
Chapter 3 .......................................................... 15
Chapter 4 .......................................................... 25
Chapter 5 .......................................................... 35
Chapter 6 .......................................................... 45
Chapter 7 .......................................................... 57
Chapter 8 .......................................................... 67
Chapter 9 .......................................................... 79
Chapter 10 ......................................................... 85
Chapter 11 ......................................................... 93
Chapter 12 ......................................................... 101
Chapter 13 ......................................................... 109
Chapter 14 ......................................................... 115
Chapter 15 ......................................................... 123
Chapter 16 ......................................................... 135
Chapter 17 ......................................................... 143
Chapter 18 ......................................................... 149
Chapter 19 ......................................................... 157
Chapter 20 ......................................................... 163
Chapter 21 ......................................................... 171
Chapter 22 ......................................................... 177
Chapter 23 ......................................................... 187
Chapter 24 ......................................................... 199
Chapter 25 ......................................................... 207
Chapter 26 ......................................................... 213
Chapter 27 ......................................................... 221
Chapter 28 ......................................................... 233
Chapter 29 ......................................................... 239
Chapter 30 ......................................................... 247
Chapter 31 ......................................................... 255
Chapter 32 ......................................................... 265
Chapter 33 ......................................................... 273
Chapter 34 ......................................................... 279
Chapter 35 ......................................................... 287
Chapter 36 ......................................................... 295
Chapter 37 ......................................................... 305
Chapter 38 ......................................................... 315
Chapter 39 ......................................................... 323
Chapter 40 ......................................................... 333
Author ............................................................. 337

# <u>Chapter 1</u>

## **#HomeComing**

Colby and his companions dragged themselves off the private jet upon arriving back in Chicago. The events of the last few days taxed them both in mind and body. Once they rested for a few days in the hotel, they decided to stay and witness the lunar eclipse over Chichén Itzá. Half expecting something extraordinary to occur, they were somewhat disappointed when nothing happened. Beyond a sudden drop in the Emassa around the area, which Pace explained was expected since the equinox passed, there was no sign of evil or agents of the Shizumu.

Colby wasn't sure what he was expecting, but there must be something they missed. Too many references to the astronomical events were presented for nothing more to happen. Grateful for a trouble free last few days and the recovery of Mr. Bodine, Colby let his heavy mind settle into enjoying the festival that accompanied the eclipse. Now he was back home and could focus on what might come next. His troubles would soon return, of that Colby was certain, but for now, they could relax and get a bit of peace. His last thought was dashed, however, when he recognized the erratic driving of Shelly's car as it arrived in the parking area outside the private hanger.

Nana exited the car and was in the heat of an argument with the security guard when Mr. Bodine commanded her being allowed past.

✳ ✳ ✳

"I thought you were coming home days ago?" Nana said. "I had the worst dreams and visions."

Nana scooped Colby into her arms and squeezed him until he was nearly forced to push her back. Before he could detach himself from her, she jumped back and narrowed her eyes. She looked him over and shifted from side to side.

"Nannie? What's wrong?"

Nana blinked and shook her head. "It's just…nothing. I suppose I'm just glad you're all home."

She grabbed and hugged the rest of the kids, even Shelly.

"Come along now. Dinner for everyone and tell old Nana about your adventure."

"Good Lord you old hag, we just had the strangest days of our lives, surviving seekers and a mad Shizumu. Only to come home and be poisoned by your cooking?" Shelly rolled her eyes and took her car keys back from Nana. "And what have I said about driving my car?"

Nana grumbled and gave Shelly her favorite single finger salute. "Your car is fine and still as filthy as I found it. As for dinner, your mother is home and cooking everything now." Nana waved the others on. "You all come along as well. Hopefully, those awful long-eared monkeys have left the property."

"Are you referring to the Dreggs?" Colby asked. "They were only looking after you and the house while we were away."

Nana huffed and waddled toward the car, winking at Rigel as she passed. "Well, next time you decide your old granny needs a babysitter, get

Professor yummy-pants here to stay behind. He's prettier to look at and probably smells better than those horrid Dreggs."

Rigel made his apologies and shrugged off the dinner invitation. He headed to his waiting taxi while taking a wide path past Nana.

Colby shook his head and packed his, Shelly's, and Gary's things in the trunk of Shelly's car. He then waved at the others as they piled into Mr. Bodine's limousine. He sat in the back with Gary, noticing his friend smirking at Jasper as he watched them get in the car. Instead of saying something, Colby shook his head and looked at Nana who sat in the front passenger seat staring at him.

Nana quickly smiled and turned back to the front of the car as they headed home, followed by the others. She kept turning in her seat to look at Colby as they made their way home. When asked, she said only that she was glad to see him returned and that he looked different.

Colby said he would explain the full measure of what happened during the trip when they got home. He didn't want to tell the story twice. Since mom was home, Colby could retell the events of their journey while she was present. Colby could share with her his visit with dad. The moment he thought of his father and the short spell that brought them together in the hidden temple below the pyramid of Chichén Itzá, his nose tingled. Colby felt a well of emotion building beneath the surface and did his best to suppress them. He couldn't prevent the glistening of his eyes.

Nana smiled at Colby and turned away. She smacked Shelly on the arm.

"Watch out for the pedestrians Shelly."

"They're on the sidewalk, old woman. Unlike you, I stay on the streets when I drive."

Colby was glad to arrive back home. Though he felt renewed and hopeful after his experiences in Chichén Itzá, he felt most secure in his home. No sooner had the car stopped in the driveway, Colby was out of the vehicle and headed toward the back door. He was so excited to share the news about seeing his father with Aria, Colby failed to notice the overgrown herbs and exotic plants that Nana had finished replanting alongside the house. If he had bothered to inspect them, he would have sensed the unnatural way in which they grew and blossomed so early in the season, and only days after being ripped from the ground and then replanted following Nana's earlier outburst. Colby's thoughts were focused only on his mother and his news.

"Mom." Colby ran through the kitchen and into the living room. Not finding Aria, Colby shouted again for his mother's attention.

"In the dining room dear."

Colby raced back toward the kitchen and turned right into the dining room. Facing his mother now, Colby stalled and pondered over what exactly to say. How would he break the news of seeing his father? Would she be happy, or upset that Colby failed to bring him home? Would she understand, or would she doubt the reality of his experience? He worried that last possibility would be the likeliest.

The vision Colby experienced in the temple was his alone. Only he saw and spoke with Jarrod, and he had no proof beyond his word that it was anything more than his own imagination. The others seemed to believe Colby's account of his experience, but there remained a lingering doubt. He could sense the uncertainty when he retold his story. Except Shelly. Perhaps she was as delusional as Colby was beginning to feel of himself.

Colby stood there watching Aria set the dining room table for dinner. A welcome home feast and celebration. Aria was smiling and moving around the table with deliberate motions, laying out the elegant and formal place settings.

* * *

"Colby dear, be useful while you stand there deciding whether or not to tell me what's on your mind." Aria kept her head facing toward the table but moved her eyes to glance at Colby as she spoke to him. "I need some cloth napkins from the buffet."

Following Aria's pointed finger, Colby went to the buffet and opened the top drawer. It was overfull of napkins, placemats, runners, and table cloths. He looked at the table before deciding which napkins to retrieve and began folding them the way his mother taught him years earlier. More than once, Colby looked up to find his mother gazing back expectantly.

"I saw something during my trip to Mexico," Colby said. He wasn't sure how to say he saw his father without making it sound like a hallucination. "There is this temple beneath the pyramid in Chichén Itzá, and I had this…experience."

Colby paused and searched his mother's face. She was paying attention and smiling, but Colby could not tell if she was only half listening to placate him or if she was genuinely interested. When Aria nodded at him to continue, he took that to mean she was actively paying attention so he continued.

"Well, it was something that I saw when I was in the temple…something more than a spell. I saw-"

"Your father?" Aria said. She smiled at Colby's dumbfounded expression. "I sensed him…for just a brief and fleeting moment."

Colby was about to ask his mother how, when the look she gave him said everything he needed to know. From the glossy sheen covering her eyes as she fought back her tears, Colby could sense the special bond his parents shared. It made sense, with the magic of Emassa, that they would be connected in some mystical way. Colby's mind began to wonder about the possibilities of such a connection but was interrupted when the rest of the family and guests began entering the room.

"Everyone take a seat," Aria said. She painted on her most cheerful smile and hid away her heartache. "I'll not be but a moment bringing everything else to the buffet."

Everyone seated themselves and carried on a quiet conversation as Aria returned with the bread basket and salad. She took her own seat leaving only one empty place.

Colby looked at the empty chair, wondering if his mother had set it thinking her husband might be coming home. Of course, she and Colby knew that wasn't yet a possibility, so he continued to stare at the place setting until at last his answer arrived with the sound of the doorbell. Someone else was coming to dinner by the look on Aria's face, but Colby was silenced with a look before he could question his mother.

# <u>Chapter 2</u>

## #DinnerGuest

Aria got up to go answer the door —much to Nana's disapproval— and a light conversation began around the table. Everyone began unfolding napkins, arranging their plates and talking about the lighter aspects of their trip.

Fizzlewink jerked his head toward the front of the house and gave out a low rumbling purr of which no one took notice. It wasn't until Fizzlewink transformed and darted across the table, that anyone paid mind to his abrupt change in mood.

The scraggly blue cat leaped over the candles and fine china on the table and jumped to the floor as Aria and her unknown guest entered the dining room. As the man looked down at the aggravated feline, a faint curl of the man's lip evoked a loud yowl and hasty exit from Fizzlewink.

"I'm so sorry," Aria said. "He is a rather derisive beast that cat of ours. I don't understand why."

The man laughed and smiled —a broad, white, toothy grin— and shook his head. "It's okay, but perhaps you might take him to be neutered. I hear that can calm the most waspish of beasts."

* * *

Aria looked at him and squinted. The tone of his voice now seemed unfamiliar to her. When he smiled at her, Aria shook off the vestiges of doubt that wrinkled her face and returned an uneasy smile.

Adam regarded the others in the room, showing his perfect smile and unassuming face. He followed Aria's lead and walked further into the room for introductions. He paused momentarily to set his bag down on the floor against the wall, after pulling his hand from inside the middle compartment.

"Everyone," Aria said, "this is Adam Votive. We met a few days ago at the training retreat." After he had smiled and nodded, Aria continued.

Aria went around the table and introduced her guest to everyone assembled at the table. Nana being first, was more than a bit terse with her greeting. Aria couldn't help but snigger when she imagined Adam suggesting she have Nana spayed, thinking her a more waspish beast than Fizzlewink.

As she made her way around the table she introduced the others, making her way toward the final two, Adam stopped and took the empty seat opposite Colby.

"Yes, well met everyone." Adam smiled and waved off Aria's confused look. "No need to bore everyone with further formalities."

Aria shook off the odd sensation she began to feel and took her seat before making small talk. More than once she felt a shiver run along her spine, but she chose to ignore the warning. Instead, she reinforced her smile as she poured herself a glass of water. Aria passed the pitcher to her mother before taking a drink to settle herself.

Not feeling water a strong enough elixir for her growing sense of agitation, Nana passed along the water and helped herself to a glass of wine. She drank deeply, her eyes scanning the room through the bottom of her glass. She settled her gaze on Adam and shivered.

Aria glanced more than once at the open bottle of Cabernet on the table. Rather than give into the growing desire for her long-time companion, Aria took another drink of her water to soothe growing tension. She noticed Adam watching her.

"So Adam was a speaker at the conference," Aria said. She hoped a bit of chit-chat would liven the mood hanging over the table like an oppressive storm cloud. "He gave an interesting talk about his work in research and development and our need for technology."

Clearing his throat, Adam dabbed his mouth with his napkin and settled it back in his lap.

Colby noticed his place was thus far empty of food and narrowed his eyes at why the man would have wiped his mouth.

"I must admit that my speech was more along the lines of humanities reliance on technology rather than its need."

"I must have misunderstood," Aria said. "You did share with us some new advances you were working on. It seemed to me you were excited about them, but could not share the details. Are they some sort of top secret project?" Aria smiled and looked to David for approval to speak. It was his company after all.

David returned a look of confusion. Though he had been unwilling host to a Shizumu, David retained the memories of what transpired over the past several years. The question in his eyes confirmed that David was completely unaware of that on which Adam may be working. He looked closer at Adam, wondering at a nagging feeling that began to unsettle his stomach.

As the plates of food made their rounds, everyone took sparingly from the overly filled platters. They all seemed to share an increasing lack of appetite. Plate after plate moved silently around the table and partaken from before they made it back to the buffet.

Each plate that passed Adam was hurried along the group without his taking a single item. As the final dish made it to his hands, Adam paused as he felt himself pass under scrutiny's eye. Nana who was fixated on his empty plate nodded for him to take something and eat. Adam smiled and took a piece of food before hurrying it away from himself.

Satisfied in appearance only, Nana raised her glass in salute to Adam as he returned the gesture and drank from his glass of water. She noticed he took no wine and began to consider the significance of his odd behaviors.

There was something about that old woman that scraped against Adam's senses. He couldn't place it, but somehow he wondered against his plan. The moment passed, however when the boy named Gary began to speak. Now was his chance to start springing his trap.

"What is this new technology you're working on if we are privy to the information? If you feel we rely on tech so much, why create something new? You must like what you do if you work at MacroTech."

Adam sat back and regarded Gary's questions. "I find the technology here a crutch. Nothing short of tools to weaken the minds potential."

Colby took offense. "It's the very potential of brilliant minds that create and innovate. Technology doesn't just fall from the sky."

Adam laughed as though Colby made a joke to which he had no clue. "You are very near understanding without even knowing. All things come from the stars, even children such as yourselves." Adam looked around at each of the kids at the table.

* * *

Colby and the others looked around the dining room at one another. A spark of realization brewing beneath the surface of comprehension.

"I detest this modern world and its conveniences," he said as he stood and placed his napkin over the single slice of beef on his plate and pushed it away. A single glint in his eye began to unfold the power laying in wait.

"These conveniences, tools as they are, help to better mankind." Colby reflexively looked down at his phWatch.

A barely audible grunt escaped Adam's mouth as he glanced at the object on Colby's wrist. "They cripple you."

A seething hatred has begun to ripple across the boundary of Colby's awareness as he pulled back his wrist and placed it in his lap. He started to type a hashtag when he noticed Adam moving, making his attention to the device peripheral.

Adam moved slow and deliberate around the table, his eyes never leaving Colby's. "What happen's when the electric power goes out? Most of your toys go dark along with the lights."

A few steps more brought Adam closer to rounding the table toward Colby. He began to feel the weight of Adam's stare, but he was unable to look away or focus on his secondary objective. He fumbled with his phWatch mindlessly.

Another step closer.

"Your food begins to spoil in the ice boxes and your microwave and electric ovens provide no means to cook. You might use gas, but even that can become unregulated or unavailable in widespread blackouts." Adam moved further still in the direction of his quarry.

* * *

Aria knew something was happening, but she could not figure it out. Something was clouding her thoughts. A part of her was refusing to act. Rising to force herself to some action, Aria grabbed the basket of dinner rolls from the buffet and began an opposing circle around the table to intercept Adam. She paused as she reached each guest at her table. The table she set for a dinner of celebration and accomplishment. She spent hours cooking and preparing a feast to share with her family and friends and this man she barely knew was spoiling everything.

But she did know him. More than just the fact she met Adam a few days earlier, but something more. As a person, she realized she barely knew him at all. The man she met at the conference was very different than the person here now. There was something else, deeper and connected but she could not place it.

"What happens when you can no longer rely on your modes of transportation. They will fail and would you go back to beasts of burden? Or would you wish yourself to where you want and transport in the blink of an eye?"

In an instant, the flames of comprehension ignited in Colby's head, and he began to stand and point his watch at Adam.

Adam was faster. With a single word, a static charge raced through the air and found purchase on Colby, causing both watches to fall from his wrists. His phWatch fell dark, and his father's timepiece lay somewhere on the floor out of sight. A low steady hum resonated through the room as Adam laughed.

"How do you perform magic without your toy, child of the stars?"

Apparently aware of an impending threat, Aria shoved the basket of rolls into Shelly's hands and moved toward Colby and David Bodine. As she approached, apprehension stirred when she noticed the confused look on Mr. Bodine's face turn to one of full recognition.

* * *

"Adam, what are you-" Aria could not finish speaking as a glancing touch from Adam silenced her.

Adam moved faster than humanly possible as he brushed past Aria to push Mr. Bodine back down into his seat before the man could rise. "Do keep your place, David. No need to stand for me, your old traveling companion."

"Adam, what is going on here?" Aria staggered back as energy built up around Adam.

Adam smiled as he watched the face of David Bodine twist in restrained agony. The pulses of red Emassa flowing from his hand and entering the man's body caused David to convulse. He reached over to Colby and placed the same grip on his raised arm.

Colby twisted in agony, frequently his touch could force a Shizumu from a body, but he had yet to do so consciously. His fear refused to react in his defense either, making his mind burn under the pressure of mental invasion from the creature trying to enter his body. That same creature would burn Jasper's dad from the inside out.

Colby searched for something, anything that could help. His memory failed, and the runes would not come to him. The pain was unbearable, causing him too much distraction to form a spell. He looked out desperately to his friends. They too were unable to use their devices and access Hashtag Magic. He reached desperately at his chest, the pain searing him from within, knocking the pendant out from behind his shirt that he wore around his neck.

Desperation saturated Colby's soul. He cried out from inside his very being for help and something heard his plea.

Nana, shocked into motionlessness, reached slowly toward the glow —

only she saw— at the end of a leather string around her grandson's neck.

A single thought separated itself from the haze in Colby's mind. As though a single drop of water fell upon a pool of oil and pushed it away, he could see what he must do. Colby's hand slid down to the pendant on his chest and the instant his skin met with the smooth and polished stone, a light flashed from his body and pushed him free of Adam's vice-like grip.

No longer hiding the thing inside him, Adam snarled and pointed toward the bag he left by the door when arriving. A single phrase escaped his curled lips in raspy response to Colby's escape. "Initiate Device EMP."

At Colby's release, the bewilderment that caused inaction from the others ended. Chaos ensued as the kids dove for the stranger who was torturing Jasper's father. They reacted with hashtag spells that sputtered and then failed. As they attempted more, the phWatches went dead at the same time a pulse emitted from Adam's bag, blacking out the entire house and beyond. The candles on the table and eerie red glow of Adam's handy-work were the only sources of illumination in the dining room.

"I brought my own little toy to the party." Adam now spoke with a familiar Shizumu voice.

# Chapter 3

## #PlayFetch

Still clutching David Bodine in his hand, Adam dragged the limp-bodied man into the corner of the room to better position his defense. He waited patiently as his adversaries gathered and regarded him. They took too long to prepare an offense.

"You are all pathetic. You have access to the greatest power in the universe and yet find yourselves utterly impotent without your electronics and this program you call hashtag magic. It is creative, for an infant, but it will not help you prevent the inevitable."

The flesh-bags were not taking his bait. The Shizumu decided to take a more direct approach. "You couldn't even interpret those obscure runes in your father's little notebook, could you boy?" He waited for the recognition on Colby's face, letting it sink in that he'd been inside the child's mind rooting around for information. "You see the point boy? You have had such knowledge of power in your hands and don't know the first thing about how to put it to use."

Colby knew exactly what the demon referred to. A set of runes etched inside the pages of his father's journal that he was yet to explore the meaning of since they were completely foreign to him. But this maniacal shadow of a formerly living being knew something now from invading his head. What else did he know?

As if hearing Colby's thoughts, the Shizumu looked deeply into Colby's eyes and parted his lips in a growing smile that told Colby all he needed to know. It knew more than Colby would have hoped. Without further thought, Colby lashed out with a bolt of energy. He could remember the runes without difficulty and drew them in his minds-eye.

Adam laughed with the voice of the Shizumu that once infested David. He easily absorbed the energy as he voided the spell Colby cast. "You'll have to do better than that."

Colby threw more bolts in rapid succession.

The quick exchange between Adam and Colby allowed Aria a needed diversion to plan her next move. She edged her way around the table, moving closer to Adam. Her hands, held behind her back and hidden from Adam's view, were pulsing with barely restrained energy. She moved ever closer, preparing her assault but never got close enough.

Before Aria could raise a hand, the Shizumu face lifted from Adam's, casting a spectral image of malevolence. The face turned in her direction. An instant later and Aria was lifted through the air and pinned against the wall next to him. He laughed at her feeble attempt. "You just stay put. You may be more useful than this one." As he said the words, he released David Bodine and sent him flying across the room, landing at Nana's feet.

Jasper ran to his father and cradled his head while Rhea followed behind. At his pleading, Rhea sat next to Jasper and laid a healing touch to his father.

Nana squatted beside the listless man as well, checking for signs of life. She sighed heavily with relief when she felt the faint but steady rhythm of blood flowing through his veins. When Nana looked around her to find the rest of the children gathering hastily constructed spells, Nana stepped away, leaving Jasper and Rhea to care for his father. She thought to join the fight but became transfixed the moment her eyes reconnected with the pendant around Colby's neck. She began to mumble and shiver.

None of the others paid Nana mind as they launched attacks on the entity now visibly radiating from Adam. Each one conjured weak and ineffectual offenses against their enemy. They were unable to focus on the strength and effectiveness of their magic. Though they had practiced some spells without the use of Hashtag Magic at Fizzlewink's insistence, they had mastered none of them. This being was far too powerful for their inefficient use of Emassa.

Taking a different approach, Darla lowered her hands and began to move toward the creature. It had made no attempt to retaliate with its own magic, only defended itself. Darla started to use the one gift she needed not concentrate on using. It required no runes or preparation. She reached out with her mind and tried to compel the thing to her will. It laughed at her.

"You think your wiles worthy of power more ancient than you could imagine little girl?" With a look, it sent a wave of consciousness back along the tethered thoughts Darla sent toward it. In less than a breath, Darla was on the floor gasping for air and crying in pain as he turned back to the others.

Shelly began chanting and invoking her ancestors. She called to the spirits of her Great-Grandmother and her mother before her. None came at her beckoning. She angered at the laughter from across the room. Again she pushed her will on the boundary between the realms of the living and the dead, not understanding what blocked her call.

Nana continued to sway and mumbled as she stared into the depths of pulsing light that shone only for her from the pendant. If anyone were to listen, they would have heard her repeating Shelly's words.

* * *

Gary, unable to use his gift on the phWatch on his wrist, tried desperately to think of someway to help. With the electronics rendered useless, he thought back to the reason and turned toward the bag Adam brought with him and left nearby. Gary crawled under the flow of power flying from his friends' hands toward the bag now laying half open near the door. Just as he neared, a blue foot landed between him and his target.

"Fizz," Gary said. He grabbed his chest and exhaled hard as he sat upright. "Where have you been?"

Fizzlewink regarded Gary and moved toward Colby. "I was trying to get some help from the monkeys in the yard."

"And?" Colby said. "Where are they?"

Fizzlewink shook his head and leveled his gaze across the room. "They said they won't get this deeply involved yet…whatever that means. We're on our own for now." Fizzlewink flexed his fingers, causing his nails to lengthen and spark with Emassa. His growl vibrated the air around him, making Colby take a step back.

"Oh, hello there kitty-kitty. You want to play?" The Shizumu snickered and launched a ball of plasma toward Fizzlewink. It went over his head and out the doorway past Gary. "Fetch."

"I'm no mangy dog to play fetch with, you half-souled abomination."

Rhea was doing all she could for Mr. Bodine. She sent Jasper away to help the others with a simple nod and look toward their friends.

Jasper turned and pushed himself up to rejoin his friends. He nearly stepped on Colby's timepiece that belonged to his father. He picked up the watch and carried it as he stepped away from his helpless father. Jasper fell in line with Colby behind Fizz, handing Colby his missing father's wrist watch. He assured Colby his own father seemed well enough for the moment. "He's better than your mother at the moment. We need to do something quick."

"Any suggestions are welcome," Colby said, putting the watch back on his wrist. A hint of defeat added an edge to the timber in his voice. "I'm out of ideas."

"Can you hold him with force?" Fizzlewink asked.

Without answering with words, Jasper released a savage scream and the full force of his rage in the form of a shield. It expanded toward Adam in an instant, pinning him to the wall. He pushed with all his strength using the vast reserve of power he accumulated the past few days. It was not his full potential by far, but it would have to do. Colby offered his own strength, but Jasper refused. He wanted this for himself.

Fizzlewink charged the Shizumu and leaped at his face, claws at the ready to shred the thing free of Adam's body. Inches before he could strike, the Shizumu retreated into Adam and pulled freely on the force Jasper was throwing at him.

Adam screamed in pain for only a moment before Jasper's shield failed and all the energy behind it was taken away and redirected at Fizzlewink.

Realization dawned on the flying feline as his eyes went wide with the impact of what Adam now used against him. Fizzlewink slammed into the oncoming blast and was thrown clear across the room. The light in his eyes was gone even before his body reacted by transforming back into the visage of a cat. When the sickening crack of bones filled the room, it was shortly followed by the lifeless thud as his body fell to the floor.

The silence that followed mingled with the shadows dancing around the room, cast by the only light source, two candles on the table. The shadows seemed to stay clear of Fizzlewink's motionless form.

* * *

Rhea barely made it to Fizzlewink to lay her hand on him and sob before the silence was broken by a renewed desire for an attack, born of the need for retribution. Rhea huddled over Fizzlewink's lifeless cat body while the others who were able, launched attacks at the Shizumu.

Gary however, found himself drawn to the device he now sensed in Adam's satchel. He looked back at his friends, fighting to free Aria and rid themselves of the powerful and unrelenting Shizumu. Thinking himself better able to assist by shutting off this device, Gary turned back to the incessant hum that drew upon his innate ability with electronics. If he could disable it, perhaps they could regain access to Hashtag Magic.

The possessed Adam, no longer content to toy with his prey, had enough of the game and launched an offensive spell. Without a word, the Shizumu released a blast of energy that enveloped everyone standing against him.

The kids stiffened, and their hands sputtered as prepared spells lost their potency and became unraveled. Unable to move, they lacked the ability to speak the names of runes or draw them in the air to focus on them. The kids were helpless.

Adam moved toward Colby slowly, deliberately, trying to unnerve his quarry. "All of this is really quite unnecessary, child." Adam's mouth moved much the way a puppet would mouth words given by another's voice. "If only you allowed yourself to see the real side of power, you might understand the absurdity of our situation."

Colby could not look away from the approaching menace. Unable to speak or even look away, Colby became entranced by the Shizumu's words. He was unable to detect the undertone of a casting as the magic was flowing from every syllable spoken.

"Listen to my words boy. Hear the truth behind what I tell you." Adam crept closer still.

Colby felt a sensation ripple beneath his skin. A familiar need for acceptance. Beneath that feeling was a desire that bubbled and churned. It was primal and restrained. A burning pit of seething that wanted nothing more than the freedom to do its will. Colby was repulsed. Not by the feeling, but his attraction to it. He could do what he wanted, make people see him for who he was and accept it without hesitation. He wanted nothing more than to just be himself but was this him.

"Do not fight what you are Colby. You have more to give than anyone ever has. Let me show you how." Adam spoke the last few words in a whisper meant only for Colby's ear. He leaned in closer and continued to tempt Colby with promises of power to get everything he wanted and more.

Colby latched onto those words and fed on them, hungry for the release of his inner self. He found himself able to move his eyes and stare into the abyss behind Adam's overtaken eyes. "What do you want from me in return?" Colby found his voice.

Adam lifted his left brow and leaned back away from Colby's ear. Apparently impressed with his control over the power, the Shizumu allowed Adam's body to loosen. The tense lines on his strained face relaxed and a reserved smile parted the borrowed lips.

"We want wrongs put right. You could help us with that star child." Adam's guest spirit had the boy now. He allowed Colby more freedom of movement. He fed images to Colby's mind of the things he wanted Colby to help them achieve.

Colby witnessed the creation of great civilizations, but they were built atop the conquered. He saw the rebirth of lost people's, long vanished from history and knowing. But this required the death and destruction of others. Hands covered in blood, Colby placed himself in the center of a vast empire built with magic and none to challenge his authority and power. He would be the immortal ruler of death eternal and life everlasting.

A shock traveled Colby's body from his wrist to his heart and head. The images ceased and in the fleeting moment of uninfluenced thought, Colby grabbed at his chest. The pendant of Bellatrix fell free.

The Shizumu-controlled Adam leaned back from Colby's sudden shift and caught site of the flash as Colby and began to realize his mistake as the power of the trinket was revealing itself.

"Mother do something!" Aria screamed. She felt what was happening, somehow knowing what others were yet to come to understand.

Broken from the spell of restraint, Nana turned to see the pendant and was overtaken by instinct. As the necklace glowed more brightly, Nana's eyes cleared, and her features shifted. Arm raised she charged the Shizumu and its host. Just as she reached her target, a dagger of pure light and energy formed in her clenched fist. Nana drove the magic blade into Adam's chest.

Clarity replaced the confused look Adam wore. "Manaba…"

The Shizumu was ripped free of Adam as Nana retracted the magical dagger from his relatively unharmed chest. It shimmered, confused and unable to retreat into its host.

Colby rushed the Shizumu, reaching out to dispatch it with his touch. "I would know your name before I send you to whatever hell you came from."

It laughed at him. "You may call me Koyaanisqatsi, for that, is what I bring."

* * *

Colby reached for the being, and as he brushed his fingers at the edge of the Shizumu's energies, Koyaanisqatsi disappeared.

Quiet returned to the room. Rhea checked Adam out as the others grabbed each other in embraces and looked around at one other and the sad state of the dining room. Nobody spoke, perhaps out of fear, or pure shock for the last several minutes they endured.

Jasper was first to speak after checking on his father's state. "What kind of name is Coin-Anna-Squating?"

A few nervous snickers and sighs released some of the tension yet hanging in the air.

"You can Google it," Gary said as the lights came back on. "I managed to stop the block on electronics."

"Is it off then?" Colby asked.

"No, I can't figure it out entirely. It's completely wicked, though."

Jasper fiddled with his phWatch. It was on. However, the app would not work. "These aren't working  yet, so what good did you do?"

"Jasper!" Darla chided.

"What? We are all defending ourselves and trying to take down this Konan-squatsi thing…all Gary manages to do was keep out of the battle and turn the lights back on."

"I said it is complicated, you witless oaf."

Aria finally had listened to more bickering than she could stand. "Enough." She moved around the table, attempting to clean up a bit. "Let's just clean this up and try to salvage something to eat."

* * *

They all moved at Aria's implied command, picking up turned over platters and spilled glasses. The food was most everywhere throughout the room except on the plates.

Shelly dropped a plate she was picking up. It shattered on the hardwood floor, silencing the conversations in the room. "It's still here."

Aria screamed. Pain rippling through the air as a phantasmic red hand tore through her chest from behind.

Everyone turned as Koyaanisqatsi ripped a similarly red spirit from Aria and dropped her panting yet conscious body to the floor. They remained frozen in shock at the sight and vitriol lashing that Koyaanisqatsi spoke at Aria. He looked across the room directly at Colby before waving his hand to form a swirling mass of light made from dark and roiling colors. As the Shizumu entered the portal, dragging Aria's half split soul with him, he glared once again at Colby with a challenge in his glowing eyes.

# <u>Chapter 4</u>

## #TakeDownShield

Colby reacted by instinct, creating a time bubble. He was too slow to stop Koyaanisqatsi from escaping with what he now understood to be Aria's Shizumu, her split soul. The portal, however, was stuck open.

Without thinking about what might happen, Colby ran for the entrance and leaped. His body sped up as it approached the event horizon of the swirling mass. Instead of entering the vortex after the Shizumu, Colby was repelled when the pendant reacted to the attempted entry.

Colby felt the stinging pain growing the closer he came to the portal. The peak of agony arrived the moment he was sent flying back the way he approached. If not for Jasper's strength and quick reaction, Colby would have flown headlong into the wall.

Helping Colby to steady his feet, Jasper held his friend firmly. "You alright?"

"Yeah, thanks. Wasn't expecting the recoil." Colby smiled at Jasper.

Letting go of Colby, Jasper stepped back and looked away from Colby's eyes. "What do you think happened?"

* * *

"Besides jumping toward a magical portal leading to who knows where?" Shelly interjected. "What were you thinking?"

"I wasn't...I just reacted to a feeling. The Koyaanisqatsi escaped with mom's...I don't know what to think."

Shelly looked over at there mother laying on the floor barely conscious and muttering. "Well, she won't be able to tell us anything at the moment."

Colby regarded the pendant around his neck as he moved closer to the portal. It began to sting him again as he approached. "Something about this thing, or maybe my time bubble is reacting to the Goddess's pendant." He stepped back far enough for the pain to lessen and stood next to Nana who regarded the artifact he now wore around his neck again. "Maybe I should remove the bubble?" Colby raised his hand toward the portal.

"No," Gary shouted. "That won't matter. This device started acting differently the moment the portal opened. It may be important." As Colby lowered his hand, Gary relaxed. "Besides, your time distortion expands beyond the portal so something else must be the problem." Gary pointed to the pendant.

"Gary's right," Darla said. "Those candles in the living room are flickering, meaning they are inside the bubble with us."

Nana finally looked away from the pendant around Colby's neck and stepped back, eyes creased around the corners and worry on her face. "I'll see how far this time thing extends." She took one more look at the pendant and moved toward the table.

Colby noticed Nana's fascination with the necklace. "Be careful. If you go outside the bubble, you may be out there a while."

* * *

Nana grunted and picked up a candle from the table. "I may be old, but I ain't lost my wits altogether." She walked from the room, holding the candle before her watching for the flickering flame to change as it passed through the boundary. Once past the border it would stop moving or go incredibly fast, depending on the type of time bubble Colby created.

Colby watched his Nana look back at him several times before moving out of view. After Nana had passed Rhea, who was looking after Adam's body, Colby went to see what could be done for the man.

"I'm sorry Colby, he's gone. My gift can't help heal the dead." She looked away and rested her eyes on Fizzlewink's body laying motionless as well.

"Great. How are we going to explain a dead man that came for dinner?" Shelly said. "Blame Nana's cooking?"

Uneasy laughter escaped a few mouths, but it was not long after the silence fell upon them all again.

"I can help with that," Mr. Bodine said as he struggled to sit upright. "What's one more spontaneous combustion case to add to the blue screen of death cases?"

At the sound of his father's voice, not the possessed under-toned voice, Jasper ran to his father's side and embraced him.

While heart warming and hopeful to witness, Colby couldn't help but feel a pang of jealousy build in his chest. He longed for a similar reunion with his own father, but the deeper into his journey with magic, the farther away that seemed to get.

He looked away and toward his mother who was also starting to stir. She pushed away all offers of help and made her way to the dining table to sit. She looked at Colby with glassy and emotionless eyes before stopping her gaze on a glass of wine on the table.

* * *

Aria picked up the glass and drank it. Emptying the glass, she immediately reached for another and poured it into the first before drinking heavily from it again.

"She's ba-a-a-ack," Shelly drawled. "Looks like someone has fallen back into her drunken ways."

Nana returned to the dining room and looked at Aria then to the portal and back again. "Leave her be for the moment, Shelly." Nana held the still-lit candle before her. "We got bigger concerns right now."

Shelly looked at the candle then scanned the room before resting her eyes on Fizzlewink laying still on the floor. "Yes, we have more to be worried about. What are we gonna do about poor ol' Fizz?"

"Bury him out back with the rest of your dead pets," Aria slurred. "Got a regular pet cemetery out by the garage."

"Shut up Ar," Nana said before turning back to the others. "Though she's right. We could likely make it out there. This time-thingy extends well outside the house."

Colby noticed his grandmother looking between the portal and Aria. He was not ready to ignore what was going on with his mother. "What is goin' on with her? There is something weird about how suddenly a Shizumu is pulled from her, and then she reverts to being a drunk."

"He took part of my soul," Aria said and sobbed into her empty glass. "The part that was disconnected and unrestrained."

Colby Took his mother's hand in his, noticing how she suddenly became more coherent. "What do you mean? Are you part Shizumu mother?"

Aria snorted. "Don't be ridiculous."

* * *

"Then what just happened?"

Aria moved her lips as though to answer, but stopped herself. "You have far more important questions to find answers to right now son. This will wait." She looked away and reached for another glass of wine. When she looked back at him, Colby's eyes met hers with a pleading for clarity. She returned his gaze with one of resigned refusal to explain. At least for now.

"Lay your friend to rest," Aria said, looking at Fizzlewink.

### 

The entire property was locked in time. The bubble Colby created, surrounded the house and yard so they had no difficulties reaching the area beside the garage where they prepared to lay Fizzlewink to rest.

The service was short but filled with tears. With the unfolding events, they had little time to spend on grieving now. There would hopefully be time for that later.

After they lowered his little blue cat form into the ground and began to bury him, Jasper grabbed Colby's arm.

"Hey, those giant monkey guys are watching us." Jasper pointed toward the trees on the edge of the property.

Colby looked up to see Conrad and a few of his companions staring back from the other side of his time bubble. Though they did not move, Colby felt they were watching everything in real time somehow. The Dreggs were a mystery and their abilities not entirely known.

"Let them watch."

* * *

Once they finished the short and impersonal service for Fizzlewink, they helped Mr. Bodine to his car with Adam's body. He would take care of everything and check-in once they contacted him with their own progress. He was of little more help until he rested, even then his power was limited somehow. Everyone agreed he would best be placed inside his company to work at shutting down whatever Koyaanisqatsi started.

Once back inside, and the house somewhat cleaned up, Colby constricted the time bubble to circle only the dining room. He tried to condense it further but was unable for some reason. He explained that it felt as though something fought back at his spell.

As those who remained in the house sat around the kitchen discussing next steps, Nana sat watching Colby's new necklace, looking away only whenever he would catch her glance.

Colby pushed the pendant away into his shirt. "We can't just leave part of mom in there with that monster."

Aria saluted with her glass of wine. "Cheers to that!"

Everyone ignored her drunkenness.

"We should close that portal," Darla suggested. "What if he comes back, or others come as well?"

Colby shook his head. "We can't. What if mom's split soul gets free? She needs to have a way back, if she can make it back."

Shelly agreed with Darla. "There's gotta be other ways out. Those things have been comin' from somewhere before that portal was open."

"Are you willing to take that chance," Colby argued. "She may remember how to get back to this portal. We can't be assured she could find or reach any others."

*  *  *

Stepping back from observing the device just inside the dining room and consequently the time bubble, Gary interrupted the debate.

"We may not have a choice."

Gary explained that after spending all this time examining the device and then observing its behavior as the time bubble was shrunk, there was a connection. He felt that somehow the device was connected to the portal, perhaps even powering it. If they wanted to close the portal they would have to likely destroy the device. If they did this, there would be little chance of developing a way to counter its effect of messing with Hashtag Magic.

"What proof do you have?" Jasper asked. His voice was clipped and doubtful.

Gary frowned and sneered at Jasper. "I know electronics and energy. That thing is flowing toward the portal. I just haven't figured out why and what powers it."

"Well, how about you figure that out before bringing a half-baked theory."

Colby looked at Jasper. "Hey come on. We are all a little at a loss here."

"Sorry," Jasper mumbled. His tone belied the sentiment of his apology.

Unmoved by his words, Gary turned back to Jasper. "Do you have anything better to offer?"

"Actually, I do."

Jasper got up from his seat and moved toward Gary. "I say we put a shield around the damn thing."

* * *

Gary snorted. "If that portal is connected to the device, that is what is likely keeping Colby from shrinking the time field. How do you think a shield would work any better?"

As the two began to bicker, Colby thought about the argument. Jasper's idea had merit, but Gary was also right. He got up and retrieved a pen and paper from a drawer and began scribbling out an idea.

"You both are right."

Colby waved everyone over once his two pals stopped bitching long enough to realize Colby wanted their attention. When they all congregated around the kitchen island, Colby explained his idea.

"What if we create a shield that can match the flow of energy from the device, but keep anything from coming back through the effecting our shield?"

The idea was promising. With Jasper's affinity for runes and Gary's growing knowledge of the device and its signals, they soon had the workings of a spell. Based on what they came up with, it looked like it would need a lot of power, but Colby was sure he could provide what they needed. He was desperate. He couldn't let a part of his mother remain with the Shizumu.

The runes were written on separate pieces of paper and laid out before the portal. When the other boys signaled they were ready, Colby dropped the time bubble.

The portal immediately started to shrink. Gary watched the device and waited to give his ready to go.

"What are we waiting for?" Jasper asked.

* * *

"Go!" Gary finally shouted.

Colby focused on the runes and fed them power. Within moments, the portal was surrounded by a field of growing energy. Focusing deeper on the final runes, Colby poured more Emassa into the construct. The shattering of glass broke his concentration, but he was already done.

Colby turned to where the noise came from to witness his mother leaning back in her chair, head shaking and eyes rolled back in a seizure. He ran to her side and felt the chill of responsibility run down his spine.

Nana held Aria's head, keeping it from slamming against the back of the chair. "Take that shield down," she screamed.

Colby turned to do as Nana ordered when a shaky hand grabbed his arm.

"No," Aria whispered. She was gaining her senses as the seizure abated. "You have to do this…no matter the risk or cost."

Colby was unsure what to do. He knew that leaving the shield up would continue to harm his mother. A part of her soul was trapped in the vortex and putting up the shield seemed to exacerbate the situation. He looked at his mother, not knowing what to do. His hand was clutching the pendant he wore around his neck.

Aria looked at the pendant and then at her mother, who stared at it with desire and fear in her eyes. Aria grabbed her mother's hand and squeezed with the little strength she had, a knowing look on her face.

"You must help them, mother. With Fizz gone, who else can guide them?"

Nana looked at Aria with a heart full of desire to help, and a look that was worried about what worse could happen if she did.

# <u>Chapter 5</u>

## #RevealAndExplain

When next Aria awoke, she became hostile. She wanted a drink, but they were nowhere near the liquor cabinet.

"What are you all doing just standing around?" Aria looked at them in disgust. "I told him it would never work." She looked through the bottom of her empty wine glass.

"What would never work mom?" Shelly asked.

Aria looked up at Shelly and for a moment looked as though she might answer. "Are you gonna just stand there looking like the Bride of Chucky or are you gonna get mommy a drink?" Aria put on a forced smile and batter her eyes. "Get momma a drink sweetie…"

Shelly frowned and turned her back on Aria. "Alcoholic. Can't we just drop her off at an AA meeting somewhere and get back to other issues?"

"Alcoholics Anonymous is for quitters," Aria whispered with a bite in her voice. "I'm no quitter, just a failure." She broke down again into fits of sobbing and passed out.

Colby shook his head at his mother's state and noticed his grandmother staring at him again. "Nana, why does mom think you can help?"

Nana didn't answer. She just stood to the side of the room, gazing at the pendant around Colby's neck. When Colby tucked the piece back in his shirt, she snapped out of her stupor. "What was that Fart-blossom?"

Rolling his eyes at her use of the moniker, Colby walked over to Nana. "What makes mom think you can help us with what's happening?"

Nana looked into Colby's eyes. The room went quiet waiting for her response and she began to fidget. "I have no idea what-"

"No!" Colby said a bit more forcibly than he wished, but it got her attention. "You know something…what is it?"

Nana shook her head and sat down across from Aria at the table. "I can't remember…it's all muddled up lately. My memory and power…it's all fractured."

Colby was already moving toward Nana when her last word stopped him. 'Fractured,' he remembered. The Goddess used that same description of her state even as she disintegrated into dust on the wind. He looked at his grandmother differently when he raised his eyes to her and squinted.

Shelly, not noticing Colby's reaction, prodded Nana for more information. "You know something old witch, now spill it. What's going on with mom?"

"This is like before, don't you remember?" Nana looked at Shelly and then to Colby, hoping they would recall. When they maintained the ignorance on their faces, Nana continued. "When your father disappeared, she acted the same way very much as now, except…"

"What?" Colby asked.

* * *

"This is much worse. I don't think this will pass in a few days like last time."

"Why do you say that?"

"Because her spirit is split. I suspect it has been since that night so long ago, but now it can't make its way back at will. I think she has been like this since that night she left with your father. When she came back alone, she was different, changed."

"Changed how Nannie?" Colby pleaded for more details. He wanted to understand what was happening to his mother and perhaps glean more knowledge about his father's disappearance.

"Her soul was split in twain. Something similar but not the same as the ancient Nefslama."

Colby grew more suspicious. They only learned about what happened to the Nefslama so long ago and their spell to release the restrictions of their magical ethics. Had someone mentioned this to Nana since they returned? Colby narrowed his eyes at his grandmother and prepared to question her knowledge, but his mother stirred again.

"I only wanted to help you see…keep you safe and keep watch on the others." Aria cried as she reached out for Colby. When he arrived at her side, she continued. "Your father said I had to be weary and ever watchful. I needed to be in many places. I couldn't do that while whole."

Aria passed out again before Colby could ask what she meant. "What did she suggest Nana. And before you deny it, I know there is something you aren't telling us." Colby retrieved the pendant and twirled it on the leather cord, taunting her. He felt there was a connection between this trinket and his grandmother.

Nana stammered and shook. Something at the edge of her tongue she couldn't quite bite into was wanting to come out, but at the same time held back by another part of her unable to recall. She was only granted a reprieve when Aria fell from her seat and started convulsing again.

Rhea knelt down and held Aria's head in her lap. Aria wasn't seizing, but she shivered uncontrollably. Rhea was at a loss for what ailed her. She placed her healer's hands on Aria's forehead and tried to pull the unknown sickness from her, but without any luck.

"She's burning up Colby. She won't last like this for long."

"What can we do?"

Rhea shook her head as she looked back down at Aria. "I can keep the fever at bay…for a time, but you have to get her Shizumu half back."

More than one gasp escaped the lips of those present. None muttered the words, but they all knew what was pulled from Aria and into the vortex.

"It's time we stop dancing around the subject Colby." Rhea sounded different. She was in a take charge mode and wanted to lay it all out there. "Your mother has been hosting her own Shizumu, split from her but still connected somehow. Until you get it back to her, there will be no answers from, or recovery of your mother."

The dining room was thick and stagnant. The atmosphere felt warm as the combined body heat of those present made the room stuffier with each added breath. Silence settled on the dense air since Rhea's proclamation. When no one responded to her statement about Aria's Shizumu half, Rhea went back to relieving her ailment.

Aria's fever eventually broke and her temperature remained just above normal without Rhea's assistance. She got up and moved to the living room sofa.

* * *

Nana's face lifted in a weak smile as she felt her daughter's face. "She'll be stable now."

Colby joined his grandmother next to Aria. "You said this is like before. Did she look so pale and weak then also?"

"No. Your mother was weak of course, but that passed quickly. This is different as I've said. I don't think she-"

"You needn't speak about me as if I weren't here."

Aria pulled her legs under her bottom and patted the couch next to her. She looked up at Colby and patted the couch again.

Colby leaned into his mother as he sat beside her. He closed his moist eyes as he settled into the embrace.

Aria stroked Colby's hair as she began to speak. "I wasn't always like this…scattered." She kissed the top of Colby's head before he sat up and looked at her waiting for more explanation.

Jarrod and Aria should never have had children, she began to explain. This part they had already heard, but Aria was explaining why. They were both full-blood Nefslama, though the remaining elders could not explain, or would not explain how that could be as Aria was Nana's daughter. Colby, of course, had his own suspicion on the subject, but only glanced at his grandmother before urging Aria to continue explaining.

She told them how the advancement of technology was making it increasingly difficult to hide their longevity and powers, limited as they were at the time. Any children would have to wait until they might find a way to leave this realm or find a sanctuary of some kind.

Aria and Jarrod knew neither solution would be likely and decided to break the no longer enforced law of the elders. When Shelly was born, the Elders looked the other way but warned of the possibility that if she or any children they had manifested power early, it could attract their enemies and awaken others.

Jarrod wanted a son, but Aria took the Elders warning to heart. For a few years, Jarrod continued to press Aria and try to convince her that they could still have another child, he had an idea. Aria relented and went along with Jarrod's outlandish spell; a spell built on an ancient text telling about splitting your magical core.

"Your father figured that if one of our magical cores were divided, that would make any future children different. They wouldn't be Nefslama exactly, so that would prevent others from taking notice."

"But that isn't what ended up happening, is it?" Colby asked.

Aria sighed as she fingered the hair away from Colby's face. "No, my boy, you were born and though at first, we thought his plan worked, you eventually attracted more attention than anyone could have ever expected."

She continued to explain how Jarrod was able to re-split her magical core, her spirit, and anchor it together with his own. This would keep her grounded, but different enough that she would not become like the Shizumu and would allow her the use of magic again. This worked perfectly until the night Colby's power manifested the first time.

"When you made that toy disappear, it sent a taste of power stronger than any have felt in millennia. That's how your father described it. He said that there was no denying that your abilities would cause a significant number of changes, but you were too young to face such responsibility.

"That's why he left, to help protect you. My soul was split so I could stay behind and keep you safe, but I could also go where he could not. I

40

could venture into the realm of the Shizumu."

Too much information pounded into Colby's head. He was forming questions again before the previous one was fully thought out. Before he could ask anything, however, his mother continued her story.

"I was unsettled at first when he left. Where ever he went caused a lessening of our bond, but soon I adjusted and recovered physically. Mentally, I have been a train wreck ever since."

"I'll say."

"Shut-up Shelly," everyone else in the room said in unison.

Shelly grumbled but moved to sit next to Colby as she reached over to hand a glass of water to Aria.

"Thank you. Where was I…Oh yes…Your father left to protect us all. First, if something happened to him, our spirit bond might break, and I would possibly succumb to the Shizumu. Also with your power manifested, others would come for you and do whatever necessary, including destroying anyone who stood in their way.

"Your father said he would go somewhere protected if he could, but a place Jarrod could watch over us and maybe help, until the day he could return. I thought that day would be when your power came back, but something has kept him from us."

Aria sobbed freely into an offered napkin as she pulled it to her face. Colby consoled her and eventually she regained her composure.

"You said you could go where the Shizumu go…or at least your split half could. Where is that?" Shelly asked.

"A prison…or at least it once was. Some found a way out of the realm where they were once banished long ago. It would seem that the boundary became weakened in the mid-1990's due to some tethering experiment of NASA.

"In their ignorance of the shield that surrounds the planet and prevents too much Emassa flowing onto the Earth, their failed experiment to harness a newly discovered energy, caused a tear in the shield and allowed more power to flow and the Shizumu somehow got access to it and broke free.

"I don't have all the details. It's tough to spy on these beings, especially when you are trying to sneak about. What I do know is that they are increasing their numbers somehow. And have expanded their realm into the Earthly one using technology."

"The internet," Darla said. "They expanded into the electronic web, a region of energy." She was quiet through most of the events of the day, though the creases in her face and moisture of her eyes said more than her voice could. Being an empath made her acutely aware of every emotion in the room. The effort of holding them all in check was draining but showed how strong she was becoming.

"That makes sense," Jasper said. "That's why the blue screen of death was so easy for them and were able to go anywhere connected to the web. They made it like a Shizumu network."

"The Shiznet," Darla laughed. She felt the joke lighten everyone in the room a bit. All except Nana.

Nana stood behind Aria, impatience and hurt showing on her face. She felt that her daughter kept this big secret all these years and never shared her burden. Aria allowed everyone to think her weak and unable to carry the weight of being a single mother. All this time she was dealing with a split soul, infiltration into a hostile realm of energy creatures, and waiting for the day her husband would return only to have that taken away as well.

"Why did you never tell me about all this, child of mine?" The tremor in Nana's voice gave away her feelings.

"Jarrod forbade it." Before Nana could interrupt her, Aria continued. "He said that you would understand someday, but for the time being, he suspected there was something about you knowing anything that could jeopardize our plans. He did not explain, and I trusted his judgment."

Nana started to protest but stopped when Aria's eyes went glossy, and her head fell back. She was having another seizure.

# Chapter 6

## #TimeShift

As Aria drifted in and out, Colby decided it best to move her. Time was not on their side, except when it was, he thought. "We need to move her into the study upstairs."

"Is that smart?" Shelly asked. "You saw what happened when she was separated from the portal before."

Colby shrugged and moved toward his mother. "We don't have much choice. She's already cut off from her spirit somehow. If we do nothing, she will continue to get worse. Up in the study at least we can slow things down."

Darla, Rhea, and Jasper having never been in the study required an explanation of the effects of the special time bubble already in place around the room. Colby's father, Jarrod, put it in place many years earlier for some unclear reason. Although it didn't stop time completely, it was near enough to help slow the progression of Aria's affliction.

"Let me help you," Gary said as he moved to assist Colby carry his mother.

Jasper crowded Gary out of the way, much to Gary's annoyance.

* * *

"I was gonna help him."

Jasper winked at Gary and smirked. "I'm stronger. Let me help with the heavy lifting while you do what you do best." Jasper nodded his head toward the device the Shizumu activated. "Figure out that thing's secrets."

Dejected and otherwise unable to argue Jasper's point, Gary went back to studying the unusual machine now sending energy through the portal.

Colby cringed at Jasper's dismissal of Gary but knew that his logic was sound. Gary would better serve their needs right now learning about the device. He smiled at Jasper and nodded as they both put arms under his mother, their skin touching as they cradled Aria.

Colby shuttered at the contact, trying not to let it show on his face. He watched Jasper from the corner of his eye and saw the reaction was bi-directional. He didn't want to make his friend uncomfortable so he cleared his throat.

"Lift on three?"

"Um…yeah, three." Jasper began to lift Aria, forcing Colby to match his movements.

"I meant on the count of three…" Colby mumbled. When Jasper smiled at him with an impish grin, Colby melted a little inside. "Let's get her upstairs and comfortable as possible in the study."

Making it up the stairs was awkward. The width of the staircase was not built for three abreast to comfortably climb. The boys squeezed together as close as possible while keeping Aria's comfort in mind. If they weren't thinking of her comfort, Nana's constant reminders on the climb up pounded it in.

* * *

Once they made the two flights to the third floor where the study was, Colby allowed Shelly to step in and support their mother with Jasper. He made his way to the door and cast his hashtag spell to open the portal through the barrier protecting the time-stopped room.

With the way open, Colby took his place back from Shelly and made contact with Jasper's arm. Jasper pulled back a bit in response. "I may need to be touching everyone I lead into the room. I only set this spell to allow myself and Shelly in."

Relaxing at the explanation, Jasper reached his hand over and grabbed Colby's arm below Aria's back. "Lead on."

Colby turned toward the door, hoping to hide his flushed face. He headed for the door but was stopped before entering. The barrier was open, but Aria's feet were not passing through the opening.

"What's the hold-up?" Nana asked.

"Mom's not passing the portal opening."

Nana huffed and waddled up behind them and started pushing on Aria's feet. It was no use. The only thing she managed to accomplish was to raise her own level of frustration and knock a chain and pendant loose from around Aria's neck.

Nana looked down at the necklace that fell. She reached and grabbed it, knowing in an instant what it was. Holding the old skeleton key in her one hand, Nana smacked herself in the head with the other.

Pushing past the boys, Nana grumble for them to move back. She stuck the key in the door and waved her hand a few times, mumbling something. When she turned the key and stepped back, the door swung open and allowed her to enter.

* * *

Inside the room, Nana turned back to the others, hands on hips and smirk on her wrinkled old face. "Well…you gonna stand there all day?"

Without hesitating further, Colby and Jasper carried Aria in and placed her on the leather sofa. After Shelly, Darla, and Rhea entered, the door slammed shut, though Colby's portal spell remained.

"How did you do that?" Colby asked.

Nana just looked at him as though he had asked her how old she was. She lifted the necklace and dangled the key in his face. "Magic boy. What the hell do you think?" She put the necklace back on Aria and stepped back. "You're mother has been wearing this thing since the night your dad left. Figures it would be the way in."

"But she has come in before, and it was just a room. She told me this weeks ago." Shelly said.

"You gotta say the words. Otherwise, you only see a dusty old room. You mother could have come in anytime she wanted."

"She just didn't want to see it the way dad left it." Colby realized at that moment just how deeply his mother was tortured by his father's absence. He wished he'd been more understanding in the past. Her use of alcohol was an escape from the pain. He didn't excuse the abuse, but at least now he had an understanding of it.

"What's that shimmering," Darla said. She pointed to the walls where the barrier of the time bubble was wavering.

Colby pushed past her and held his hand toward the weak area. "Something's wrong with the bubble."

"So do something," Shelly said. "You got the whole time control thing going now to go with your growing gifts." Shelly sounded terser than she meant, but with his continued growth in power, Colby made her feel more insignificant than usual.

"I wouldn't suggest that?" Aria said as she stirred and struggled to lift herself upright. "You haven't the knowledge of your father's spell work to begin to change what has started."

"What's going on mom?" Colby asked.

"I must finish my story, then you will begin to understand."

Aria sat up on the leather sofa, pulling an afghan blanket close and smelling it. She closed her eyes at the memory of her husband as she breathed in his faded scent.

"There's still something I don't understand," Colby started. "Several things actually, but first is why you didn't go insane like the Shizumu who split from the Nefslama ages ago and why you always acted so erratic and drank all the time."

Aria sighed and looked down at the afghan that still held her husband's scent. "First, you should know those old tales of the origin of the Shizumu are inaccurate. Stories do change over time, but truth be told, they came about after the transit between the realms from the Nefslama home to Earth.

"They didn't live there, between the realms, the idea was created there from the Nefslama who suffered a weakness of will to balance their hearts for the good of all. That's how your father explained his theory. Perhaps when you find him, he can tell you more."

Nana grunted, drawing Aria's glare. "There are few others still among the Nefslama who may eventually remember the truth to those stories and more." She looked back at Colby and smiled. "As far as my swings of mental fortitude, let's just say it is due to having a part of your soul ripped out from your being and unable to find it."

"Do the Shizumu tempt your other half?" Colby asked.

"No," she said. "But that isn't what I'm referring to. It was the loss of your father's presence. Imagine what it would feel like to have a big piece of you torn away without knowing where it is and how to reach it. The constant pain of loss and longing for it to return invades all other thoughts, making it impossible to focus. Can you understand that?"

Colby immediately looked at Jasper, remembering when he disappeared from his life so many years ago without warning or reason. "I understand completely." Colby smiled at Jasper who returned the genuine expression.

Colby turned back to his mother who acknowledged his understanding of her dilemma. "I can tell you how greater the sensation and fullness upon its return will make the wait worth the pain."

Aria smiled at her son and looked over to Jasper. "When this is over, I look forward to sharing our hearts joyous reunion stories."

Shelly realized something as she did her best to ignore the mushy sentimentality exchanging beside her. "Now I know why Colby is the one…why he's different."

Colby turned to Shelly, horror on his face as she prepared to out him before he was ready. He wasn't yet even confident about Jasper's feelings or what it all meant.

Seeing Colby's worried face and mirrored anguish on Jasper's, she gasped for a moment and went wide-eyed. She collected herself and gave Colby a reassuring look. "You were conceived under different circumstances than I was."

Relieved and yet confused, Colby sat up and regarded Shelly's proclamation. "What are you getting at?"

"Mom's spirit was released and linked to dad's, so you are a different sort of magic user. Not entirely human, witch or warlock, or whatever…and not quite Nefslama or Shizumu descendent, you're something new."

Aria agreed. "Yes, I was split at the time, and we were also in a time bubble. This time bubble actually. I assume your father put it in place, but it has been deteriorating since your sixteenth birthday." Aria looked at the sofa and caressed the supple material. "As a matter of fact, it was on this very couch."

"Oh gross!" Shelly and Colby both got up from the couch and stepped back. Pursed lips and wrinkled up noses, they shook the images from their minds.

"I did not…need that visual," Shelly said.

Aria laughed along with everyone but Shelly and Colby. As heartening as the moment of joy brought to the room, it was just as quick to become weighed back down as Aria's laughter turned into sobs.

Rhea moved in quickly to check for the return of Aria's fever. "Her temperature seems normal."

"So what's causing these sudden mood swings?" Colby said.

Nana regarded the question before tilting her head and smiling. "You know she is of that age now…"

Aria's last sob choked in her throat as she lifted her head toward her mother. Sad drooping eyes became replaced by a narrow glare and lowered lip that showed Aria's bottom teeth.

Colby saw the look on his mother's face and backed away. He knew from experience that anytime you saw mom's lower teeth outside of a smile, it meant she was pissed.

"Are you insinuating I am starting menopause mother?"

"It's a possibility, and with the other malady-"

"I am not going through the change mother. The only thing wrong with me is the part of me linked to my missing husband." Aria turned to look at Colby. "And he's only missing because we didn't listen to the elders and stop after Shelly."

Colby shook from the verbal blow to the chest. Now he had the truth of it; his mother blamed him for his father's disappearance.

"Don't you listen to her Fart-blossom, she's going through the change alright. Mental-Pause."

Aria was taken in by her own words. As though each syllable bounced off Colby and slapped her back in the face, Aria stung from the backlash. "I'm sorry son, I'm not myself. I didn't mean-"

Colby shook his head and moved in to give Aria a quick, if not awkward, hug. "I know mom. I'll find Dad and get him home no matter what it takes."

"When you find my other half, I will be able to help you. Without your father, I will never feel whole." Aria had faded into unconsciousness before Rhea shook her head to Colby.

"She seems fine from everything I can tell. This is beyond my limited talents for healing Colby. You need to get her soul back together."

Colby let Aria go and turned to thoughts of the spell he knew resided in the journal of his father's. The spell to rebuild the shield circling the planet and filtering out the Emassa could restore things to normal. This option, however, meant the lives of his friends required being sacrifice as well as his own unless he could find another way. His absentminded wandering kept him from realizing that he was holding the journal and tracing the surface of the wheel of time inlaid on its cover. The result of this action was what brought him out of his stupor.

The power of Colby's inadvertent spell pulsed out from the symbol on the journal cover and seeped into the barrier surrounding the room. The ripple that cascaded around the perimeter accompanied a dizziness felt by everyone in the study.

Everyone grabbed hold of the closest thing to steady themselves. For Colby, that was Jasper's arm. They stood there holding each other steady for a few moments after the wave settled, wordless.

Nana cleared her throat and pointed at the barrier when she got Colby's attention.

He smiled nervously at Jasper before letting go and moving over to see what Nana was trying to tell him. "What's wrong?"

"This doesn't look good. I think the time bubble is breaking down faster than before."

"What are you saying? Do we have time to find mom's split soul? Can't we fix it?"

Nana shrugged but said nothing as she moved toward the window. She averted her eyes from the pendant hanging around Colby's neck.

Colby caught a side glance from his grandmother as she walked away. There was something she wasn't saying, and she seemed especially interested in the old pendant that ancient witch gave him. He started after her when the room seemed to shift, and everyone fell to the floor.

* * *

"Oh dear," Nana said from the window.

Colby and the others joined her and soon saw what she was concerned about. Outside the window, it was Halloween, last year. Two goblins ran through the side lot and on the yard perimeter lurked the Dreggs.

"Hey, that means I'm about to start snooping around up here." Jasper headed toward the door to the hall. "Shit, here I come."

"Jasper! Get that door closed, and Colby close your portal." Nana ran toward the door. "He can't be allowed to see us in here."

Colby leaned against the window sill to push off toward the door, and his hand made contact with the barrier. The room shifted again, but in what direction they could not yet tell.

"It's not Halloween anymore," Rhea said from the window. "Looks like we're close to where we left from. Jasper's dad is just getting into his car."

"Okay," Colby said in the middle of the room. "Nobody touch anything."

"You're the time-bubble boy," Shelly snapped.

Colby rolled his eyes at Shelly. "Jasper, can you bring my journal over here please."

Jasper grabbed the journal and ran to Colby's side. They sat together on the floor across from one another, Colby thumbing frantically through the pages while Jasper watched.

Shelly narrowed her eyes at the sight of them and shook her head as she turned back toward her mother. What a mess she thought. Shelly wondered at how long they were going to be stuck in this place.

* * *

"Can't we just leave?"

"Normally, yes," Colby said. "But since the time shifted, we don't want to leave before we've even entered."

"Huh?" This came from all the girls and Jasper. Only Nana seemed to follow Colby's logic.

"He means, that we don't want to run into ourselves out there before they had a chance to enter the room. We could throw everything out of whack!"

"Oh yeah like on Doctor Who," Shelly realized.

Colby stopped looking through the pages and slammed the book shut. He dipped his head in defeat.

Jasper placed his hand on Colby's shoulder. "How can I help. Maybe if we join energy, it could fix the barrier?"

"That won't do, dear boy," Nana said. "I'm afraid that I should never have entered this room in my fractured state."

Colby was more than a little confused by his grandmother's use of that particular phrase. That was until he watched her eyes drift down to the pendant he was absently fondling at that moment. Her fractured reference brought back the last few moments spent with the Goddess, the witch, the elder known as Bellatrix.

# <u>Chapter 7</u>

## **#PendantReturned**

The Shizumu had used Bellatrix's power against her, but somehow the old witch, the Goddess, Bellatrix, she knew what was about to happen. She let herself be destroyed intentionally.

Colby and the others watched in helpless horror as the events unfolded and the magic was drained from the old woman. They may have been able to dispatch the Shizumu, but it was too late.

As Colby held the frail and dying woman in his arms, she passed final words to him and spoke in broken phrases. The one thing that stood out was her repeated use of the word fractured. This was the last whispered word as her body was reduced to dust and scattered to the wind.

Colby returned his thoughts to the present, holding the pendant in his hand which laid over the open journal in his lap. He glanced over at his grandmother, who again tore her eyes away from the artifact. Colby shook his head in doubt.

"What's wrong," Shelly asked as she sat down next to her little brother. When Colby shook his head, Shelly would have none of it. "Don't give me that crap. Something's bothering you. I can tell these things you know." She gave him a googly-eyed look and wiggled her fingers around as though casting a spell.

A slight laugh was all he could manage. "There is nothing in this journal that I understand so far to help fix the time bubble. And I don't know enough of the magic on my own to do anything but make matters worse." He fumbled with the pendant and looked over at Nana. "I think this has something to do with it."

Shaking her head, Shelly grabbed the leather strap from Colby's hand and twirled the pendant before her face. "Nah, this thing is just some old piece of junk jewelry."

Nana moaned and complained of a headache as she watched Shelly whirl around the necklace. Once Shelly and Colby noticed the reaction and Shelly stopped, Nana sat back up, relief showing on her wrinkled old face.

"Maybe not," Colby answered. "Think about how odd Nana has been since the whole magic stuff started. It's gotten way worse since we got back from Mexico."

Shelly thought about it and realized Colby was right. "And what was all that ripping the garden to shreds about? Then suddenly it was replanted and now growing like super-fast. She was also against you 'sparking' her magic, remember."

Colby nodded. "I don't think I ever needed to. I think there's more to our old Nannie than meets the eye."

"You think she's Bellatrix don't you?" Shelly said with doubt, but her eyes betrayed her own thoughts.

"There's only one way to find out," Colby looked at the pendant and then Nana. "But what happens if she is?"

* * *

"We may not have a choice. Looks what's going on Curds, we can use all the help we can get. Even if she is completely batshit crazy, having the power of an Elder would be a plus."

Nana inched her way closer as Colby and Shelly spoke in hushed tones. She eyed the pendant longingly and no longer turned away from it. So transfixed on the powerful stone that called to her from a leather thong held in Colby's hand, she failed to notice they stopped speaking.

"I recognize that," Nana whispered.

"I should think you would, ya nutty old witch. It's belonged to you for longer than the days have been counted." Fizzlewink jumped into the room through the door, not using the portal spell since he knew another way.

"Fizzlewink?" Colby said.

Nana snatched the charm from Colby while he was distracted.

"You see him too?" Shelly said. "Good because I was thinking I would start getting haunted by every dead pet in the city."

"I'm not dead…yet. I was in the form of a cat remember." Fizzlewink shook the dirt from his clothes and frowned at the room of onlookers as he tried to clean up after digging his way out of a grave.

"What's that got to do with anything. I tried to heal you. You were gone." Rhea was already fussing over the cat-man, checking his health.

"Nine lives? That old tale has a bit of truth behind it." Fizzlewink pointed at Nana. "There's a lot we all have to learn about the truths behind myths and magic."

Nana looked up to find all eyes except Aria's fixed upon her. "This is mine. I made this for a spell so very long ago."

"Nana, are you…you?" Colby wasn't sure who to expect as he watched Nana coddling the pendant.

Nana stared at the necklace and stroked it. Her only response was to hum and nod then smile broad and toothy at Colby.

"Oh yeah. Not at all weird," Colby said.

"Hey, at least she isn't tearing things up and rambling like a nutter."

"Shelly, those aren't her fake teeth. She has real teeth now! You don't see that as a bit strange?"

Fizzlewink jumped in between the siblings. He chose to ignore their waving hands and pinched noses directed at the ripe scent of manure and dirt that clung to him. "That's nothing of her full power. We'll have to watch her for things much more subtle than growing new teeth."

Colby breathed through his mouth and coughed. The scent was not much less pungent and left a film of dirt on his tongue. "What are you saying, Fizz? And can you say it from over there?"

Fizz shuffled back from Colby but made sure his narrowed lids and half raised lip expressed his feelings. "Let me go bury you out back and see how well you smell after a resurrection and digging your way out?"

"Who resurrected you?" Rhea asked.

"Oh for the love of Sheba," Fizz said. "Nobody. It's a very ancient and complicated spell I placed on myself a long time ago. Anyone could do it with enough power and talent."

"You mean we could live forever?" Jasper asked. He looked over at Colby and smiled.

"Not exactly. The spirit continues, but if the damage to the body isn't too bad, the spell can replace damaged tissue and regenerate the body. It isn't something that wouldn't have worked since long ago. I think that Colby's growing power allowed it to work again now." Fizzlewink nodded a muted thanks to his charge.

"Too bad, we could have charged a fee for burial and resurrection and made a lot of money," Darla finally said. "I know my little sister has a hamster in our back yard she'd give up all her saved allowance to get back."

Shelly frowned at Darla and sprayed a bottle of perfume at Fizzlewink as she passed him. "First of all, that didn't work out so well in the movies. Second, not a chance in hell I'd let a bunch of snot-nosed rug rats begin burying their dead rodents and goldfish out back." She emptied the bottle spraying the stinky feline. After frowning at the empty bottle, she threw it in a bin and walked around looking for something else to spray. "It stinks enough with one cat coming back from the great beyond. Can you imagine how bad it'll get with more?"

Fizzlewink was not amused. "It doesn't work that way-"

"Not the point smelly cat." Her attempts at downgrading the offensive aroma made things worse. "It smells like the cross between a pasture and Chicago cab in here now."

"What was the point?" Colby asked. "Oh yeah, what's gonna happen with Nana?"

Fizzlewink twisted his head slowly to face the old woman who sat quietly in the corner, admiring the trinket on a string she snatched from Colby's hands. "I'm not certain, but time is not something we have working for us by the looks of your mother." Fizz regarded Aria, gasping and thrashing on the couch.

Colby threw out his hands and forced Emassa out through his fingertips. The resulting energy flowed out in all directions and burst through the time barrier surrounding the study. He realized what he did a moment too late.

"Oops."

"Really?" Shelly said. "That's the best you got? Oops. You didn't just step in a fur-ball or spill a glass of juice cheese-curd. What did you just do?"

"I just reacted. I went to freeze time, hoping to reinforce the barrier, but it just went right through it."

"Outside again," Jasper confirmed from the window. "You know if you keep this up, having a pet resurrection gig in the back will seem mild compared to a yard the defies time and gravity and weather and-"

"Thanks, Jasper, I get it." Colby sat back and put his head in his hands after checking that Aria was ok. "I'm completely at a loss."

"I can guide you." The voice was accompanied by a firm grasp on his shoulder that defied the frail and aged appearance of Nana's hand.

"Oh look, the old bat has returned from obsessing over her precious."

Nana's head spun around faster than a blink as she spoke. "Shut your trap, ghost whisperer. I'll deal with you later."

Colby watched for the first time as Shelly backed down from anyone. The color drained from her already powdered face as she sat down and shut her mouth.

Nana turned back to Colby. "All you have to do is tell me this is mine once again." Nana held the pendant before Colby's face. "Say the words, and I can help."

Colby looked into different eyes as he stared at Nana's face. Already the wrinkles seemed to retreat, and clouded cataracts dissolve. Who was this woman if not his crazy old granny? He could tell it was still her, but there was more to her now. She seemed more substantial in presence but not quite put together. Fractured.

"Say the words to present me with my charm," Nana said with a hint of failing patience.

"It's yours. Take the stupid pendant already." Colby just wanted to be done with the thing and figure out what was going to happen, his own patience wearing thin.

Nana smiled wider for a moment before hesitation pushed her lips into a pucker. She slid her feet back in turn as she backed away from Colby and waited.

Everyone waited. By now the entire room of occupants was entertaining their own wild ideas of what would happen to Nana once she took the pendant. But nothing was going on, at first. Then Nana sat with a resounding thump on the floor and began to sob.

"Oh great," Shelly said. "Now I'm getting a little freaked out. She never cries."

Colby frowned at Shelly as he moved slowly toward his grandmother. The floorboard creaked more loudly the lighter he tried to make his steps. It didn't matter in the end as Nana was completely self-absorbed in her self-recriminations. Colby heard her whispers clearly now that he edged closer. She was blaming herself for everything.

"Nana?" Colby whispered. "Nana, are you okay?"

* * *

She looked up, tears pouring over as the moisture welled in her bloodshot eyes. "It's coming back to me…memories of the horrible things we did…I did."

Colby was unable to determine how best to console her. On the one hand, this was his Nannie, the woman who was responsible for the better part of his upbringing. The other hand held the knowledge of who she really was, Bellatrix the Goddess and mythical mother-witch of the Mayan people.

He still wasn't sure how all this worked with the Emassa and the Elders, those few that remained. It looked, however, that he would soon be finding out. As he pondered the situation, he felt the massive tug on the ancient magic of the universe before he turned back to watch what happened next.

Nana, still blubbering and rocking herself on the floor, stiffened at the sizzling arch of power that flashed around her hand. She opened the white-knuckled fingers that wrapped around her coveted prize pendant and used the other hand to shield her old eyes from the onslaught of light radiating from the polished rune stone.

The leather thong burned away as the pendant rose into the air above Nana's palm. It pulsed and hummed faster-and-faster as more power pulled through Colby and into the awaiting spells now activating.

Colby gasped for air as more and more Emassa was channeled through the core of his power. A faint sizzle added to the hum of the stone as the stench of burning skin and singed hair wafted off of Colby. He was helpless to stop the flow, not because he lacked the knowledge, but because he didn't have the strength. That was until strong arms wrapped around his aching chest from behind, pouring relief and power into his depleted core.

* * *

Ripples of alleviation matched those of the muscled arms Colby ran his fingers across and sighed a deep and satisfying breath. The instant they came in contact with his own body, Colby soaked in the feel of Jasper's arms around him. Colby melted into Jasper's body holding him from behind, collapsing as the last yank of eternal power was shifted through their combined sources of Emassa access.

Colby spared only the briefest smiling glance at his friend before the growing crackle of energy and light drew his eyes toward the frantic old woman beside him.

The pendant chose that moment to burst outward toward its intended target. Nana was its maker, or at least a version of her was. The charm recognized her and flowed without reserve for the center of its predetermined destination.

Time swung wildly in all directions as images of Nana, of Bellatrix in truth, from the past, present, and future coalesced. The thunderous clap that sounded as all those images joined and slammed into Nana's chest knocked everyone onto their collective asses.

Nana's eyes cleared and brightened as she blinked away the stars in her vision. She looked at her hands, arms, legs, and body. Though the disappointment at recognizing the shape of which her body had taken in this life showed on her face, the surprise in her voice meant she was glad she had a body at all.

"What do you know…it worked!"

# <u>Chapter 8</u>

## #Manaba

Nana turned to everyone in the room. Her glee-filled smile began to falter as her eyes cleared and she saw the children in the room before her. That part of herself which now rejoined to rebuild the whole, shook deep within her chest sending a shudder throughout her body.

Looking at each of these exceptional children and the same time feeling the disturbance in the flow of Emassa, Bellatrix began to manifest a dominating presence in the forefront of Nana's mind. Two distinct occupancies in her head, both knowing they were each part of the whole, but neither one willing to surrender to the other.

Bellatrix saw the star children before her as a tool, but Nana allowed her to see them as loved ones. All the broken yesterdays that Bellatrix lived in her multi-time split-presence existence, they all began to close in on her mental existence and show her what those deeds of hers in the past have wreaked over the eons.

It was too much to bear. Nana jumped up from the floor with an agility beyond what someone of her age should have. Without stopping, she pushed past the kids and proceeded to pass right through the barrier without hesitation.

* * *

Immediately after her passing through the barrier, Colby noticed that Nana shimmered in and out of view before disappearing. This confirmed the changes in the barrier and what was happening with the time distortions with two bubbles in place. He wasted little time in getting up to follow her out.

Once he opened his portal to exit the study, Colby resealed it and followed after Nana down the stairs. He knew where to follow her because he could still feel her pulling Emassa from him. He continued to fill his center with power to keep the flow steady enough to remain sufficiently robust enough to walk. The consumption of his energy was constant and strong which worried him about what his newly reconstituted grandmother slash mythical Goddess could do with all that magic.

On his way along the trail of energy tethering him to his grandmother, Colby did his best to block out the throb that developed as a result of the buzz running around his head. So focused on blocking out the noise, he ran past an excited Gary sitting by the machine the Shizumu left behind.

"COLBY!" Gary yelled again but this time reached out and grabbed his friend. "What's going on?"

"I can't stop now. I gotta go after Nana."

Gary watched him as Colby kept going and out through the kitchen. He looked back at his new toy on the floor and grumbled. "That's fine. I'll just stay here and do all the technical work. Just finding out how to get your mother back, nothing important like chasing a half-crazed old bat. By the way, your dead cat just came by…"

Had his hearing been unimpeded, Colby would still have been too preoccupied to hear his friends' sarcastic words. He kept moving through the house and out the back kitchen door before spotting Nana in the side yard near the border of his impromptu time shield.

* * *

Colby felt the tugging on his Emassa easing as he neared her. Once he came to stand next to Nana, the forced pull of power all but ceased.

"I'm sorry I had to do that Fart-blossom. I have adjusted the flow so you'll hardly notice my draw on the Emassa through your link."

Relief shattered the apprehension Colby felt moments before when he heard Nana use her pet name for him. He cared little about her using him to access the source of magic. Colby melted into her embrace when she turned to him with open arms.

"I'm still me sweetheart. There's just a little bit more to me today than yesterday." She started to hum.

Colby hummed along to the old song. "But not as much as tomorrow." He sang the other words to the melody.

Nana laughed. "I'll not say it's gonna be an easy adjustment, but we can talk on that later. Right now, we got more important things to handle."

Colby followed Nana's eyes as she turned to regard the time bubble Colby erected outside the house accidentally. "You mean things like this? I just don't know what I'm doing."

"Yet," Nana assured him. "I can help with that."

Nana stepped back and took Colby's hand in hers. "What we need here is not a time pocket, but one for concealment."

"You call it a pocket, but it's a bubble."

Nana's lips pursed as her head snapped to face Colby. "Don't contradict me when I'm instructing."

Colby stepped back and regarded the harsh tone and manner that came from Nana. She never scolded him like that before. He relaxed a bit, however, when Nana lightened her features and gave his hand a little squeeze.

"Sorry, my boy. I'm still adjusting to the wrestling match going on in my head."

"Will you be ok?"

Nana waved off concern. "Right as rain soon enough. I just have millennia of dirt under my nails, and it'll take a while to clean it out."

Colby tried to look as though he understood what she was talking about. But it seemed no matter the manifestation of Bellatrix over the eons, she must have always been a little bonkers. So he just smiled and nodded before turning back to the problem.

"So what is the difference between a pocket and a bubble?" Nana asked him.

Colby thought for a moment before voicing his answer. "A bubble is a sphere?"

Nana smiled and patted Colby on the fanny. "Almost right. They naturally move toward a sphere shape but can be forced into another. What else?"

"A pocket exists outside of normal space I think."

"Don't think…know."

Again Colby noticed the sharp edge to Nana's voice, but he assumed that was how Bellatrix was used to teaching magic to the youth of her own time. Colby tried to think what answer she wanted but only shrugged.

* * *

Nana huffed and waved her hand. The ground rose up and began to shift. The grass faded away, and the rich brown soil turned into a dull gray as stone replaced the dirt. Where there was once flat grassy yard, now sat a stone bench crafted from the earth with the wave of an old woman's hand.

"Sit," Nana commanded. "Your father should be here teaching you these basics before sending you to me, but that can't be helped I suppose." Her voice shifted between the crackling hiss of old age, to the resounding and authoritative vibrato of a Nefslama elder.

Colby sat down and waited patiently for Nana to tell him what she expected him to know. He was nervous because of Nana's unpredictable mood but excited to learn something new.

Nana looked at Colby for a moment before considering how best to explain to him what she knew without thinking about such things. She reached down and pulled a leaf from the ground and held it before Colby's face. She then slid the foliage into the front pocket of her housecoat.

"That is a pocket. Somewhere to store something to keep it safe, or dry, or hidden, and so on. It is as you say outside regular space in a way. It is concealed in the folds of the fabric." Nana smiled as Colby's face brightened with understanding.

"So a pocket doesn't exist outside of normal space, it resides in the folds. Then space, being a fabric of sorts, can be torn and that's how the Nefslama traveled to Earth from another dimension."

"Who's the smartest Fart-blossom around," Nana said. She rustled Colby's hair and smiled. "Now how does a pocket become a bubble?"

Colby thought for a moment before turning back and smirking. "You make it expand beyond the folds of the space fabric."

"Part right. You can create a bubble by accident or by design." Nana withdrew to her own thoughts briefly before turning her attention back to Colby. "I would suggest avoiding the first way in the future, my boy."

"So how would I go about creating one by design?"

"A bubble in time," Nana said with a wink. "You have already done that by mere instinct, but without control. That will come with more understanding of your affinity to time and space magic. Other bubbles may be used to conceal something. Any time you wish to do something that would disrupt the normal flow of space or time, a bubble is required to curve the flow back along its natural path.

"We could talk for weeks on this subject alone and not have scratched our asses on the fine points. We have far too much to worry about right now so let's skip ahead, shall we? I will give you the runes to transform your time bubble here into a concealment shield. You put those into your little gizmo watch thingy and let 'er rip!"

"Isn't that cheating?" Colby asked as he looked at his watch. "I mean I should be able to do this without Hashtag Magic."

"Nonsense. Any charm, pendant, wand or enchanted device is a shortcut. Just because you have to use your computers and gadgets doesn't mean you are cheating. Different tools for a different age my boy. Now just put these in your do-dad there and let's get back to work."

Nana drew out the runes in the dirt at her feet while Colby watched. When she was done, she looked at Colby as though he should know what they were.

"Well…aren't you gonna put these into your watch and conjure the time bubble you hastily erected earlier?"

* * *

Colby shrugged. "Hashtag Magic is down since that Shizumu, Koyaanisqatsi, left through the portal."

Nana laughed and smirked at Colby. "First, that isn't his name more than a description of what he represents. Imbalance of life from war and destruction mostly. Second, that Tinkertoy he left behind is not blocking your computer magic anymore."

Colby checked, and sure enough, the watch was working and connected to the primary AI server. "How did you know, some kind of witch sense?"

Again Nana laughed. "Only the sense to listen to my friends when they need me to listen." It was evident by the blank stare that Colby didn't understand what she was talking about. "Gary was trying to tell you he managed that much with the device as you came running out after me."

Now Colby felt a pinch in his chest for having ignored Gary. In fact, he hadn't considered his friend being left behind with the device while the others were all upstairs in the study.

"I'll stop to talk with him when we go back in the house." Colby looked at Nana and realized she was referring to something of her own experience not listening to a friend. "What happened when you didn't listen to a friend?"

Nana looked at Colby without expression of emotion. She slowly turned the other way and lowered her head. "It was the biggest mistake of my very long life thus far and the reason I split myself across time." She turned back to Colby, tears flowing from her eyes. "Against the advice of a wise and dear friend, I helped create the shield that filters the Emassa."

"You sacrificed your children to block out the Emassa?" Colby just blurted it out. He jumped from his seat and spun around on Nana still sitting on the earthen bench.

The place crumbled to dust as Nana stood and stepped back from Colby. After only a few small shuffling steps backward from Colby, Nana's face twisted in contempt as her lip raised to one side and her eyes narrowed.

"You were not there, child. You have no idea what was happening in this world when the first sacrifices were made. Those children chose their fate for the sake of those lives that would be saved for future generations."

Nana cut the distance between her and Colby in the blink of his eye. He cowered under the force of power she willed upon him with her cold stare.

"The Koyaanisqatsi, life out of balance, was too far gone to simply ignore and do nothing. For many uncountable human generations, we watched and kept our way to not interfere. The time came when we could no longer look beyond the effects the Shizumu were having on the human race. We had to act; so we went to war."

Colby exhaled as Nana backed away. He hardly realized he was holding his breath until the pounding in his ears became unbearable. When Bellatrix took over, it was like riding a freight train down a toboggan slide. Excessive force and power radiated from Nana's body and barreled toward whoever was in its path. The other effect was the power she used funneling through him. It was like a gas pocket caught within his chest above his heart, and someone was trying to pull it out all at once.

Colby forced himself to remain standing as he caught his breath. He knew that Nana was battling with this other side of herself. He had his own battles and understood the difficulty she was facing.

"What happened before the war?" Colby wanted to keep her talking in hopes that it would calm her down.

* * *

The Bellatrix side of Nana grunted and shifted her weight. "For millennia we lived on the edges of humanity, fostering their development. There were many jumps in advancement and some great progress, but inevitably the Shizumu infested mankind with their own dark desires and base instincts.

"The humans we encountered when first we arrived in this world were of good nature. They were kind and caring for everyone and everything. They lived as one with the world and respected life as well as the natural giving of life required for their own survival. That changed when the Shizumu tempted a young man with power and knowledge. That led to desire and jealousy as well as all the other deadly sins as you may know them.

"We left that part of the world and headed west. Eventually, the whole of what is now Europe and Asia became corrupt and barbaric. The council of Elder Nefslama was weak and unwilling to do anything about the Shizumu scourge so we left for the Americas where we found a peaceful people, but that too did not last either."

"The Shizumu followed you here?" Colby asked. He felt the anguish that showed on Nana's face. The feeling of helplessness rebounded back along the line of power that ran between them. "You couldn't have stopped them from coming."

Nana bit her tongue and held back her irrational need to thrash out. Instead, a bitter laugh escaped her clenched teeth. "We could have stopped a great many things, had we learned from our own past. The further from the lessons of failure you travel along the road of success, the blinder you become at seeing the folly of ignorance that follows." Nana saw the blank look on Colby's face and tried another witty statement. "You must heed the trails you blaze in the name of advancement lest they lead you back into the fire."

"What's that supposed to mean?"

*  *  *

"It means that you should never forget to fix past mistakes, or they'll come back and bite you in the ass." Those words were heard from Nana's unmistakably sarcastic voice. "Now let's fix this bubble of yours."

Colby entered the runes into his phWatch and worked out how they would combine with others to form the cloaking shield around the property. Time would return to normal everywhere except in the study, but the Stevens' home and yard would prevent anything magical from being detected outside the remade bubble.

"Get the lead out Fart-blossom, Nana's got stuff to do." She looked over at the new hole in the yard next to the garage. "You think that mangy dwarf-mage cat could have filled his grave back in?"

Colby stopped just before casting the hashtag spell. "What did you call him?"

"Dwarf-mage…this is gonna be an adjustment getting all these memories back. Some are better than others, particularly where the Shizumu are involved."

"You know you aren't responsible for the Shizumu. They chose their own path." Colby cast the spell and extended his arm out and palmed the bubble. The energy rippled along the bubble and converted it into a concealment shield.

Colby accepted the hug from Nana as they both watched time running at normal speed outside the yard.

Nana looked at Colby and sighed. "I could have done more to stop them in the beginning when they first manifested. Instead, I went along with the rest of those old fools in choosing to ignore the situation and hope it went away." Nana wiggled her finger at Colby. "That never works you know."

* * *

"So instead the Shizumu got stronger and grew in numbers, but how?"

Nana turned away from Colby and looked around the yard outside the bubble. Her eyes were locked with a Dregg hiding in the shadows beyond the tree line. "You really don't understand where all this started do you?"

Colby looked in the direction Nana watched. He saw Conrad staring back at his grandmother. Several others also lined the perimeter of the yard. "What's going on Nana, or Bellatrix. What am I supposed to call you?"

Nana turned back to Colby. "I'm still your Nana and always will be." She pulled Colby into another hug. "We have a lot to prepare for and too many distractions." She let him go and went back to examining the bubble as they walked back toward the kitchen door.

"What are we preparing for?"

"Manaba," Nana answered.

"That's what the Shizumu called you."

Nana laughed, but there was no mirth in the short outburst. "That was not a name, but a warning my boy."

"So what does it mean?"

Nana turned back to Colby and looked him directly in the eye and pointed toward the Dreggs before standing up straight. "War returns with her coming."

# <u>Chapter 9</u>

## #BurntSausage

Gary sat up against the wall and huffed in frustration at the puzzling device sitting on the floor before him. The actual purpose of the instrument eluded him, though he felt there was something familiar about its design. He was certain he never saw anything like it, yet at the edges of his understanding, there was something tugging at his awareness when he stared at the thing.

It didn't help that he was distracted by thoughts of what was happening both upstairs and out in the yard. When Nana passed by, she stopped only briefly and looked him over, nodded, and headed out back. When Colby followed shortly after, Gary's friend didn't even stay long enough to hear about his progress.

When Jasper suggested that Gary should stay behind and figure out the electronic device, it felt like a dismissal. Gary knew that he was best assigned the duty of figuring out how the machine worked and what it did, but that didn't stop him from feeling as though he took a few steps back from Colby. He felt like he was being replaced by Jasper now that he was back in the picture.

Where has Jasper been all these years while Colby needed a friend? Just when Jasper left Colby alone, Gary showed up. Gary was there every time

Colby needed him somehow sensing unknowingly that he should show up. Gary couldn't think of a single time that he wasn't right there the moment Colby required his support except now.

Colby and Gary had always been there for each other. Colby and the Stevens were more family to Gary than his own parents. Gary's mother and father were always off somewhere, and he never saw them. In fact, as Gary thought about it, he had trouble even picturing their faces. The harder he tried to envision them, the blurrier the visions got to the point he started to have a headache.

Gary held his head as the throbbing subsided. He felt the trickle of blood run down from his nose before he saw it drip on his bent knees. He jumped back when a tissue appeared before his face.

"You might want to concentrate a little less if it's causing nose bleeds Mr. Connor," Rigel said.

"Rigel! When did you get here and how?"

Rigel shoved the tissue closer to Gary until he took it. "Only a few moments ago. As to how I took a cab."

Gary wiped his nose and then wadded up the tissue to stuff up his nostrils. "No I mean how did you get past the time bubble?"

Rigel raised his left brow, acknowledging that interesting things were happening around the Stevens' home. He stared at the portal and then the device on the floor. "There was no time bubble as you call it, only a shield to obscure what lay within."

Gary shrugged. "Colby and Nana must have fixed it then. They went out back a little while ago."

"And where are the others?"

"A lot has happened since we left the airport. Long story short, Mrs. Stevens got her soul sucked into this portal by a Shizumu dude that was wearing some guy's body from MacroTech. He's dead, and Mr. Bodine took his body to stage a coverup. The others are up in Mr. Stevens' study hoping the time bubble protecting it will help Mrs. Stevens survive until we can figure all this out."

Rigel rubbed his chin but remained otherwise expressionless. "Indeed. And what are you doing here, besides mumbling about your parents."

"I wasn't…I'm trying to figure this thing out."

Gary pointed at the device and turned to look at it. Something changed since the last time he gazed at the machine. There seemed to be a pattern of color swirling on the LED touch screen on top of it.

Gary moved closer, but as he did the movement on the screen subsided. Gary pushed on the screen and flipped a few of the switches he already determined were decoys. Nothing happened. "I don't get it?"

"What seems to be the issue, Mr. Connor?"

"The only thing I've been able to determine is how to shut off the part of this thing that blocks electronics." He pointed then to the swirling vortex of light near the wall. "As far as anything else it does including that portal, I just can't figure out the mechanics."

Rigel turned from the device to Gary and looked at him carefully before responding. "Do you not feel the Emassa?"

"What?"

"The power of all magic. You should be able to feel it coming off of this contraption."

* * *

Gary paused to consider Rigel's words. Rather than attempt to answer a question he simply didn't understand, he moved closer to the device. Gary held his hand over the screen as though checking for heat over a flame. Before backing away, he checked the corner of his vision to see Rigel staring at him, inspecting him.

"I don't have Colby's gift. I don't feel the Emassa like he does."

"My mistake. I thought you all had access to it now directly. But you are wrong on at least the first count. You have Colby's gift with computers it would seem."

Gary was confused by the statement or was it a question he didn't know. "Anyway, I can still use the Emassa. So if this thing uses magic, that would make sense why I've been having such a hard time with it."

Rigel shook his head and sat back on a chair at the dining table. "What were you thinking about when I entered? Oh yes, your parents. Tell me about them."

Rigel immediately saw what he was expecting. The moment he mentioned Gary's parents, the screen on the device began to swirl with color. It also appeared that Gary's face seemed to drain of color at the same moment.

"What do you mean?"

Rigel leaned forward. "Just tell me the first thing that comes to mind when you think about your parents."

The portal faltered and grew for a brief moment before settling back to its previous state. The device, however, displayed an increasingly erratic pattern of color and light on the touch screen.

* * *

Rigel raised his left brow and continued to watch the device, Gary, and the portal.

Gary turned to the portal, a brief sound drawing his attention. He thought he heard someone call his name. He was prepared to dismiss the notion as a result of his stress and aggravation until he heard it again.

"Gary," the faint voice called.

"Did you hear that?" Gary asked.

"I don't hear anything." Rigel leaned closer to Gary. His eyes remained transfixed on the young man rather than the portal. "What do you sense?"

"I don't sense anything," Gary was frustrated at Rigel. "I 'hear' a voice whispering my name."

"Gary," the voice whispered again.

Rather than argue with the pestering Professor, Gary moved closer to the vortex. "Hello?"

"Gary, come to us."

The voice felt familiar, yet Gary couldn't place it. The pleading tone called him closer.

"We need your help son."

"Mom? Dad?" Gary said before realizing. He turned to see Rigel staring at him, but it seemed he did not hear Gary's words. He turned back to the portal and knew instantly what he must do.

Now that Hashtag Magic was up and running again, he was able to throw a spell at it. **#OpenForPassage.**

The portal shifted to a swirling purple then widened before the swirling stopped and was replaced by a pulsing angry red color.

Gary, not ready to test the passage himself picked up an apple left laying on the floor from the earlier excitement, and threw it into the portal.

The apple flew past the event horizon and disappeared while emitting a sizzling hiss.

"That didn't sound pleasing," Rigel said.

Gary jumped at the sudden proximity of the professor now standing directly behind him. He got up and went for other objects if nothing more than to put some distance between Rigel and himself.

"Maybe it isn't meant for food to pass? I'll try something else." Gary took a fork and prepared to toss it in when Rigel took his wrist and stopped him.

"Let me see that."

Rigel took the fork from Gary and added a piece of sausage from the table. Stabbing the sausage with the fork, he pushed it halfway into the vortex and then pulled it back out. The end of the sausage that returned from beyond the entry was shriveled, and blackened then turned to dust and fell away.

"Looks like this isn't meant for physical transportation."

# <u>Chapter 10</u>

## #DialUpModem

Nana and Colby walked past Nana's regrowing plants and both looked at them and shook their heads as the approached the back door.

"Can you help fix the time bubble around dad's study?"

Colby was hopeful after the success he had adjusting the shield around the house. Nana gave him the necessary runes, and now that he understood them, he hoped that something could be done for the destabilizing spell surrounding the room his mother lay suffering inside.

Nana paused when they entered the kitchen from the back door. She went to the sink and poured a glass of water from the tap.

"I'm certain that there isn't anything wrong with the spell. It is your father's work and unlikely to have a fault in its construction."

"Yeah, but maybe I did something to mess it all up?"

"I don't think so Fart-blossom." Nana halted her speaking as she grabbed her head and sighed. She moved to a stool and sat down. "I'm forgetting something."

* * *

"What is it, Nana?"

"So much is fading in and out. I know who I am and was, but the many are fighting to become the one."

Clomping on the back steps from upstairs accompanied Shelly's voice. "It's just the old parts of your brain failing to become one with your tongue." Shelly entered the kitchen and went to the fridge. She pulled out a pitcher of water and set it on the counter.

"Why are you down here?" Colby asked. "Has something happened with Mom?"

Shelly shook her head. "No, she's still a drooling slug. Rhea needs something to drink and eat. That girl's gonna burn herself out." For a moment there was a hint of admiration in her voice. But then she looked at Nana. "Too bad the old witch isn't firing on all cylinders. We could use the help up there."

Nana lowered her hands and turned to Shelly, fire in her eyes. She raised her right hand and drew a rune with her finger, flames licking after her nail as she went. The rune hung in the air before her until she whispered to it.

Colby sucked in his breath as Shelly shimmered into a wispy apparition. "What did you do, kill her?"

Nana laughed. "Blessed no. This is my modern mix with the ancient version of a time-out. That saucy little she-devil...she needs to learn some respect."

Colby shuddered, but he sort of understood. "I'm gonna go check on the others."

Nana just smiled back and waved him along. "You do that Fart-blossom.

I'll be along when I've collected my-selves." She turned to where Shelly vanished.

The kitchen went dark around Shelly. She no longer felt the counter beneath her hand or the floor beneath her feet. She could make out the wispy outlines of her former surroundings, but they were now ghostly impressions. She reached out to them and connected with nothing. When Shelly turned back from watching Colby leave, her eyes locked with Nana's wicked grin and she screamed.

"That won't solve anything, my dear," Nana said. She picked up a knife and then an apple from the basket next to her. As she sat there peeling the apple, she waited for Shelly to calm down. When at last the silent tantrum abated, Nana joined Shelly in the spell.

Nana faded from normal vision as though she was dissolving. Shelly thought she was disappearing from view until her form stepped closer and suddenly became opaque.

"Are you ready to begin showing some respect for your old granny now?"

"What have you done to me?" Shelly controlled her tone, through clenched teeth.

"Teaching you how to have a private chat without others overhearing. You have inherited the ability to sense shifted realities from me. It's time you learn to do something with that gift beside talk to dead folk."

It was the first time Shelly heard there was something useful about her gift beside being a medium. "Is that what you want to talk about? Why do we need the secrecy?"

"The demonstration is part of your lesson. The secrecy is what I need to tell you about your brother and his friend."

* * *

"I don't think that Jasper and Colby's…well it isn't our business."

"I'm not talking about Jasper," Bellatrix said using Nana's mouth. "It's Gary that is a bit off if you ask my discerning eye."

"What do you mean? I can see the jealousy simmering now that Jasper is taking much of Colby's attention away from him, but Gary is…well, just Gary."

"Is he?" Bellatrix asked. "Is he just Gary, as you say?"

Shelly gasped. "Do you mean that he is a Shizumu spy?"

Bellatrix laughed and shook her head. "Nothing quite so obvious, otherwise I'd have seen it sooner and that would be too simple an explanation. No, what I sense is far deeper and somehow obfuscated from my vision."

"What then?"

Patting Shelly on the hand, Bellatrix began describing how to perform the spell to walk between realms of perception to her granddaughter. Once she was certain Shelly had the hang of the enchantment, Nana returned and the spell shifted them back into the corporeal plane.

"Use that and do a little…eavesdropping."

### 

Gary couldn't get the image of the incinerated sausage out of his mind as he worked through possible rune combinations. He wanted to attempt altering the portal. There would be no way of following after the Shizumu and Aria's spirit if they all got cremated as they passed the event horizon.

* * *

Drawn to the mixture of lights on the display, Gary leaned in closer to the device. There was a pattern there. It was faint, barely noticeable, but then Gary had Colby's gift with computers and electronics. Thinking about that, what Rigel had said, Gary paused to wonder why he seemed to know this as inherent. He did draw his ability from Colby, but why.

This was a question to answer another time. Right now Gary noticed something deeper in the patterns from the device. Raising his phWatch before him, he entered a hashtag spell. **#Translate**.

Squelching and beeping filled the room. Gary covered his ears against the onslaught of noise emanating from the now prevalent flashes of patterned light on the device's screen. He turned to see Rigel laughing.

"What's so funny," Gary asked. He kept his hands against his ears. "What?"

Rigel gesticulated his response by moving his hands against his head and lowering them.

Gary realized he still covered his ears and could not hear Rigel's answer. He removed his hands but cringed and the noise still screeching from the box.

"What are you laughing about?"

"You."

"Whatever." Gary turned back to the device and added a new spell. **#Quieter**.

The noise remained but was now subdued and bearable.

"You know what this noise is then?"

* * *

"That is the handshake signaling of a dial-up modem," Rigel said.

Gary turned back to the device. "That's really old-school."

"A matter of one's experience I suppose." Rigel was neither amused or insulted by the age reference. He was thousands of years old. Old school to him was the invention of the wheel.

"So what does it mean?"

"Well back in the stone age of computers, it would have said that the device was waiting to establish a connection from another instrument," Rigel smirked.

Gary had an idea. **#AnswerTheModem**.

After a few final buzzes and beeps, the noise stopped, and the screen displayed a symbol, The Wheel of Time, Colby's logo for the Hashtag Magic app. The symbol faded and lines of runes scattered across the screen before they scrolled past.

"Again…not what I was expecting." Gary scratched his head and looked at his phWatch. The symbols rolled across his display as well. Then the screen went black, and his phWatch rebooted.

"What has happened Mr. Connor?" Rigel asked the question, but in such a way that implied he suspected the answer.

"Um…I think I just uploaded Hashtag Magic to the Shiz network."

Rigel laughed. "Interesting label for the place."

"What?"

"Never mind that. What are you going to do about entering the portal?"

* * *

Gary thought about the question and then looked at his phWatch. "Well, I suppose we could find a way to transfer our consciousness?"

Rigel shook his head. "That would leave you vulnerable to the Shizumu who might be lurking just outside."

"Not if we protect ourselves somehow."

"There are few things a Shizumu is not crafty enough to get past."

"I know of something they would never get past." Gary smiled, but then grimaced when he thought about how Nana would react to his suggestion.

Gary headed toward the kitchen, when he walked past Nana and Shelly, they gave him an awkward smile. "Have you seen Colby?"

"Oh didn't he come talk to you?" Nana asked.

"No," Gary said. His face gave away his frustration with Colby's ignorance to his need for attention. "Never mind him then. I'll be outside." Gary headed out the back door.

"I still don't see anything?" Shelly said.

Nana smiled and returned to the sliced apple on the counter. "You will. It's much easier to see the truth in things when you aren't observed watching them happen."

# Chapter 11

## #StirConfusion

Colby walked back into the study and found himself headed directly for Jasper. When his conscious mind took back control, he took a full turn toward the window to feign interest in what was happening outside.

"The outside shield is fixed. How's my mom?" Colby took the water pitcher he brought from the kitchen and poured a glass for Rhea.

"She is stable, but it will be exhausting work to keep up with her if she doesn't start to get better soon." Rhea drank the contents of the glass in a single turn. When she finished, she handed the glass back to Colby for a refill.

After getting another drink for Rhea, Colby sat down by his mother and began patting her forehead with a damp cloth. Though he wore the concern over his mother's predicament on his face like a mask, his thoughts were of Jasper and the growing connection that was distracting them both. He looked over toward the desk where Jasper sat and smiled.

Rhea watched Colby through the bottom of her emptying glass and followed his line of sight. When she saw the subject of his split attention, she coughed on her last swallow of water.

* * *

Colby was oblivious to anything else in the room and did not hear Rhea. He continued to gaze at Jasper, the light from the window casting an ephemeral backlight to his striking face. When Jasper turned and cast a sheepish grin back at Colby, a shudder ran through him.

Jasper rested his eyes on Colby for only a moment before snapping out of his own daydream. He turned to Rhea who held an unreadable expression. Flushing heat flowed down his forehead and across his face. Jasper turned away from Rhea and hustled to the door.

"I'm gonna go check how Gary is doing with that machine." Jasper barely met Rhea's eyes as he exited.

"Just swallowed wrong. Not gonna choke to death or anything." Rhea turned back to Colby who was now acutely aware that she and Darla were also still in the room.

Colby turned away and began mopping the no longer present sweat from his mother's brow. His heart was thumping in his chest so hard that he couldn't hear Darla's voice, but he felt her standing in front of him. Colby tried looking up at her, but his nerves were on edge, and Colby felt the blood rushing to his face. Though he knew Darla was aware of his true feelings for Jasper, it was another thing to be embarrassed in front of her. That now included Rhea. So drawn into himself and his feeling of rejection and humiliation, Colby failed to sense the Emassa spreading out from his fingers.

The power flowed off his hand like liquid. It reached his fingertips before free-falling down onto his mother's forehead. There the emulsified magic soaked into her pores and caused her skin to glow. Aria's eyes began to move beneath closed lids much as they would if she were in REM sleep.

Colby's eyes focused on Darla to witness her horrified expression. He cast a glance toward Rhea to find the same shock on her face. Without looking down, Colby scooted from holding his mother's head in his lap and pushed past Darla and Rhea, giving no mind to their protests. He left the room, picking up speed as he passed the threshold of the barrier surrounding the study.

"What just happened?" Darla said as she joined Rhea already checking on Aria. "What did he do to her with that leak of Emassa?"

Rhea checked Aria's pulse and probed her overall wellbeing using her magic. "I'm not sure, but she seems to be completely stable now and resting. I'm surprised considering how embarrassed he looked when he saw us witness his exchange with Jasper."

Darla waved Rhea's comment off. "He'll get over it. I'm more worried about how Jasper is gonna be acting. He's just not yet ready to give Colby the kind of friendship he wants."

"I don't think Colby understands what he wants either." Rhea stepped back from Aria and pulled Darla by the arm. "I think it's safe to leave her for a bit. Let's go see where everyone else has gone."

"You know time works different in this room, what's the hurry?"

"Yeah, it goes slower in here. They've been gone longer than you think."

Everyone was gathered in the dining room when Darla and Rhea joined them. Nobody spoke as they looked around, noticing evidence of the events that occurred leaving a mess of food and dishes scattered, no visible sign it even happened remained. The room was immaculate.

"Time must be moving much slower up there for you guys to get this all cleaned up so well," Darla said.

"We didn't clean the room," Jasper answered. "We just found it this way." He looked at the one odd thing in the chamber. Nana was sitting at the table talking to Shelly in hushed tones. Shelly glanced at him with a knowing in her eyes but quickly turned back to Nana.

Colby moved toward Jasper then but could say nothing before Gary interrupted.

"Never mind the room. I've made some progress with the device that Shizumu left behind."

Everyone gathered closer, and Nana allowed Shelly to break from their conversation. Although Colby was interested to know what they were talking about, it was evident from Shelly's avoidance of him, that she wasn't going to tell him. Those two never spoke in low voices; that sent a shiver along Colby's spine.

"The device is a portal as we all know," Gary started. "But where that portal goes is the big question." He moved the device to the center of the now cleared dining table, much to the gasps of those around him. "It's safe enough to move. The device is drawing power from a crystal in a compartment here on the side. When we want to shut it off, all we need to do is remove it, but if we want to go after Mrs. Stevens, we need to leave this thing on for now."

"So how do we get in? That portal opening is barely large enough for a grapefruit." Jasper spoke with doubt hanging on every word. He looked at Gary as though he wasn't helping the group. "This is supposed to be your specialty, Connor."

"I'm getting to that Jasper," Gary snapped. "We can't just jump into the portal anyway, so the size of the event horizon is not relevant."

Colby moved closer to the vortex of swirling light and mist as he listened to Gary describe the device. He began to lift his hand and push his palm toward the portal, feeling the energy on his hand. As Colby reached closer, a tingling started to affect his wrist. It felt as though thousands of minuscule pinpricks were assaulting him from around the watch band he wore. The timepiece began to slide on his wrist away from the vortex.

The room grew quiet as Gary stopped speaking and all eyes were on Colby. This drew his attention away. He waved off concern as he took off his father's watch and massaged his wrist. Nodding at Gary to continue, Colby wondered at the odd behavior of the watch.

"As I was saying, we can't just jump into the field." As a way of demonstration, Gary picked up a fork with a piece cf sausage on the end. Repeating Rigel's experiment, he showed the others what would happen when organic matter passed the event horizon. The sizzling and charred link and fork were enough to get his point across.

"So what is the alternative?" Colby asked. "Is there a spell to protect us that you found?"

"No. There is no spell to allow our physical forms to enter the portal that I could discover."

"So, in other words, Gary, you've not helped at all." Jasper rolled his eyes and sat back, folding his arms over his puffed out chest.

"Jasper, shut up," Darla said. "You haven't let him finish." She turned to Gary. "You have more to share I hope."

"Yes Darla, I have more to share if I could finish without being interrupted." Gary glared at Jasper who snarled in return. "We have to each send our consciousness into the portal while our bodies remain behind."

Now that he had everyone's attention, Gary was able to explain how he discovered the device would allow energy through the portal as it would the Shizumu. The consciousness was nothing more than a for of energy in his summation so they should be able to transfer themselves that way.

* * *

"Should be able to? That isn't very reassuring," Rhea said. "Have you tested this?"

"Well…no, but it is the best I got unless you want to split yourself from your soul and send a Shizumu form in."

"No," This came from Shelly before Colby could open his mouth. "No one is going to perform that spell." She looked directly at Colby.

Colby felt oddly comforted by Shelly's protective stance. He also noticed the exchange she had with Nana and the odd timing of her finally speaking up. "Shelly's right. We can't do that and leave ourselves open to Shizumu influence."

"And what if this mind transfer thing does work," Jasper said. "What does leaving our bodies here help if they decide to attack. This could be exactly what they want."

"It is not likely all they wanted, but sometimes you have to give your enemy what they want to fool them into giving up what you are after." Rigel sat quietly in the corner until now. "Is there something you're forgetting to mention Mr. Connor?"

Even Fizz perked up. He sat brooding over the developments with Nana and discovering who she was. Now, understanding more of the powers converging and Rigel's comment, he could put aside his own issues momentarily.

Jasper turned to Gary. "What did you do?"

"Um…I sort of uploaded Hashtag Magic into the Shiznet. It was an accident."

"What?" Colby looked at his phWatch and focused his mind on the

Emassa. He could sense the trail of energy being pulled from all of the devices in the room and leading to the portal. "How?" he demanded.

Gary told them.

"Figures. Colby needed you to do one thing, and you still messed that up."

"Jasper!" Darla said.

"No Darla. We're all upstairs trying to figure out how to keep Mrs. Stevens' body around, while he was down here giving away our magic."

"Oh really Jasper," Gary seethed. "You just joined this group recently after being an asshole for several years when you abandoned your best friend. Now you're back suddenly while your father was the 'unwilling' host to our enemy?"

Colby remained transfixed on the argument, not saying a word.

Shelly and Nana watched him.

"Well, at least my father is free of the Shizumu now and is helping us. That's more than I can say about your parents that are never around. Not even they can stand to be around you!"

Gary turned to Colby, anguish in his eyes. His stare pleading for support, but Colby offered none. Gary's face twisted in rage as he stood. Seeing the watch Colby coveted of his father's on the table, Gary grabbed it and threw it at the portal as he turned to run from the room. Gary never turned to see the timepiece reach the entrance and rebound in a flash of light and sparks.

Rigel, already standing, reached down and retrieved the watch for Colby. "This is what they want you to know. They will break you all down if you let them." Reluctantly, he handed the watch to Colby.

"He had it coming," Jasper spat.

"That is enough Jasper Bodine," Nana said. "You will deal with Gary As Colby has dealt with your past behavior."

"Well all this testosterone and posturing aside, are we really considering sending our minds into that thing?" Darla pointed at the portal.

Colby shrugged. "I don't see any other option. We'll just have to find a means of protecting our vulnerable state in this realm while we travel to theirs."

"Gary had an idea about that as well," Rigel said and smirked. Then he looked at Nana. "But he doesn't think everyone is gonna like it."

"Spit it out yummy-pants," Nana said, knowing that Rigel disliked the nickname.

Rigel grinned and nodded at the jibe. "Gary suggests we have the Dreggs, stand guard."

# <u>Chapter 12</u>

## #DreggOrigin

"Absolutely not!" Fizzlewink said. "I can deal with a lot of the crazy going on here lately, but those beasts in the house is quite another matter."

What exactly his problem with the Dreggs was, Colby knew. He hadn't explained it to the others since it was Fizzlewink's painful story to share. But the look that Colby now saw on Nana's face told him there was more to be said about their history.

"They will provide security around the perimeter of the house," Nana said, "It will not be necessary for more than one to remain inside and watch over your sleeping bodies."

"What?" Fizzlewink yowled. "You can't be serious? You know what those monsters did. Who knows what-"

"Enough dwarf-mage. We will speak about this privately later."

The look Nana gave Fizz silenced his unspoken words, but he did not look pleased from what Colby could tell. He felt for the furry little man, but need outweighed his desire to agree with Fizzlewink. "How do you know they will even help?"

* * *

"They will do as I command, as all my children obey." Nana winked at Shelly and left the room. "I'll take care of the guards, you all prepare yourselves for your journey."

"What do you suppose that means?" Darla asked, looking at Shelly.

"Let's just get some pillows and blankets together so we are not laying on the hard floor when we go to sleep," Shelly said. "There are some air mattresses in the garage with the camping stuff."

"I'll go check on your mother and see where Gary went." Rhea left the others and headed back upstairs where she suspected Gary stormed off. She checked everywhere on her way up, but there was no sign of him. She didn't find him in the study either.

Putting Gary's issues aside, Rhea focused on her worry for Aria. The woman was pale and her skin clammy. Though her heart rate was stable and breathing steady, she would continue to fade if they did not rejoin her spirit-self to her physical body.

"She'll be fine while you're gone, my dear. I'll see to that."

Rhea was startled by Nana's sudden appearance by the window. She had not heard her enter, nor did she see her there when she came in. "Were you there when I entered?"

"Never mind that child. What is your assessment of my daughter's current state?"

Rhea squinted at Nana as she shuffled closer. "She's stable for now, but there's no way to determine how much time we have. I should stay with her."

"Time…interesting concept. Anyway, you are needed far more by your friends than here with my daughter. There is strength in numbers, especially you children."

"Don't you mean 'Star Children'?" Rhea asked. "That is what you elder's keep calling us."

Nana was surprised by Rhea's question, and though she tried to disguise it, Rhea caught the moment she hoped for. "It's an old title linked to old ways. We shall endeavor to correct that."

Rhea wasn't going to let her off that easy. "The title of those sacrificed to shield the Emassa? Would that title not still apply if that is our purpose as well?"

"Things change my dear, and I'm afraid the choice, this time, is not in my hands."

"Whose choice is it then?"

"Uncertain. Enough of this. The time spent in this dusty old room has left the others awaiting you downstairs. Off you go."

"I was hoping to find Gary and drag him back downstairs."

"Gary will be where he's needed, when he's needed. He always has been."

###

The living room was staged much like a teenage girls slumber party. The few blow-up mattresses they had were augmented by water rafts and cushions from the furniture. Blankets and pillows added to the piles, turning the room into a huge bed of sorts.

"You guys have been busy," Rhea said. She noticed Gary standing in the corner pouting. Rhea smiled a moment until she saw Nana staring at her from the kitchen door. "How did she get down here so fast," she murmured.

Nana smiled and went back into the kitchen.

"This room looks like a harem chamber," Fizzlewink said. He walked around on the soft bedding lifting his feet in a paw-paw motion before sitting down.

"Don't get comfortable fur-ball," Shelly said. "You aren't coming with us."

"I am-"

"Not going," Nana said from the kitchen. "Come in here Fizzlewink. It's time for our little chat."

Shelly sent an unusual look of sympathy toward the little blue man as he sulked his way toward the kitchen. Strange things were going on, and Colby was watching them unfold with little interest. The only things on his mind were helping his mother and Jasper. One of which he tried to put aside, but he couldn't stop thinking about Jasper mainly as he was sitting only a few feet away.

"Focus on the reason we are going into this Shiznet place little brother," Shelly said as she sat beside Colby. "We all need to work together to remain focused, and you're the center of it all."

Colby shook his head thinking he heard Shelly wrong. "What did you say? The center of what?"

"Just keep yourself thinking about getting mom out of there. The rest can wait until she is safe."

"What are you talking about?" Then Colby thought about her odd behavior after Nana's little spell. "Does this have anything to do with you and Nana suddenly acting differently around each other? What did she tell you?"

"Nothing you need to know," Shelly said.

"Shelly?" Colby persisted.

"Just figure out the Hashtag Magic spell we need to get out of our heads and into that portal. It has to rely on the strengths of us six that are going in."

"So it's just up to us kids now," Jasper joked. "Why is it the adults always seem to leave us to take care of this hocus-pocus crap?"

"I don't think my parents even know what's going on?" Gary offered.

"Say, where are your folks these days? They just drop you off at your pal Colby's again so they could go off to wherever again?"

"Jasper, that's enough," Darla said. She turned to Colby. "Why aren't you sticking up for Gary?"

Colby shrugged but never looked up from his notebook. "I suppose there's something to what Jasper says, albeit not in the nicest way." He went back to scribbling runes for the required spell.

"Do you believe Gary's parents have something to do with this?" Rhea whispered.

Colby looked up then and at Gary who stared back. "I don't really know what to think about his parents. I can't even picture them when I think about it."

Gary turned from Colby and directed his glare at Jasper. "Well, at least I still have both my parents.”

Before Jasper could get up, Shelly pulled him back down. “Stop baiting each other. This isn’t helping.” She shook her head at them both and looked at her brother. “What have you got for the spell so far?”

Colby handed her the list of options he could think of, but they meant nothing to her. Turning them over to Jasper who had a greater knowledge of the Runes from his game experience, he would match Colby’s words to symbols.

“The first few wouldn’t work because you haven’t set something strong enough to anchor our minds. But this third one might do it if we had something to use as a focal.”

“A focal for what?” Gary asked.

“When we enter that Shiznet, we need to know where we are going right?” Jasper waited until everyone agreed. “We need to focus on your mother since she is who we want to find.”

“We could use her rune name,” Colby said.

“She has her own rune?” Rhea asked. “How is that possible?”

“There are runes for writing in the old language just as there are separate ones for spell work. I found mom’s personal rune on the back of an old photo last year.” Colby drew the symbol and passed it around for everyone to study.

Jasper held it last. “This should do it. We all focus on this rune as we complete the hashtag spell and separate mind from body.”

“That simpler?” Gary asked. “That sounds too easy.”

* * *

"It's not that easy Gary. Have you ever tried focusing on one thing so hard and finding your thoughts jumping from one thing to another?" Jasper saw Gary's understanding as well as everyone else's. "Yeah, we have to clear all thoughts and think only of this symbol."

The room remained quiet as they all thought about that.

"Maybe you should make more copies of that rune so we can all study it a bit more before we go?" Darla asked.

Colby nodded and drew out more copies for the others. "Okay, but then we need to get this trip started. Type the hashtag spell into your phWatches and let's get ready."

Colby uploaded the runes to the primary hashtag server and let it prepare the construct that would be called as they each sent the spell on their devices. In a few minutes, they would be leaving their bodies and entering a virtual world parallel to the internet.

### ###

Fizzlewink sat at the counter waiting for Nana to address him. Not long ago he would have been hoping for the crazy old bat to stop talking and give him a plate of fish. Now that the truth of who she truly is came to light, he was confused by the feeling of devotion that stirred within his chest.

"The Dreggs are here Fizzlewink," Nana said. "I hope there will be no unfortunate misunderstandings with them."

"But they killed my people," Fizz cried.

"No, they did not," Nana answered. "They were born to from them."

Fizzlewink looked at her doubtfully. "I saw them departing the settlements, leaving the husks of my people behind."

"Yes, you only saw them leaving. Those husks were such as those any creature would crawl free of when they go through metamorphosis." Nana waited for the dawning of understanding to cross Fizz's face. "Yes, they were transformed into the Dreggs. That was always the Nefsmari's ultimate purpose."

Fizzlewink's eyes widened at the shock of hearing the truth. His people were still alive, changed, but alive. Then he thought of himself. "Why did I not change like the rest?"

Nana turned to face him with that question. "Because you were meant for another purpose perhaps. Then again maybe it was because you were the first of your kind and a favorite." Nana turned, back away. Watching the Dreggs arriving outside she continued. "There is many a task remaining for you to perform before I can allow the reunion with your wife and children."

Fizzlewink was preparing to question further when the static in the air distracted him.

Rigel burst through the door. "The kids started their spell, but something has gone wrong!"

# <u>Chapter 13</u>

## #IntoTheVoid

The six kids were sitting in a circle when they all sent the hashtag spell and joined hands. In the center of the circle the children sat, was placed the device holding the portal open to the Shiznet. While a hazy outline of each youth was pushing out from their bodies and toward a swirling disk around the vortex, an angry red light pulsed from the event horizon.

"They are being blocked from entering," Fizzlewink said. "The Shizumu were there waiting for someone to try entering their realm."

Nana just nodded and moved closer, careful not to touch any of the children. "Interesting."

Rigel and Fizz looked at Nana, seeing her now as Bellatrix. Neither of them knew what to make of her transformation or the fact that she was just observing. It was Rigel who eventually stepped forward, ready to cast a spell.

"Hold," Bellatrix said. "The spiteful creatures have planned for that and will hurt the children."

"Then what are we to do?" Fizz asked. "They can't enter while those things are there can they?"

*　*　*

"Of course they can enter. The problem is the enemy getting out once they cross the portal threshold." Bellatrix waved her hands before her lips as she whispered an incantation. The wisps of Emassa flowed through her flickering fingers and into the portal.

A burst of red light came from the vortex and held just before the disk swirling around it, the one gathering the consciousnesses of the children. A final angry flicker and the red light collapsed back into the portal and was gone.

The crystalline forms of the six kids joined the disk as it then freely sank into the vortex. As the last of their collective minds passed beyond the physical and into the Shiznet realm, they fell back on their pillows. Their hands remained clenched as a circle of sleeping bodies joined in a dream.

"What did you just do?" Rigel asked.

"The only thing I could Rigel. I made the portal one way."

Nana waved off the arguments that ensued. Both Fizz and Rigel protested that the kids would not be able to return, but Nana ensured them that would not be the case. The children had the combined power to open the portal back as long as they worked together.

"Yes, but will they work together?" Rigel asked. "They were bickering all day, and the rivalry between the boys is…unhealthy."

"That will settle itself." Bellatrix looked at the portal and cringed slightly. "Now if you boys would be so kind as to entertain our guests in the yard. I'm going to check on my daughter."

Bellatrix left and headed up the stairs without waiting for a response. Her orders would be carried out as always. Her form faded back into the old hunched façade of Nana as she began climbing, her old bones creaking in time with each wood step. The effort of regaining prominence in her own head and body was exhausting both mentally and physically.

As she entered the dusty old study, Nana looked around and wondered how things were so different in these modern times based on Bellatrix's memories. Distinct in some, but much the same in others. The struggle for power was the primary theme of human and Nefslama kind. All self-proclaimed intelligent races were guilty of placing themselves above all else. Bellatrix grew tired of the fight, and Nana felt the same. As she huffed out a heavy sigh, she watched her daughter working through a battle of her own.

Nana sat next to her sleeping daughter, wondering how all the choices in her many lives led to this point. She was once again whole, but pieces were missing. As those pieces came back, sometimes in droves, it was overwhelming to remember the atrocities she committed in the name of saving the world from the Shizumu threat.

Memories of creating the Dreggs was only the start of what plagued her. Images and visions of genocide, complete destruction of entire cultures that were infected or worshiping the Shizumu, tortured her. Even when she realized that course was too much and a final solution was required, it led to the first of the children being sacrificed to the shield.

Nana cried. Her eyes poured forth waves of tears for each sweet-faced child that flashed before her minds-eye. She knew they were not actually killed, but freed to exist in the Emassa. This knowledge did little to sooth her thoughts on what eventually might come to happen yet again.

Colby was the answer, Nana thought. Bellatrix planned this long ago, even so much as helping manipulate Jarrod and Aria into having a boy child against the will of the elders. She did not realize at the time what they were doing, but now the rejoining of all her lives and memories spoke the truth of her and her conspirator's long played plans.

* * *

Colby was learning what he would need. This venture into the Shiznet was just another test for him to pass. Once he returned, for he must, another clue would be granted from the journal she spied resting on his father's desk.

### 

The entry into the Shiznet was rough. Colby wondered if his body had become a lump of dough sent through a pasta crank. As his mind remained whole, he felt phantom limbs and body being pulled and stretched to infinite lengths. At the peaking threshold of imagined pain, it all ceased, and he felt whole but was afraid to open his eyes.

When he heard the voices of his friends, Colby began to relax. His eyes fluttered in response to his demand for sight. Colby realized that he wasn't physically opening his eyes. Perhaps that is what made the effort difficult. When he stopped forcing the matter, he found his sight return smoothly.

"Don't force it," Colby said to his friends. They all stood in the circle where they began this journey. "Just desire to see and relax."

As the others were beginning to acclimate to their disembodied states, Colby began to look around. They stood in a transparent version of his living room. The device in the center of them all was there as well. It had a stronger appearance than the rest of the space.

Colby released Shelly's hand, breaking the circle. He wanted to touch the device that looked more substantial than it should. The moment the ring broke, Colby watched the virtual world around them shift.

The artificial floor dissolved, sending the six youths plummeting into a swirling mass of red fog. Their screams echoed in contrast to the preening laughs of the phantasmic menace reaching for them from beyond the perimeter of the tunnel they now traversed.

* * *

All sound ceased as they came to a halt, falling in a jumbled mass on what seemed solid ground. Despite the grumbling as they all removed themselves from the pile, each appeared to be unharmed. They had no facts about what would happen to their physical bodies while in this virtual state. Feeling no pain was a relief, but still not a certainty.

"My guess is that it's like a dream right," Jasper said. "If we are threatened too badly we would wake up?"

"Don't you usually wake up when you feel yourself falling?" asked Darla. "I didn't wake from that fall, so I don't think this is like dreaming."

Colby was afraid Darla was correct. It would be more like being trapped in a coma or similar, except their minds were now far from their bodies and completely cut off from one another. And now they were even deeper into the Shiznet based on the change in topography.

They all looked around to find walls and doorways, beyond each was a different landscape. They each had an opaque, realistic look to them once you ignored the subtle underlying digital framework and shifting characters.

"It's a completely virtual world or several of them," Gary said. He moved toward the closest doorway. Beyond Gary saw what he imagined as his home. He swore he almost heard his mother's voice calling to him. The pinch on his arm changed his assumption.

"Gary!" Rhea said and pulled him away from the doorway. "Don't get too far away until we know where we're going."

Gary looked back over his shoulder at the doorway to the voice of his mother.  He watched as the scenery beyond changed into a familiar hallway at school. "Fine, but it looks like the paths are changing."

# <u>Chapter 14</u>

## #Labyrinth

"How are we supposed to know where we're going?" Shelly asked. She touched Colby's shoulder and nudged him. "Can't you send some spell to search out a path to mom?"

Colby smiled inwardly at her suggestion but smirked at the hand on his shoulder. Shelly is not a touchy-feely person. So either she's frightened, or up to something. He wasn't sure which, but for now he would concentrate on her idea.

"Gary, from what you've learned of that device, do you think we could map out the Shiznet?"

"Maybe, it depends on what you have in mind."

Colby met Gary at the virtual version of the device that remained in the center of the room. They debated for a few minutes on what it meant having the thing there with them. Too many theories led them to move past it and focus on figuring out their new environment.

Gary theorized that he and the others were in some kind of hub or central point of passage in and out of the Shizumu realm. From there six portals or ports existed for networking out into the Shiznet. Each one of those paths could lead to an infinite number of others if they passed through other hubs.

They needed a way to test their theory. Using their shared knowledge of computer networking, they devised a set of spell orbs they named 'pingers.' These pingers would traverse the labyrinth of paths and send back location information to a master device they called the mapping node.

Once the mapping node was created, Colby linked it to everyone's virtual phWatch in case they got separated. They would each find their way back to this hub where they first entered. He then began creating pingers and sending them out through the six doorway ports. Displaying their progress on a master map projected in the center of the room, they all could see the digital reality unfold. It was already immense and still mapping.

Colby felt like he was playing a retro arcade game as he stood watching the movement of small blinking dots on the display screen. They fingers worked their way around a network of paths that crisscrossed, ran parallel, or reached dead-ends and doubled back. The diagram expanded as the path-seeking spells snaked around the unknown landscape. With every moment the map extended.

"This place is huge, it must go on forever," Rhea said. She pulled her hair back when Darla noticed her chewing the end of a braid. "How will we find your mother in all this?"

Colby smiled and stepped back from the map. "I've been thinking about that." He lifted his hand and spoke a word into the virtual wristwatch he wore. He called out the rune symbol for Aria's name in the air, where it hovered and shone with his unique purple magical-light. "Remember us all thinking about this as we entered the Shiznet? We will use it to track her down."

* * *

Explaining how he imbued each pinger with a proximity spell for her rune, Colby created a way to have the mapping also identify the location of Aria's Shizumu-like half. Once there was a general direction to follow, a destination could be determined.

"So what do we do in the meantime?" Shelly asked. "Anyone bring a deck of tarot cards?"

The light giggle was a relief to most, but Gary was not amused. He was still distracted by the voice he heard coming from one of the ports. Something told him it was his mother calling him. She was telling him to come find her and leave his friends to their own task.

At one time, Gary would have immediately confided in his best friend, Colby. Now, as he looked aside at Colby and Jasper talking over the Shiznet map, he ground his teeth. Colby would tell him it was his imagination. They were here to help Colby's mom, not Gary's.

Gary was twitching and pacing the room waiting to get moving. He had to do something, anything besides sitting around. Giving into his desperation, Gary directed a spell at the device. A red dot appeared on the Shiznet map.

"There's mom!" Colby cried. "Let's go get her." Colby pulled Jasper along, both smiling and eager to get moving.

The girls followed after them. First Darla then Rhea, stepped through the port and out into the labyrinth maze of virtual reality. Shelly followed behind, turning to see what was keeping Gary. He was gone.

They finally departed, leaving Gary free to go his own way. Colby didn't need him to find his mother. He had Jasper now along with the others.

Gary sensed there was something here for him; for him alone.

* * *

The voice was stronger now that he was free of the central hub room. He paused to check for a discernible direction. He looked at the Shiznet map to check on the progress of his companions. They stopped shortly after leaving their starting point.

His hand started shaking, and he swallowed hard. If they doubled back to find out what was keeping him, Gary wouldn't be able to see what was calling his name. He didn't know if his parents were involved with all that was happening, but they were always gone. If they were here, perhaps they required his help.

Gary worked through a possible spell without thinking it out. **#RandomizePaths**. The moment he released it, Gary regretted the impulsive act. He watched the holographic map projected from his watch in horror as every path previously outlined was altered, including his own chosen route.

"No, no, no…This can't be happening." He rubbed his temples and thought he might fix what he started. **#ReleaseMagic**.

Again, no sooner had Gary released a spell, it backfired. The Hashtag Magic that was attached to the virtual device on his wrist began streaming out from the display and into the surrounding pathway walls. He disconnected himself from the Hashtag Magic app and couldn't get it to respond any longer. In his panic he headed back the way he came, only to find the doorway now gone.

###

Colby reached both hands up to his chest and grimaced. "Something doesn't feel right."

Shelly pushed past the others and stood beside Colby. "What is it?"

Rubbing his temples, Colby grimaced from a throbbing that beat against the back of his eyes. He grunted as it subsided. "Holy crap that hurt, but it seems to have stopped." While his vision cleared, Colby gripped his wrist where his father's watch normally was. "It feels as though I've lost something, but I can't think of what it might be."

"It's this place," Darla said. She stepped around the group, looking at the shifting lights all around them. On the surface, it appeared as though they were entering a long series of hallways, but she could feel the malice just beyond the artificial walls. "I can feel them watching us."

Colby raised his phWatch and adjusted the angle to look at the map. "There's no doubt they know we're here, so let's just keep moving." Seeing the fading and flicker of his map, Colby moved his wrist again hoping to clear it up. "Something's wrong with the map."

Jasper checked the map from his device as well. "It's changing." He looked around, checking the others had the same issue. "Hey, where's Gary?"

Shelly saw no one else noticed before that moment, Gary wasn't among them. Only Shelly seemed unsurprised by his absence, but nobody sensed her knowing anything more than the rest of them. "He was behind us before we left the place we entered the Shiznet. Maybe he got cut off when the paths started changing, but I'm sure he'll find us." It was a weak reassurance, but acceptable to most.

"We need to go back for him."

"No Colby, we need to find your mother." Jasper blocked the way back. "Gary can take care of himself. Besides, how do we know he didn't go back home?"

Darla and Rhea shook their heads in agreement while Shelly stepped back toward the wall. The colors began to flare and swirl, but no one took notice.

* * *

"Step out of the way Jasper," Colby said. "Gary wouldn't just abandon us."

"Really? Then where is he?"

As the boys squared off and their tensions rose, so rose the speed at which the swirling masses around them moved. Colby and Jasper didn't notice, but the girls did. Darla grabbed Rhea just before a plasmatic red hand took hold of her shoulder. They screamed.

Shelly reached for Darla as she was dragged back screaming from searing pain as the phantasmic red hand scorched the skin of her ankle. Grabbing hold of Darla's hand, Shelly called for Rhea's help. "You need to perform a spell to get her free."

Rhea, momentarily stunned by the spectacle playing out, reacted too slowly and was not ready when the hand of another beast shot forth from the melting walls to grab at her. Rhea stumbled and fell as a clawed and calloused red hand took hold of her ankle. She reached for her phWatch by instinct, but the floor meeting her side was faster than her hands. She slammed into the ground.

One after the next, each of the kids was tripped, pushed, or thrown to the ground as the large arms stretched out from the walls. Tossed and pushed around in the tunnel and adjoining pathways like pinballs.

Colby covered his ears against the ringing that began when he hit his head on the ground. He looked around to see his companions in similar positions along the way, each reacting to being banged about. As the ringing abated, it was replaced by a whispering annoyance at the edges of his perception.

Reaching out to swing at an imaginary gnat or another annoying insect, Colby's hand connected with something.

* * *

"Ouch," Shelly said and returned the slug.

Colby rubbed his arm from where his sister smacked him. "Sorry, I thought a bug or something was buzzing in my ear."

"Right."

Colby shook his head. "Can't you hear that?" the buzzing morphed into a whisper. Voices began spitting words at him that stung his ears. Rising to his feet Colby looked around. "Anyone else hearing this?"

"I hear something," Darla admitted. "But it's the sting that hurts."

"Words," Rhea said. "The words hurt."

"I hear and feel them too," said Jasper. "Where are they coming from?"

Shelly heard nothing for some reason, but she was the first to see the source. "The walls, faces are coming out of them."

As the last of the reaching arms retracted into the surrounding walls, the twisted features of angry faces began to protrude from the surfaces. The mouths moved with every word that flowed and gained substance with a light wispy red smoke. The trails of each insult and trolling comment found an easy target in Colby and his friends. Only Shelly seemed resistant to the taunting.

"Let's get out of here," Shelly said and grabbed Colby. "Lead the way little brother."

Colby shuffled ahead, followed by each of his friends as Shelly hurried them along. She stood back looking at the receding faces as one of the verbal assaults hit her arm. It bit, but she brushed it off. "You'll have to do better than that to get under my skin."

* * *

Shelly turned toward her party and followed them down a new passage, not knowing where it would lead.

# **Chapter 15**

## **#AntiVirus**

They wondered aimlessly for what felt like hours. The further along they went, the less sure Colby was they were heading the right way.

"I don't think this is right."

Colby held up his hand indicating a halt to the others. He lifted his other hand and tapped the face of his phWatch. When the map flickered into existence above his wrist, the shifting now became apparent.

"Damn it!"

"What's wrong?" Shelly asked.

Colby sighed and released the map before turning to face his sister. Meeting her impatient stare, Colby prepared himself to admit what Jasper already shared; Gary might be working against them.

"The map…it's changing."

Jasper hooted and slapped his chest. "I knew it. Didn't I say he was up to something?"

* * *

Colby rolled his eyes but didn't respond to Jasper. He turned away and began the workings of a spell in his head. He knew there was nothing in the Hashtag Magic app to start from so he had to think of something new.

The shaky voicing of bickering and complaints fell off the edges of his ears. Colby wasn't ready to accept Gary's possible deceit, nor was he in the mood for listening to what the others had to say. They weren't helping matters and Colby was getting more agitated every moment.

While his new spell —what he thought might work— was as ready as it was going to get. He began entering it into the Hashtag Magic interface before finally focusing on it and calling it forth. **#NewMap**.

A newly spelled map hologram flickered into existence before Colby's eyes. The path taken by the seeking orbs began to appear as twisted lines, crisscrossing and doubling back on themselves. The labyrinth was changing, and there was little doubt as to why.

Colby's vision rippled as a sheet of moisture formed from the ache forming in his chest. His longtime friend and confidant had somehow corrupted the spell they created to navigate the Shiznet and find Aria's split soul. Gary betrayed him.

Light pressure on his shoulder alerted Colby to Jasper's comforting presence. Pushing back the wellspring of pain from Gary's act against his efforts, Colby wiped his eyes before dismissing the map with a simple hand gesture.

"What has happened," Jasper asked.

He already knew the answer, but hearing the truth from Colby's lips was the confirmation he needed. Jasper wanted to feel justified in his dislike of Gary. He wasn't prepared to admit his feelings originated from jealousy of the bond Colby shared with his rival for attention.

* * *

"The map is useless," Colby said, the timber of his voice shaky. "Gary has somehow corrupted the spell. We have to find another way to my mother's spirit."

"I think we should go back," Rhea said.

Colby spun around to face Rhea, dagger-eyed and fists clenched. "How do you suppose we find our way back any better than forward?" The power of his magic charged the air around him as it danced along his arms from his fists.

Rhea shuffled back several paces to the relative safety of Shelly and Darla. When Shelly pulled her behind and stepped forward, Rhea felt no more safe from Colby's angry stare.

"Put those away," Shelly said, pointing to Colby's energy filled hands. "We're all on the same side here."

Shelly tried her best to sound authoritative, but against Colby's raging magic, she knew instinctively the damage he could perform. She eased her way forward, keeping her eyes on the slow dissipation of energy from her brother. Before she managed to close the distance more than a few feet, Colby found a target for his anger.

Colby twisted back toward a previously empty passage as he felt the icy tingling on his neck. There, along the walls, large bulges of muscle and mangled limbs extended outward to block their way. Once fully-formed, the troll-like apparitions fluctuated from the energy filled digital beginnings into fully materialized creatures. They blocked the way back and now began to form on the opposite side, blocking the way forward as well.

As he saw the threat surround them, Colby made up his mind and gave no time for further debate. He lashed out for the closest adversaries, the ones blocking their forward path. Emassa built up around his arms and hands as Colby pushed from his reserves and prepared his attack. In a deliberate lunge, his arms pushed forward, releasing the deadly assault.

Power coursed through him and into the beastly trolls barring Colby's way. The creatures fell back several paces but did not fall. Colby pulled deeper within his reservoir of Emassa, draining it by nearly half before releasing it back into the stream of assaulting bolts now leaping freely from his hands. His efforts were rewarded by an echoing static crack.

The first troll halted its movements as the bolt of energy penetrating its chest began to cause a red glowing webbing to spread outward. The widening fissures continued to crack as the center of the troll began to crumble and fall to the floor.

A final push of power from Colby sailed forth and into the forward path-blocking foes. The resulting burst of light and crack of energy sent particles flying through the air as one-by-one the trolls crumbled to the ground.

"Come on!"

Colby waved his friends forward and past the piles of wasted trolls. As they passed him, Colby looked ashamedly into his friends' eyes. His temper nearly caused him to act against them. Though he did not, the threat of him losing control still simmered below the surface of his tightly-wound emotions.

The last of them rushed past him, and Colby began to follow before taking a closer look at movement near his feet. As he squatted down to examine the pile that remained of the first troll, he noticed the tiny cubicle form still flickered. It looked to him as though it was a small pixel of the creature. When it shifted and combined with another, then another, Colby confirmed what his inner voice already suspected.

* * *

"We need to move, NOW!"

Colby stood and ran after his friends. They did not question him until he caught up with them, continuing to run headlong into the unknown passages.

"What's wrong?" Shelly asked. "The other trolls did not look to be moving that fast? And you destroyed the other ones."

"They're not destroyed, exactly. When I looked closer, they just seemed to break down into tiny pixels of the whole. Then they started to shift back together."

"Crap on a cracker," Shelly said.

Colby nodded at Shelly's comment. "What's worse-"

"It gets worse?" Rhea asked.

Though she spoke to Colby, Rhea remained safely behind Shelly. When Colby looked at her apologetically, she smiled weakly but remained where she was.

Colby felt hurt but understood Rhea's trepidation. He threatened her with his earlier temperamental outburst, and for that he was sorry. A trust had been broken, and that is not something easily rebuilt.

"It took half my reserve of Emassa to reduce those things down to 'pixel-dust.' And as I now try to refill my power, it is taking a great deal more time than normal."

Jasper and the others laughed—albeit nervously—at Colby's pun, but they all knew the 'pixel-dust' would soon be reformed into the virtual trolls again. Once they were whole, it wouldn't be long before they started pursuit. Even now the strange virtual world around them began shifting, and a haze of mist began to lower the visibility of what lay ahead of them as they ran headlong into the unknown.

The shifting in the Shiznet was no longer confined to changes in the maze of passages and corridors. The strange virtual world expanded and morphed as Colby and his companions moved through a veil of digital mist that moments ago blocked their progress.

Stretched before them was a landscape that none would have imagined finding in this realm of their enemy. Rolling hills of dark red grasses and blooming wild flowers, cascaded downward into a valley spotted with trees and other plants. Varying shades of red in hues and brilliance impossible to imagine met their bewildered gazes.

Colby stepped forward so he might get a better view. From the height where he stood, he could also see a river of sorts snaking down the slopes, disappearing beyond a far plateau. When he listened carefully, he could hear the bubbling of the waters. There was something else there, the chirping of a bird.

"Do you hear that?" Colby said.

Shelly stepped up to her brother and listened. "I hear a bird."

"I hear it also," said Darla.

The others moved closer to listen for the soft twittering. They looked at one another, confusion apparent on their faces. This place was nothing like what they expected to find. It held a serene beauty that was in contrast to the evil that they associated to the Shizumu. For several minutes the kids looked around and examined their new surroundings while slowly descending the hills toward the valley.

"I can also feel emotions from the bird. It's happy."

* * *

"That isn't possible," Jasper said. "This is a virtual world."

"Well someone forgot to tell that to this place. I can feel a mix of emotions all around us." Darla put her hand on Rhea's shoulder for support. "It's almost intoxicating."

As they reached a small clearing of sorts, Colby noticed that the birds' chirping grew louder. He looked around at the small trees that surrounded the glade they now stood in. The planting of the trees seemed somewhat artificial. This thought itself made him laugh being as though this entire place was a virtual realm.

"What's so funny?" Jasper asked. "I don't see anything to laugh about here."

Colby looked around and pointed to the symmetrical beauty of the trees and how they grew here in this odd little grove. He pointed to the solitary bird that he spotted again sitting on the branch of a nearby tree. When he turned to Jasper, however, his smile faded as he saw something akin to terror in his friend's eyes.

"What's wrong with you? Can't you-"

"I don't like this place," Jasper said. "Let's just keep moving."

Jasper looked up at the bird scowling. Lifting his right hand, he displayed a bird of his own to the twittering creature. When the bird's song suddenly changed, Jasper wasted little time drawing a spell with his extended middle finger. **#SilentBird**.

The spell formed a blue orb of light and sailed toward the virtual finch. Just as it hit the animal, the spell turned red, and the bird exploded. Its pixels spread out among the trees but did not fall to the ground. Instead of being drawn back to one another, the pixel-dust began cloning itself, each speck creating a duplicate of the original bird.

* * *

"What just happened?" Darla asked. She began to feel a change in the emotional state of the creatures and the world around them. "This doesn't feel good."

As the last of the cloned birds reformed, they all started twittering and chirping frantically. They all launched into the air and began flying in a circle around the group.

"What was that spell you sent?" Colby asked Jasper.

"A spell to silence that damn bird. But it changed from blue to red as it made contact."

Colby sunk his head realizing the extent of Gary's betrayal. "It isn't just the spell map that is getting manipulated; all the Hashtag Magic is probably at risk."

Shelly let out a mirthless laugh. "Good going, I think you just retweeted that bird." She kept her eyes on the swirling mass of flying rage building above their heads. As she watched, she noticed them beginning to fly faster and driving lower toward them. "Guys?"

Nobody was listening. Everyone else was quickly trying to form spells, watching them all be twisted into something else moments after they were cast.

"Guys?" Shelly kept her eyes skyward while trying to locate someone, anyone, to get their attention.

"HEY!"

All of them looked at Shelly now, and as she slowly lowered her head and then leveled her eyes at them, they didn't need to look up at what she was warning them about. They heard the frantic chittering of a thousand angry birds.

"RUN!"

As single-minded as they all turned to run, so did the birds break into a united dive toward the fleeing human avatars. The screaming of the girls, including Shelly, was drowned out by the screeching call from the agitated avifauna of the Shiznet. They dove in concert, circling the running kids and darting between extended limbs while pecking at them.

Colby led the others by shouts alone as they were unable to keep their eyes on one another, protecting them from the scratching claws and pecking beaks. The wounds they received were superficial, but they stung terribly. As they ran, Colby failed to understand that they were being forced along a path of the birds' choosing. They were being herded. Every time Colby or one of the others attempted to change course, a flock would charge in from above to force them back the way they first headed.

Ahead, Colby saw an outcropping of large stones. Before he could head toward them, A new flock of birds cut off the route so he headed for what appeared a sunken entrance to a cave.

"Follow me," Colby yelled without looking back. "We can put up a shield to keep them from flying in after us."

Colby jumped into the cave, rolling as he landed hard transitioning from the soft red grasses to the dark rocky ground inside the cave. He looked back toward the entrance as the others dove in and covered their heads expecting the birds continued assault; none followed.

Pain shot up Colby's left side as he struggled to stand. A gash on the side of his leg from the knee down his calf sent throbbing through to his bone. As he hopped to a bolder to take a seat, Rhea ran over to lay her hands on the wound.

* * *

"This is bad. I'll have to use a spell to close the skin."

Rhea looked at Colby and waited for his nod of approval. Their magic was being manipulated, and it was risky trying anything for fear it being turned against them. Rhea feared her spell might do the opposite of what she wanted.

As she looked closer, she noticed the debris in and around the cut. She needed to clean it before proceeding. Being as though they entered a virtual world, they didn't pack any sort of provisions. She decided her first act would be to get some water. **#Water**.

The spell began to form, flickering at first as the runes she conjured hung in the air above Colby's wound. She relaxed her will of intent on the spell and watched through squinting eyes and a turned head as the water fell. It landed on Colby's cut and ran down his leg, clearing away dirt and pebbles.

Relieved over the results, Rhea straightened her slumped shoulders and began to form another spell.

"That seemed to work ok. Let's try another." She looked into Colby's eyes. "This may sting a little." **#Peroxide**.

He did his best to remain composed, but with the biting at his leg coupled with the bubbling foam that followed, Colby had to bite his lips while grunting away the pain. The ache increased as a red glow formed around the edges of the split skin. Colby screamed.

Jasper turned from guarding the cave entrance. "Do something. You're killing him."

Rhea quickly called for water again and rinsed away the conjured peroxide. As the solution was removed, the red light faded along with the pain.

"Let's not try that again," Colby said between ragged breaths. "Just close it up."

Shaking her head, Rhea started to put her hand over the wound. "I can speed up healing, but that will leave a nasty scar, and it can still get infected. Virtually anyway."

Shelly sat next to Colby and squeezed his hand. "If only we had some anti-biotic or something but what can you do in a computerized world?"

Colby turned to Shelly. "What did you just say?"

Shelly repeated her words wondering what Colby was asking. "There's nothing we can do here if our spells get hacked."

Colby smiled at Shelly and turned back to Rhea. "Try an anti-virus to wrap your spell."

Understanding began to form with Rhea's smile. "Show me."

Colby used his finger to draw on the dirt floor of the dark cave. He showed Rhea how to start her spell with an anti-virus and firewall function that called her unaltered spell from within. This would allow her to stitch his wound while preventing the outside manipulation in theory.

After a few more checks of her work and a nod of agreement from Colby, Rhea called her new spells. **#AntiVirus** - **#Firewall** - **#DisinfectCleanStitch**.

Once her three spells fired into existence, Rhea used her will to join them together before guiding the compiled work down over Colby's festering injury. She held her breath in reaction to Colby's sharp intake when the spell touched his skin.

* * *

The enchantment settled into his wound, and Colby released his own breath as the stinging eased and his skin began to pull together and bond. It worked.

Colby took another deep breath and ran his hand over the fresh pink skin on his leg. He looked back up at Rhea in time to see the color drain from her face and her eyes roll back as she fainted. His thoughts immediately turned to Gary and if he was somehow involved in what was happening.

<u>**Chapter 16**</u>

**#BetrayFriends**

Gary wandered around, looking for the missing doorway for some time until giving up. Now he sat alone in a patch of red grass, wondering what he'd gotten himself involved.

The smell of burnt bacon and toast filled Gary's nostrils. Eyes closed, he sat up and breathed deeply through his nose to collect the sense of normalcy.  That feeling began to fade after he opened his eyes and looked around the room. His surroundings —though toned to reds and culturally themed to his heritage— was very much like Colby's. In fact, take away the few things that were more to Gary's taste and it was Colby's room down to the geeky bed set.

Gary jumped from the bed and ran for the door. He stopped and backed up after passing a mirror on the wall. One cursory look at the Batman onesie pajamas and Gary turned around to change clothes. Again he found everything a carbon copy of Colby's, but another sniff of food cooking cleared any doubt from his mind. Gary finished changing and dashed out the bedroom door running directly into an empty chamber, except for a pedestal in the center where a woman stood waiting.

The door slammed shut behind him, trapping Gary in the round room. The echoing of the latching metal door, reverberated around the room leaving glowing runes in the wake. The woman smiled at Gary in the glow of the magic emanating from the walls surrounding them.

"Come closer so that I might speak with you, child."

"Mrs. Stevens? Is that you?"

The woman laughed. "Not exactly, child. I am a Daphne"

"Who are you?" Gary asked. "Where am I?"

The woman laughed again. "Who am I? The question is more about who you are…or are not is more appropriate."

Gary noticed the woman's dull red hair and glazed eyes. Her head twitched somewhat when she wasn't speaking. Not Mrs. Stevens. This lady might be some wraith or Shizumu creature trying to trick him. He went on the offense. **#DissipateWraith**.

The degraded double of Aria Stevens, one of three Daphne, reached out and grabbed the magic spell conjured by Gary. She giggled as the magic wrapped around her arm and licked at her skin.

"That tickles."

Gary tried another spell, then another. None of his magic worked on the creature.

The Daphne was no longer laughing when she sent a jolt of energy that hit Gary in the stomach, forcing him to buckle over and fall. She smiled.

"I have to thank you for bringing this lovely little magic tool into my friends' home, or what's left of it anyway," Daphne said. "I'm sorry that…no that's not right. It's unfortunate I had to immobilize you, for the moment, but I have infinitesimal patience, and you must do something for me." Daphne waited for Gary to look up. "If you ever want your parents."

Gary tried to speak. "…Parents…what have you…where?"

Tittering accompanied Daphne's shaking head. Her unruly locks of dark red hair bounced around her face. "Don't speak little…thing. Just listen."

Daphne laid out a task for Gary. The device that brought them into the Shizumu realm was required, and he needed to take it to a particular cave construct and prepare it for the arrival of his friends. There he would only need to flip a few switches and let the device do the rest.

"I won't hurt my friends."

"Oh, it speaks again," Daphne said. "You won't be hurting them…much, and if you ever want to leave here and be a real boy with real parents, then I suggest YOU DO AS I SAY!"

Gary flinched at the woman's acrimonious and loud reaction. "What do you mean 'real'?"

"Oh dear little boy of clay, do you not yet know what you are and why your memories are so clouded?" Daphne tittered again. "Why don't I just show you. Shall I?"

Daphne waved a hand toward the pedestal in the center of the chamber. The air swirled and a wispy mist condensed until it began to shine and images play on its surface.

Gary saw himself playing in a room with Colby. Moments later he was saying goodbye and headed toward the school. The next images displayed him entering the school basement through an old cellar door inside a shed around the back of the building. Gary watched himself over again, similar scenes playing at various ages of his past. All the clips ended with him entering a chamber in the basement of the school and sitting down next to the spot he now occupied.

"What is this you're showing me?"

"Why, it's your home, young golem. This place is where you go when you are not with the boy Colby. When the master dismisses his pet, he must go somewhere." Daphne moved her arms about, pointing out the chamber and frowned. "Why he would send you back here is beyond me, but I'm a little nutty myself so who am I to judge." A chuckle escaped Daphne's lips as she grinned and tilted her head.

"You're lying. This is just a Shizumu trick."

"Am I?" Daphne said. "Think about it a bit mud-boy. You'll come to realize I speak truly. You are a creature created to serve the boy in some manner, and your parents are an illusion set up to anchor your existence. Or his delusion, I haven't yet figured that little bit out."

Gary began to object, but a nagging at his memories began to beg attention. He was focusing on the displays of the past the crazy woman played for him and realized he could not find a different ending to any of them. Though Gary never saw himself sitting in this room, he couldn't see himself in a home with his parents either. He couldn't recall a single visual memory of his mom or dad.

Daphne saw the battle for truth in the little boy-thing's face. "You'll come to accept reality. You're a creation, just like me. Except I have free will, you do not."

"I do as I please."

"Ha, at the whim of your master." Daphne waited for Gary's face to turn when he saw the spark of truth in her words. "You've done nothing but for the benefit of Colby Stevens. But now you can do something for yourself."

Gary said nothing for several moments before turning to the woman who impatiently tapped her foot. "And I'll see my parents again."

"Still not getting it," Daphne huffed. She shook her head and figured the golem would work that out on its own. "Sure, but you have to do as I tell you."

"Why should I do this?"

"Justice. Let me tell you a little story."

### 

Gary made his way along the red landscape, following the path taken by his companions. He stopped and looked at the strange alignment of massive rocks in the center of the glade, but was pressed to keep moving when the twittering of angry birds reminded him of his duty.

He left the stones behind and headed toward the cave where the Shizumu controlled flock was herding the others. It wasn't the birds alone the Shizumu controlled, it was the entire realm. During his time with the ghostly creature or illusion, he wasn't yet sure; Gary learned just what the Shizumu did with all their time locked away in this prison.

Before the Shiznet evolved into the current virtual reality hybrid realm, it was little more than an endless void that drained away the strength and power of the Shizumu. A pocket universe created by the Nefslama as a prison to hold their shame for eternity. That was what the woman called the Shizumu, the shame of the Nefslama.

Over the countless ages, the Shizumu learned to build some resistance to the draining effect of the prison. They also learned to work together, which was something they never did in the past for they are usually the embodiment of clear need for a host or vessel.

Uniting their efforts, they began learning to manipulate the energies the prison siphoned off and redirect it to affect their environment. The world the kids now explored was hard won, but now the Shizumu had complete control over everything. Taking control became possible a decade ago when a sudden burst of Emassa followed by a spell, opened their prison allowing the escape of one Shizumu.

The leader of the group who wanted revenge. This individual being spent the next ten years plotting and planning until he was finally able to gain enough power to merge the pocket universe with modern technology.

Gary was unable to find out the Shizumu master plan, but he was smart enough to know they needed something from Colby. The woman told him that his friends would come to no harmed. However, if Gary wanted to see his parents again, he must keep the other star children separated and trapped in the Shiznet.

As he neared the cave created to hold his friends captive, Gary began to feel a tug on his spirit. He didn't feel guilty as he should, nor did he explore that realization. What Gary felt was a sense of closeness and bond such as the pull of two magnets in proximity to one another. Except he was feeling the pull from multiple sources.

Gary's immediate thought was of his parents. Perhaps the Shizumu decided to free them and let them reunite. But as he entered the cave, his hopes faded. All that greeted him was five recesses in the back of the cave, each holding one of his companions deep in a trance, just as the woman said.

Daphne admitted that the Shizumu used the stolen Hashtag Magic to lure the children into this specially created cavern where they would immediately fall into a trance and begin dreaming a new reality while they stayed within.

* * *

A whispering Gary heard was the mumblings of each captive in their alcove, each immersed in their sub-world. After setting down the vortex device in the center of the cavern, Gary walked from one dreamer to the next. He wondered what secrets any could hold that might help the Shizumu with whatever they planned. A chattering from the woman in his thoughts reminded Gary he had a mission to accomplish.

Returning to the device that brought them all here, Gary waved his hand over the top to activate an interface. He then took a stylus from a holder on the side and began drawing a hashtag spell on the virtual display. **#ConnectJasper**.

A jagged beam of red light leaped from the device and hit Jasper Bodine in the forehead. Jasper rocked back on his heels and shook as his thoughts became separate images on Gary's display. The device was joining with Jasper's dream-state, allowing Gary to manipulate what was happening easily.

Gary repeated the process with the rest of his friends. Each one reacted the same as Jasper when they became mentally linked to the device. Visions of each person's inner thoughts-of-self came flooding forward and into the machine where Gary could twist them and use them to find out what each was hiding. These secrets were the information the Shizumu instructed him to retrieve.

A few adjustments on the device allowed Gary to create a separate display for each dreamer. Now he set upon them with single-mindedness required to get what he wanted, his parents freedom. With a few adjustments more he locked on his victims and began the process of creating a virtual world version of a role-playing game.

# <u>Chapter 17</u>

## #DivideAndConqure

Forming some water and splashing it on Rhea's face, Darla was the first to confirm what happened. "It was tiring just using the magic to create water. Rhea exhausted herself healing you Colby."

"It's this place," Jasper said. "And whatever that little traitor Gary did."

"Enough about Gary, Jasper," sighed Colby. "We don't know that he didn't get lost, or taken by the Shizumu even."

"Well if they took him, then let them keep him."

"I said enough."

"Gary aside," Shelly said while squeezing Colby's shoulder. She looked at Jasper and frowned. "What do you mean about this place?"

"I'm feeling more tired by the minute," said Jasper. "It's like I'm half asleep."

"That explains how you usually seem," Darla said. "You walk through life half asleep. Imagine the actual thinking you could do if you were awake?"

* * *

Jasper rolled his eyes at the comments. "Have none of you been noticing the drain on our magic?" He turned and pointed at the birds now sitting quietly in trees well away from the cave entrance. "The birds just stopped following and sit guard out there. They must know something we don't otherwise they could have flown in here after us. Why is that?"

Everyone now stood looking out from the cave entrance. One lone bird squawked at the kids' presence. Each one could feel something like an invisible barrier that buffered them from the outside and pulled on their power.

"Come to think of it," Shelly said. "I could use a nap."

Darla yawned and stretched. "Me too."

Rhea nodded and sat down on the ground.

Colby limped back to his boulder and rubbed the cramp from his right leg. Wanting to get on with their search, he had to figure out what was next. Looking back, and deeper into the cave, Colby was beckoned by a familiar feeling, though he knew it would likely weaken their magic more.

Though Colby and the others seemed more tired than expected, they sat quietly preparing for their next move. Colby had no idea what to do next, but he'd think of something. *Yawn.* All he needed…*yawn*…was a little catnap.

It wasn't long before they were all asleep. None of the companions were aware that their bodies began to drift apart and each into a recess along the wall. A red glaze of energy washed over them all as they became entrenched in a shared dream state.

A quick burst of energy shot through them all and they found themselves back on the cave floor. The teenagers sat in their circle, grumbling about hunger and what they were going to do now. None complained of being at all sleepy any longer. None had any clue they were all asleep, and something was guiding them into a dream within their virtual experience.

Each of them attempted calling and storing magic power regularly; it was an exercise that already proved good practice. Now Colby and friends found that there was little to no access to Emassa flowing in this realm and their reserves were all they had. Some had more capacity than others to store magic power, and that might become a liability. Rhea was already dangerously low on Emassa and Colby getting wounded confirmed that they were not impervious to injury in this modified former Shizumu prison.

"We need to go deeper into the Shiznet," Colby said while moving toward Rhea. He took her hand. "You're going to need this I think."

Rhea took a sharp breath as Colby released a portion of his stored magic and let it flow into her core. While his hand shone purple, the unique color of his magic, Rhea's pulsed blue as it took only the type of power she could use. Colby was a hybrid and thus able to use both the magic of the Shizumu and Nefslama. He also had the white power that accompanied his use of time magic, but he had yet to explore that source of energy fully.

"Thank you, but I fear you may need more magic in this place than the rest of us," Rhea said. She rubbed her head after the swimming sensation caused from receiving Emassa so quickly from Colby.

"I had some to spare. Besides, I can still pull in and store Emassa, albeit slowly and requires some concentration."

"How can that be?" Jasper asked. "I can't feel the link at all."

Colby shook his head. "I'm not sure. I feel a connection, but it isn't direct."

Jasper raised his right brow but said nothing while looking at the others. They returned questioning looks also but did not share them. The cave entrance became still and quiet.

Colby, unmoved by the odd looks and wordless questions, stood tentatively before putting more weight on his injured leg. A brief wince and muted grunt were the only indications to the others that he was in pain. Colby waved off their worried faces and turned toward the back of the cave. A red glow fought against the choking darkness that reached out from the depths.

"I'm gonna take a look," Colby said.

Shelly ran up to Colby and grabbed his arm. "I don't think we should go any further into this…place."

Shrugging off Shelly's hand from his shoulder, Colby moved further into the tunnel leading deeper into the cavern. Struggling to walk with as little a limp as possible, he refrained from turning back to hide the wincing and tearing eyes of his face.

"I have to see what's down there."

"Colby wait!"

He was out of Shelly's reach when the darkness enveloped Colby. He was no longer visible, nor could the shuffling steps of his injured gait be heard. Colby was gone.

"I'm going after him," Shelly said before jogging off into the darkness.

Darla, Rhea, and Jasper remained in the outer cavern tunnel. They listened without making a sound. After several minutes, and no sign of

Shelly or Colby returning, the three remaining youths turned to each other and silently agreed with slight nods. One after the next, they each made their way toward the back of the cave and stepped into the shadows. Each companion disappeared into the unknown darkness, separated from one another.

### 

Gary dismissed the spell showing a bird's eye view of an empty cave entrance. Turning around in the round room he sat in; he regarded a shadowed presence in the corner with a slight nod.

"I've done as you asked. Where are my parents?"

Barking laughter echoed in the cylindrical chamber, driving Gary to shuffle back landing on his butt and pressed up against the wall. The voices that led him back to this room promised he would be with his parents again as long as he did as they instructed. Doubt stirred in his mind as he rubbed his right calf that he now favored.

"You wish to see your parents together again?" the specter asked. "We promised this, and we shall keep that pledge, but first you must do as we have demanded."

Betraying his friend was the last thing Gary ever thought he would think of doing. But Colby was relying more and more on Jasper and less on him. Separating them to show Colby he didn't need Jasper was selfish, but it served a purpose for both Gary and the Shizumu.

Gary moved toward the device that brought them all into this virtual realm. Now that he had direction on how to use it correctly, Gary called up the display and located five pulsing dots in the matrix. They were all separated in virtual dreams within a virtual realm. They were each alone to face whatever the Shizumu had planned for them.

* * *

"It is already done. Colby and the others are no longer together. Will you bring me to my parents now?"

"Not yet. You have more work to do."

The Shizumu waved a host of its comrades into the device. They were entering the dreams to unleash whatever torment they wished upon Colby and his friends. All but one.

Gary remained silent as the Shizumu floated nearer. As he pondered what these creatures might use to attack his friends, his only consolation was that they were not actually in the Shiznet and probably slept peacefully back in the real world. He closed his eyes and tried to focus on his body and those of his friends, safe back at the Stevens' home.

# <u>Chapter 18</u>

## #MoreLies

Nana sat back from Colby's injured leg, a first aid kit lying open beside her. The wound began to close and heal before she managed to clean it. She insisted on using mundane methods to clean and dress the injury, explaining to Rigel that her magic might interfere with the spell the children used to enter the vortex. As it turned out, for the time being at least, the children were capable of taking care of themselves. The memories she regained of Bellatrix's former lives, however, reminded Nana to take nothing for chance.

Looking over at the other children, Nana found only minor cuts and scratches. Gary was the only one who showed no physical sign of injury, though his face occasionally flinched from what she presumed was caused by pain. Nana looked him over carefully but found nothing to explain his discomfort, but there was something about the boy that was off. She never noticed it before regaining her full consciousness; with all her returned power and knowledge she could see more than before. Gary was not what he seemed.

Rigel watched her examine the boy. "You notice it as well?"

Nana turned and squinted at Rigel. "What though? Do you know?"

* * *

"I'm unable to ascertain what makes him different," Rigel said while shaking his head. "I had hoped you might glean something from the boy."

Turning back to Gary, Nana touched his forehead. "Now is not the time to delve into that mystery. I mustn't meddle with this magic that puts them in such a state." She turned back to Rigel as she stood and adjusted her wrinkled housecoat. "There is someone who might know." She gave Rigel a knowing look. "The old man who played Runes with Colby."

"I have no idea where he is. He hasn't shown himself since before last Halloween."

Nana motioned Rigel toward the kitchen with a wave. She turned to face Fizzlewink, who sat quietly watching her every move since discovering who she was and is again. When he moved to follow them, Nana pointed back toward the children and stared down the little blue man.

"You stay and keep watch over the children."

Nana turned away and waddled into the kitchen, walking past Rigel who looked over to Fizzlewink with pity.

"Never mind the cat and get in here 'Yummy Pants'!"

Rigel took the seat Nana pulled out from the counter and waited while she put on a kettle for tea. Though she was very much the same eccentric old woman he met months ago, he also now saw the ancient elder who he met eons ago when the war with the Shizumu was at its peak. She was a force to be reckoned with no matter the personality that chose to show itself, so he patiently waited while Nana took her time.

Without looking back at Rigel, Nana continued to prepare a tray of tea and cookies while she spoke. "I think you have known me, well the other me, for a very long time."

* * *

"I have known-"

"That wasn't a question child. Don't interrupt." Nana turned to him with the tray and set it down before beginning to set out their cups. She began to pour out the tea. "I am just returning to myself, or what can be assimilated into who I am at present. I have quite a mess of memories floating around in my skull, some not very pretty. One of those memories involves the old bastard I need you to go find."

"Jenkins?"

"If that's what he calls himself these days. He and I have a long history. He may not wish to get involved."

"He already is."

Rigel explained to Nana about his pact with a group of Nefslama who wished to see an end to the struggle with the Shizumu. They wanted their power back. They were led by two of the remaining elders, Jenkins being one of them. He contrived a plan to broker peace with the Shizumu or put them down once and for all. That plan involved Colby, but the full details were not shared. Jenkins and Pace were the only two who had all the details, and they did not agree on the plan.

"Those two never could see eye-to-eye, especially when it came to matters of family. I remember Pace told me some of this in Uxmal, but I didn't know you're part in the farce."

Rigel continued his lie explaining that for his part, Rigel was to acquire anything that could lead them to Jarrod. They would track him down and have him reverse what he did to bind Colby's full potential. The details after that are where the sharing stopped, but the others only saw that they could have their access to the magic back, so the details did not matter. Rigel, on the other hand, remained guarded about his actual interest in Colby and his magic.

Now that Rigel became attached to the boy, he could no longer see Colby as merely a tool. This line of thinking was similar to what Pace had when last they spoke in Mexico. The boy needed to retain his power and was the key to a different way of resolving the conflict.

"How will Colby accomplish what so many before could not? Did Pace tell you what he saw?"

"It was unclear. All he could say was that the boy would realize a different path and put an end to the war with the Shizumu."

Nana grumbled and grabbed a cookie before dunking it in her tea. "That old fortune teller and his cryptic bits of information. He saw, you can bet on that, but it's likely there are multiple outcomes, and undue influence could change things drastically." She popped the cookie in her mouth and wiped her hands on her apron.

"So why do you want Jenkins here?"

"Ha! I don't want him here really…he can be useful. And if he thinks he can endear himself to the boy, he may reveal something useful." Nana paused and stared out the window. She watched as the Dreggs milled about beyond the barrier protecting the property. "Just go find him so he can tell us about the Connor boy."

"Where do I start? Back at the park where they played Runes?"

Nana swallowed and wiped away a tear, never turning around. "Go to the island south of the Chicago Loop. You will find him with Daphne."

Rigel puzzled at first, took a moment to understand where Nana was sending him. "You mean the three statues in Daphne park on Northerly Island? Why would he be there, that place is completely void of

Emassa…for some reason." Rigel knew more but stopped himself.

"Just go there. If he isn't present, he will show up sooner or later. He always went to guard her." Nana saw something in Rigel just then. A memory perhaps, or perhaps nothing. She narrowed her eyes before grunting and shooing Rigel away.

Rigel left without asking questions that he was certain would go without answers. His certainty became supported by the muffled grumbling he heard as he exited the back door of the Stevens' home. He walked past the barrier and paused before Conrad.

"Move aside mongrel," Rigel whispered then departed in a flash of energy.

Nana's mind was waking from a sort of spelled amnesia self-imposed by the spell she created eons in the past. At first, when Bellatrix's pendant caused the merger of minds and ended the spell, Nana was overwhelmed by the history of countless lives coalescing with her own. Though she soon understood the spell and what was happening, she now saw it as a curse. Along with her entire history, came the horrors she committed.

Daphne. That particular memory was among the first to resurface. And it did so with a tightening in Nana's chest. It happened so long ago, but it felt as though it were happening all over again as the memories piled upon her old mind. The one who became three to try and please Bellatrix. Everything went horribly wrong, and Jenkins —his current name— blamed Bellatrix.

Now the man was back along with her memories of their last encounter. This reunion wasn't going to be pleasant when he arrives. Remembering Daphne and the events related to her tragic accident, brought with an understanding of why she is continually drawn to that park. Why she often found herself there staring at the statues.

* * *

Nana would sit for hours in that small meadow, chatting with the three sculptures. Passersby would look and giggle at the crazy old bat talking to herself. Nana laughed along with them, not understanding her compulsion to visit with inanimate artwork that mysteriously appeared in a park devoid of magical energy. Nothing odd in the least there; Nana would laugh at herself back then. She was no longer laughing.

The part of her that was Bellatrix knew something was not kosher.

Of all the atrocities that Nana now recalled from Bellatrix's memories, the tragedy of that young girl was top of the list. She would have to deal with that soon enough if Jenkins decided to make an appearance. As she looked in the mirror at her haggard and wrinkled reflection, Nana realized he might show up if only to relish in her fall from youth and beauty.

The hundreds and then thousands of years she spent in self-seclusion were hard on her magic. At one time she used to focus her power on the beauty of nature, life, and rejuvenation. While living out multiple split existences, her magic remained focused on maintaining two lives. When her outside world life would end, she used that special magic of life to create a new incarnation within the womb of a barren woman that prayed for a child.

So often she heard those prayers of the childless and hoped to help them, but her curse required her magic to sustain the spells that kept her safe to prepare. Now the time had come, and she was no more prepared for what is expected of her than the day she secluded herself away in the Yucatán. After all her failures during the peak of the War of Souls, the name that was given for the conflict against the Shizumu, Bellatrix had no better plan now than when the war started.

The war with the Shizumu placed a heavy burden on every one of the elders, Bellatrix especially. She was tasked with a way to drain their power and make them impotent. This spell resulted in a wraith-like creature that could not hold magic but was able to draw it out of other beings. These abominations were later called Seekers.

After another string of trials and errors, Bellatrix eventually came up with a way to create an army of sorts or at least a personal guard for the Nefslama survivors. She required volunteers for a metamorphic spell, and those who came forward were among the Nefsmari, a hybrid race of blue skinned people bred to be guardians of children and muses to the artists of the world. Once word spread that this change would protect them from the Shizumu, nearly the entire race went through the procedure.

The few Nefsmari that remained were ostracized by those who mutated until they relented or went into hiding. This biased and hatred is what led to the belief Fizzlewink carried about the Dreggs destroying his kind.

Bellatrix found herself at the center of all that was wrong with the world of magic, and the bubble was collapsing on her. Now with the War of Souls raging and the Nefslama falling back, she concocted her most heinous solution of all. To block out the Emassa and render the Shizumu too weak to resist eternal confinement, the innocent magical souls of children were needed. That spell backfired also when it took not only their magic but their souls as well.

The great magical barrier that surrounded the planet required regular sacrifices to maintain the dampening of Emassa that kept the Shizumu weak. Over the eons, the elders looked to alter the spell. There was never a way to change what was required. The shame coupled with the loss of innocents —though they always volunteered— divided the elders and scattered the surviving Nefslama across the planet.

The meddling of scientists has weakened the barrier prematurely and likely allowed the Shizumu the strength to begin escaping and carrying out whatever horrors they've had millennia to plot and scheme. They have targeted Colby. His father knew and did something yet to be fully understood. And now the reminder of what happened to poor Daphne centuries ago has some spark of alignment with current events.

Nana needed to tell her daughter what was to come. If what she felt had happened to Colby the day Jarrod left was correct, it would fracture Aria further than when the man left her. Enough children were given to the stars in vain to suppress the Emassa. No more. Not her grandson. Not her Fart-blossom.

She would wait for some reinforcement. As much as the side of her that was Bellatrix resented needing the involvement of an old…acquaintance, she needed his help. Rigel would soon return with the man who played himself off as Jenkins. A reunion being ushered in by desperation.

# <u>Chapter 19</u>

**#Betelgeuse**

Rigel always found the void of energy on Northerly Island unnatural. As soon as he crossed an imaginary line into the meadow, the hairs on his arms and neck would stand on edge. And then there was nothing, no magical force at all. Before Colby came back to his power, the magic in the world was still there, but barely a trickle. This place, however, had zero access to Emassa. He was uncomfortable though he knew the lack of magic was necessary.

"Shake it off old boy," Rigel said to the wind. He nodded to a young couple that passed him, giving an odd stare, and carried on toward the sculptures of Daphne.

As he approached, he had a clear view of the garden. No Jenkins. Thankful he thought to grab some fruit on the way out of the house, Rigel found a spot in the center of the garden and sat down to wait. He took in the beauty of the Daphnes and relished in the sound of lake waves breaking against the shore. The buzz of bees hurriedly begging off the pollen from the first flowers of spring lulled him into closing his eyes.

"It's quite peaceful, is it not?"

* * *

Rigel jumped at the sound and immediate proximity of the deep voice. He usually sensed anyone or anything that got too close. Rigel was unaccustomed to having someone sneak up on him.

"I do not remember when I brought her here or when exactly, but it suits her."

Trying to compose and hide his surprise, Rigel smiled and stood. "Um, yes quite so Sir. ..."

"Oh let's not play at that game servant of the Witch. You are here to see me I imagine?"

Rigel, surprised again, furrowed his brows and leaned in closer to the man. "Do I know you? I mean I suppose you are Jenkins, but you look different than I remember, though familiar."

"Ah, well that would be the face I wore until just recently. Or perhaps you know someone of my family line."

The man had family that still lived. This information was an interesting development. The man he assumed this Jenkins actually was lived as a recluse and details of his life after he disappeared with these statues was unknown. If the old man started another family, this might change things in Rigel's plans.

"Why the change? If you don't mind my forwardness."

"I haven't worn this face in. . .well it has been rather long indeed. I had sworn never to wear it again until the day the old witch returned, and I would encounter her yet again." Jenkins waited for the light to sparkle in Rigel's eye of understanding. "And so she has merged with the present, so I adorn a face from the past."

"The family you speak of, are they many?"

* * *

Jenkins turned to regard Rigel. He looked through him as though peering into his being for a clue as to why the man would ask about his family. "Not any longer. I left my family long ago when I could no longer bear the sight of that old witch in Uxmal.

"I assume you speak of Bell-"

"Do not speak her name in the presence of my child!"

Rigel did his best to appear gobsmacked. He looked around and saw no child; then he looked at at the statutes. The thought finally occurred that there was a reason why he always visited the gardens.

"Jenkins, do you mean that the Daphne are your children?" Rigel asked knowing the answer but continued playing his own game. "They are but statues."

Jenkins shook his head. "Not children, child, of sorts. These are not merely statues, but that is not something spoken about openly." Betelgeuse looked sideways at Rigel. "And since I dropped that face you can stop calling me Jenkins in favor of my actual name. That moniker is Betelgeuse."

Another surprise that Rigel for which he was not prepared. Of course, he knew of Betelgeuse but assumed that the elder had long since passed on. To realize he had been working against this man all this time, Rigel began to doubt his typically exceptional perception.

"Don't feel so bad my boy, although you should have suspected something. After all what kind of name is Jenkins for an elder?"

Rigel smiled an agreement. "But what did you mean by 'child'? There are three statues here of Daphne; are you saying one of them is your child?"

* * *

"Three are one and one is three. That is the curse and blessing of Daphne."

Rigel only listened at first, but something told him not to bother asking what the old man meant. But when Betelgeuse mentioned a curse, Rigel couldn't help but remember Bellatrix and her concern over seeing Betelgeuse.

"Did Bellatrix curse Daphne?" Rigel wanted to hear one of the Elders admit their faults.

Betelgeuse grabbed Rigel's arm and pulled him out of the meadow. "I told you not to say that name."

Once the two men were clear of the gardens, Betelgeuse released Rigel's arm and sat down on an empty bench. As Betelgeuse composed himself, Rigel took those few moments to regard the changes in the man that he previously saw as a facsimile of Jenkins.

Gone were the white hair and wrinkled face. The same youthful teeth and clear eyes welcomed the rest of himself. The face Rigel looked at now was that of a man in his prime, and looked very familiar. Of course, familiarity among a desperately low numbered race of immortal people is commonplace.

"Bellatrix is not directly responsible for the state Daphne is in now, but it was her influence that caused this tragedy."

Rigel just sat there quietly with Betelgeuse. He didn't know quite what to say, so he just sat there and admired the quiet beauty of the statues that were once Daphne. There was something odd about the way Betelgeuse hovered over these statues. Rigel knew the truth about the woman this man believed still trapped inside the lead and silver lined sculptures. What bothered Rigel was the fact that this great Elder was too blind to see it himself.

* * *

He wasn't prepared to sit around here all day, and a sliver of disturbance in the air nearby told Rigel it was time to get moving. Rigel decided then to point out something different about the sculptures.

"Forgive me Betelgeuse, but has something changed with the sculptures?"

Betelgeuse stood and stared out at the statues that were once his daughter. His face tightened and his eyes narrowed, while his hands balled into fists. Betelgeuse moved up to one of the statues and placed his hand just above the surface and closed his eyes. When a magical charge left his hand, it sparked and fizzled out. His eyes now opening wide, Betelgeuse mouthed the word no.

Without turning to Rigel, Betelgeuse stormed out of the park, and as soon as he passed the threshold, he disappeared.

"Oh, bloody hell! I'm losing my patience with this game." Rigel ran toward the perimeter and turned back to the glade, looking for something, before leaving the island.

As Rigel left, the statues shimmered the same instant a backlash of energy entered the meadow. The illusion fell and the places where the statues once stood years prior, were empty of the likeness of Daphne and filled with wildflowers and weeds. Except one where a woman stood watching.

Stepping forward from the spot where moments ago a powerful spell fooled the Emassa using old Nefslama, but not Rigel, a young woman watched Rigel leave and smiled obediently.

"I suppose this charade had to end eventually," the woman said, brushing the windblown hair from her face. She picked a leaf from her locks and looked at it with pursed lips before incinerating it with glaring eyes.

"That'll be enough of the laurel leaf hair as well. It's time I saw a golem about his task."   She turned toward the direction Rigel went before vanishing in a red swirling vortex.

# Chapter 20

## #BeginTrolling

Gary continued the task set for him by the strange woman that promised to take him to his parents. He took to the task better than he expected. Once Gary began devising ways to manipulate the dreams of his so-called friends, Gary relished in control. They never even bothered to look for him when he separated from the others. Now he'll teach them a lesson. Rhea was his first target.

"Let's see what you can do now, little healer," Gary said.

He needed to make these manipulations as real as possible, so they didn't realize it was a dream. The more the Shizumu could get from them. Gary sent Rhea into a hospital ward full of injured people. He set Rhea in the middle of a panicked and crazed emergency room as instructed by his stalking wraith.

Rhea fell to her knees from the spinning in her head. She was just in her room a moment before, and now she found herself in the middle of screaming and injured people. Fluorescent lights flicker above her head while lights flashed, alarms sounded, nurses shouted, and more people flooded into the already crowded room. Rhea clutched the sides of her head in confused retreat and wept at the carnage surrounding her.

* * *

"Do something you silly child," a nurse scolded.

Rhea looked at the nurse as she continued, looking back at Rhea only to snare and point toward the increasing backlog of injured people arriving. Her instinct for healing kicked in, and she got up to help. A man — middle-aged— drew her attention first.

"Let me see what I can do for his injuries," Rhea said to a triage medic.

"Ya think!" the medic snapped. "Where do they get you kids these days?"

Rhea stared at the medic and blinked. "What is that supposed to mean?"

He huffed back at her question. "Slow-witted and full of questions, not what we need here. Look if you can't heal these people, then get the hell out of here because you're useless otherwise."

Through teary eyes, Rhea turned her face away from the toxic attitude thrown at her. She had to heal these people. That was something Rhea could accomplish, but the medic was right; it was the only thing she was capable of doing. She wiped her eyes and laid her hands upon the man's blast-scorched chest. A warming sensation stirred in her core and began to spread out toward her arms. As the energy began to channel to her healing hands, it fizzled and faded to nothing.

"Get out of here! You can't do anything right can you?"

"I can't do this; I-I don't understand." Rhea looked at her hands. No Emassa was forming. Though she could feel it stirring from her reserve of power stored at her core, the magic was depleting before she could get it to her hands and work her healing spells.

### 

Now that Rhea was well into a good trolling session, Gary switched his attention to Darla.

Darla walked down the halls of school looking for someone, but she couldn't remember who. She then caught sight of her cheer teammates and ran to follow them outside to the football field. There was a game starting, and her squad was there to rally the fans and cheer the team. Darla was head cheerleader and used her empath abilities to rile up the crowd regularly.

The crowd grew silent as Darla made her approach. All eyes were on her, and Darla looked down at herself to make sure she was dressed. She saw nothing wrong with her outfit or appearance. The emotions she tried to sense were foreign. That was until she sensed hate.

Darla walked past her squad, feeling the same animosity directed at her as from the fans in the bleachers. There was a definite air of disdain that hung over her, blocking out the sunshine with how thick it became.

A cup of soda flew past her as she took her position, preparing a cheer. Darla couldn't understand what was coming over the crowd. They always loved her and her pom-pom squad and the cheers they perform. Now she was being greeted with thrown cups and booing.

"You suck!" someone shouted from the crowd.

Darla tried her best to ignore the heckler and began a cheer. Her squad followed along with little enthusiasm. This behavior was not like her squad either, Darla thought. She tried to use her ability to elicit peace and fun from her girls. Nothing happened.

Quite the opposite happened. The more Darla tried to affect change in the moods of those around her, the more hostility she was rewarded.

"What is wrong with everybody?" Darla asked.

* * *

"You're the leader; this is all your fault. They don't like you." Her nearest squad member stood —hands on hips— and mocked Darla.

"Yeah," Another girl said. "I don't think they ever did like you. We sure don't."

Gary laughed at Darla's sniffles. The girl who used her charms to make everyone grovel and follow her was getting a good taste of reality. He turned his back on Darla and entered Shelly's virtual dream.

###

The overbearing and dominating Shelly was next on Gary's checklist. There was a special sort of feeling for evening the score with her that Gary didn't understand. There was no direct source or memory for this feeling he had, but Gary held a desire for payback. Shelly talked to dead people, so Gary was going to give her some spirits.

Ghosts swam through the air, moaning and pleading for Shelly's help. As she spun around inside her mind, the dizzying effect overwhelmed her senses before she collapsed on the floor. When Shelly pushed back the voices enough to force open her eyes, she found a familiar place greeting her, the diner.

Every seat, every booth, every stool, all occupied by a specter demanding service. Shelly looked around to see that she was the only waitress on shift. Without thinking, she scrambled to her feet and hurried behind the counter. Grabbing an apron from a shelf, Shelly went about starting to take orders.

From one patron to the next she moved, not thinking about what they ordered, only focused on getting each check fixed to the spinning order wheel in the window that led to the kitchens. Shelly filled the wheel, double and triple slips clamped in the same spots; she spun the wheel around until the last order was taken. She breathed deep and bent at the waist.

A bell rang. The order ready bell meant it was time to get back to work, but when she stood straight and turned to retrieve the plates she froze. The chef, Bruce, stood empty handed and glared at her.

"What do you expect of me to fill these orders?" Bruce said.

"Bruce?" Shelly stood there, nothing else to say. The last time she saw him was during the attack at Bellatrix's house in Chichén Itzá when Bruce was revealed as a traitor. She was unsure what happened to him, but now she realized she must have killed him.

Shelly looked out at the patrons, all looking at her expectantly. She looked then at the slips and saw the orders she wrote but had not registered at the time.

Contact my wife. Find my lost love. Apologize for me to someone. All these wishes, the final wishes of tortured souls and Shelly was expected to fill all these requests.

"This is your specialty, isn't it? The freak goth girl who talks to ghosts, you need to fill these orders. I can't help you with that."

Shelly took the slips that Bruce pulled down from the order wheel and then shoved toward her. She couldn't look him in the eye, knowing she likely ended his life with her violent reaction to his betrayal.

But she then remembered how he betrayed her; how he betrayed everyone from the beginning. She looked up at Bruce and saw Gary's face for a moment, then attacked Bruce.

### 

Gary ducked out of Shelly's dream just before taking the brunt of her rage against Bruce. She would be busy for a long time taking her anger out on his likeness. Now Gary would have some real fun torturing Jasper.

Dust settled to the ground and left Jasper facing a pitch black slate board. He held a thorn covered piece of chalk in his hand that he could not release. The pricking into his fingers just at the threshold of his tolerance for pain made him wince.

Voices pelted his eardrums from behind him. Commands for answers echoed through his head. When Jasper tried to turn back, hoping to stall or at least see who hounded him, searing pain was his only reward.

"Answer our questions boy!" shouted a commanding and demonic voice.

Jasper tried to focus on one of the questions, but the more he attempted to separate one question from the next, the more cluttered his thoughts became.

"Concentrate," Jasper chided himself.

The questions continued. Geometry, Physics, Chemistry, increasingly more challenging and persistent came the requests for his understanding of things he could never grasp. He was not smart, and he knew it. It wasn't a matter of applying himself; he just lacked the ability to comprehend complex ideas unless they were strategic in nature. Jasper was the embodiment of strength and was always useful in a fight. That was what his father told him as a young boy. But he heard another chiding now from that familiar voice.

"Are you thick as a board, boy?" his father said. "Why are you so stupid?"

Jasper squeezed his eyes shut while his shoulders raised. He tried squinting out the voices, but they persisted. Not only his father, but every authority figure, teacher, coach, or trainer he ever had was now hounding him. They were picking past his tough exterior, exposing his lacking intellect.

Pushing from his storehouse of power, Jasper flooded his skin with Emassa, strengthening it against the stinging of their words. The more the voices pelted him with insult, the more energy he used to push them away. When he opened his eyes to look at the chalkboard, he saw the blank slate before him, waiting for an answer to be chalked out. What was the question they wanted answering?

Now that Jasper was well and rightly flustered with having to think and answer questions, Gary was free to move on to his final victim. Colby.

# Chapter 21

## #AlteredDream

Gary found Colby standing at the center of a small plaza. Colby stood there, unaware of his surroundings or Gary's presence which Gary was relieved of but confused. This vision was not the program dream that Gary sent Colby. It changed from what the wraith had instructed.

Small buildings circled the plaza, each one two or three stories, and they appeared ancient. Old construction of stone but precision that rivaled modern building techniques. Gary was awestruck by the beauty until he noticed the thick mist that rolled just beyond the rooftops. It was receding, and with its retreat, the fog gave way to a chorus of clashing shouts and cries. Just outside the Plaza, a war took place, and it was converging on the spot Colby stood.

Gary's feet shuffled as he stood behind a pillar, hiding from his friend. He held back from calling out, torn between his loyalties and the jealousy that drove him to betray his friend's trust. As he prepared to cry out, Gary noticed Colby begin to snap out of his dazed state. Gary exhaled and stepped back into the shadows.

Colby woke to the cracking of magical energy thrown around him. A concussive wave of power threw him to the ground. Colby turned to face a man screaming out in agony as a red glowing creature forced its way into his chest. Red light poured from the man's eyes, mouth, ears, and nose. The Shizumu was burning him alive from the inside. Colby reached out to try and force the Shizumu out, but as his hand touched the other man, the screaming stopped, and Colby watched as his suffering ended in a pile of ash.

Colby retched before turning back to see the same fate enacted upon multitudes of people all around him. He twisted around onto his backside and scooted back against a wall.

"What is happening?" Colby cried out. "Where am I?"

Colby huddled there against the wall watching the battle enter the plaza. He saw first hand how the Shizumu fought to take the bodies of the people in this city. Colby struggled to make sense of when this was and where. Somehow he must have accidentally traveled through time. A firm hand on his shoulder shook him to awareness.

"Have you quickened boy?" the man asked.

"I-I, do you mean, have I got magic?"

The man looked at Colby with a tilted head. "Magic? You know we do not approve of such a base term to label our abilities such as the mortal fodder of this world."

He grabbed Colby by the collar and pulled him to his feet. "Stand and fight or go cower in the lower reaches with the weak and useless children."

Colby felt both frightened and angered by this man. He didn't know what was going on, but he wouldn't be spoken to in such a way by this stranger. He was not weak.

Colby released a blast of energy from his body that knocked the man back, but not as far as Colby would have thought. Something was inhibiting his magic. He was weakening.

The man looked at Colby again and laughed. "I hope you can do better than that. Now get out there and help put these demons into the void."

"The what?"

"The prison chamber deep in the bowels of the netherworld. What do you think this war is about boy? They discovered our plans to imprison them and attacked before we could act first."

Colby realized he was in the past when the Shizumu were first captured and locked away. "What were they doing before? Why are you, we, trying to imprison them?"

"They are evil and against the natural order of things, isn't that enough?"

"No, it is not. What makes them bad?"

The man paused, perplexed by Colby's question. His face pinched and eyes widened. "Because they are not like us."

Colby stepped back from the man who looked at him with disgust and walked away. The man disappeared into the mist that hung around the battle still waging around him. Colby needed to know more about this conflict. He ran for the center of the plaza and began reaching out to those who were being attacked by Shizumu. He would separate them and try to stop the conflict.

Colby gave no clue he was concerned about messing with the timeline, Gary thought. How could they have gone back in time, only moments ago they were traveling through the portal into the Shiznet induced dream. Something was wrong, but he couldn't focus on why he felt odd about their situation. He refrained from getting involved for unknown reasons. So he just remained hidden in the shadows and watched.

The more Colby forced his touch upon those around him, the more energy it required. He pushed Shizumu away from around him and pulled others out from invading the physical bodies among the fighting mass. The more he immersed himself in the battle, the more intense the raging became. Soon Colby found himself unable to separate the Shizumu from their prey. He could not muster enough strength, though he was surprised he did not deplete his reserve of Emassa.

People screamed and burned to ash around him. Colby could not stop the carnage by forcing the Shizumu out. His spells were well powered, but once released became impotent. Each time he tried to transport himself to the next victim, he found himself sent to the wrong spot. Something didn't want him to interfere. Colby couldn't accept the role of bystander. However, he couldn't be everywhere at once. Or could he?

Colby calmed his breathing and closed his eyes. He stood once again at the center of the plaza but this time concentrated on something other than the fighting. His hands came up before him as he opened his eyes and began drawing a hashtag spell that only he could power. **#HaltTime**.

Now would be the first time since Mexico that Colby would attempt this spell purposely. It happened by instinct before; now he hoped that his focused will and the hashtag spell would allow him to repeat the high magic. This time, Colby felt the huge draw of power on his core. That special place deep within his body where he could store the magical energy Emassa for later use. Why his earlier use had no discernible depleting effect yet, this time-spell did. Colby couldn't explain why. He didn't care. He pushed harder until the spell was sufficiently fueled and then released it.

A blinding flash of white light interlaced with red and blue streaks radiated from Colby in every direction. Everything halted. Smoke froze in the air from the many fires. Shizumu dimmed or shone brighter as they became locked between the pulsing of light that made up their energy-based forms. Not a single thing moved around Colby.

Gary stepped forward from his hiding spot, astounded at witnessing his friend's massive spell take hold. Then he realized he wasn't frozen in time along with the others. But Gary wasn't the only one unaffected by the spell. He saw movement along the far side of the plaza. A single Shizumu shifted into existence near an archway. It was accompanied by a woman. They were drawn to Colby's spell. Gary started to run out and warn Colby, but he never moved a step.

Halted mid-stride, Gary found himself unable to move. A firm grasp on his shoulder twisted him around until he was face-to-face with the woman. He didn't know her, but she looked like the Daphne woman, but different, older.

"You shouldn't be here. Go!" Daphne tossed Gary aside, and he vanished through the ground where he would have landed.

Daphne turned to her Shizumu companion. "This has begun to unravel. We need to force the children to draw themselves fully into the network."

"Is that wise?" the Shizumu asked.

"This boy," she started and pointed to Colby. "He has managed a true spell within this dream. If we do not cut them off from all access to Emassa, they could destroy this place."

The Shizumu laughed. "Our wish is for this place to be destroyed, why were they brought here in the first place if not to destroy our longtime prison?"

Daphne smiled, not a sweet smile, but a grin that did not reach her eyes. It came from her damaged psyche. "They will destroy it once all of those responsible for the War of Souls have been trapped within. Then they will destroy it, and themselves with it."

"That was not what Rigel-"

"I have changed the rules," Daphne interrupted. "Rigel, though I love him, is a fool and will suffer the same fate as these precious children if I don't take over."

The Shizumu questioned Daphne's instruction, but would not give it voice. Instead, he asked what her wishes were and set out to obey. First, he had to send his allies in to attack the Stevens boy and drain him of power, then, when the time was right see to the closing of the portal inside the Stevens home.

Daphne left the Shizumu to his task. She took one more look at Colby as he collapsed on the cobbled street, nearly drained of power. Even as weak as he was now, Daphne knew he had more magic than she, even if he didn't know it himself. She dared not risk him ruining her plans by happenstance. She jumped into a portal just as the illusionary world began to fade around Colby.

Colby was weak and didn't trust what his eyes showed him at first. The images of war dissolved but there remained several Shizumu. They stood up and surrounded Colby, but stayed out of arms reach until he stood up to face them. Now that he was upright and spent from his spell to stop time, Colby realized his folly. It was all a rouse to get him to use up his Emassa. Now he was vulnerable, and the Shizumu were here to finish him off. Colby thought of Jasper and how he wished he had his friend beside him. He needed his strength.

# **Chapter 22**

## **#BattleBoys**

Jasper scratched the chalk across the blackboard, trying to write out the answers to endless questions thrown at him. The words he wrote were nonsense and disconnected from coherent thought. He wrote without focusing on the words. His thoughts were of one thing. He thought of his friend Colby. How he was the smart one. Colby could answer these questions. Jasper wanted Colby by his side.

The chalk cracked as it hit a space between bricks. Jasper focused his mind and saw that he now faced a wall instead of the slate board of a classroom. Jasper turned to look behind himself for the first time since this nightmare began. The absence of voices taunting him was a relief, but Jasper sensed he was still somehow threatened. When he saw Colby surrounded by Shizumu, however, thoughts for his wellbeing vanished. Colby was in trouble.

Jasper ran toward the nearest Shizumu while drawing a spell on his arm. **#BatteringRamArm** and **#EnergyShield**. As the spells formed they wavered a moment until Jasper locked eyes with Colby, then he smiled. The spells energized and formed. Jasper's arm became augmented by a long energy-rod extending five feet ahead of him while a shield of plasma formed over his body. He increased his speed and ran headlong into the first Shizumu.

* * *

The Shizumu scattered after witnessing the assault on one of their own. Before Jasper could reach Colby however, the enemy sent a new illusion to each of the boys. The boys became separated by a wall that stretched infinitely above them. As they faced the wall on opposite sides, footsteps behind them drew their attention. As they turned, the hairs on the back of their arms stood in reaction to a static charge of Emassa building, but it wasn't coming from themselves.

Colby managed to dodge the first blast, but the second assault from Jasper hit him in the leg where he already nursed a wound. As he rolled away from the attack,  Colby grabbed his bleeding leg.  The viscous red fluid flowed freely from his wound, but when it hit the ground, it disintegrated. As odd as his bleeding seemed, Colby didn't have time to ponder it because Jasper was preparing another assault to send his way. But he did not use a spell.

"Hashtag; You can't even walk let alone use magic," Jasper shouted.

The words materialized in the air between him and Colby then converged into a beam of light that knocked him back down in mid-rise.

"What the-" Colby started.

Another hashtag trolling comment escaped Jasper's lips and sailed toward Colby.

"Hashtag; Your nothing more than a battery."

More insults and taunting words flew from Jasper and hit Colby, keeping him from rising to his feet. Just as he was nearing his limit and preparing to give up, Colby heard one of the spells as it neared him.

"Hashtag; How can you be the hope for peace?"

* * *

Colby lifted his hand. Sweat soaked his hair and dripped off as his head rose. Colby's eyes tilted up to view Jasper between his bangs that hung wet and stringy. The insulting beam of power froze in the air before Colby's palm as he continued to rise and watch Jasper take a tentative step back.

"What did you last say? Peace?"

Jasper did not reply, but his reaction told Colby more than he expected as he watched the skin of his friend begin to pixelate and contort.

"What are you? I know you aren't Jasper. Are you a Shizumu troll?"

The thing that was Jasper continued to transform and was unable to voice a response more understandable than a gurgling and throaty howl. Its mouth widened and several teeth jutted out to form lower fangs. His ears grew larger and began to taper into a point at the top which sagged outward growing coarse hairs. As its eyes bulged and nose flattened, the truth of what it was became apparent. When the beam of light repelled back from Colby, hitting the creature, the remaining disguise of Jasper ultimately fell away revealing a massive troll. It roared.

"You are no peace," the troll shouted. "You are nothing."

Colby wiped his eyes and flipped his drenched bangs back over his head. He squared off his position and looked the troll in the eyes.

"If you were hoping for peace from me, you should not have attacked. Hiding behind words is the hallmark of a coward."

The troll narrowed its otherwise full eyes on Colby. Rather than back down as Colby hoped, it became enraged and renewed its verbal assault. However, it was in another language. At first, it seemed gibberish to Colby until he recognized some of the odd squiggles that appeared in the air separating him from the massive beast. They were runes, and they were forming a spell. Colby barely reacted in time to deflect the brunt of the attack. What he did feel was unexpected. He felt fear.

When Colby erected his weak field of energy to protect himself, it allowed some of the troll's magic past. It was not an attack of force or deadly strike; it was as though the monster put all its feelings into a spell and sent them out to attach themselves to his foe. The creature wanted Colby to feel as it did, deficient, reviled, feeble, all this and more.

Colby required no spell from a monster to feel these things. He felt them often enough on his own, but why from this creature in the realm of the Shizumu. Why was this thing. . . 'trolling' him? That gave Colby an idea just in time for the next attack.

### 

On the other side of the wall, Jasper held his ground against the bulking mass of a beast which assailed him. Jasper didn't take the time to listen to what the spells were doing as he poured his waning energy into bolstering a shield to protect himself. Once he felt that he was safe enough, Jasper allowed himself to relax a small amount. It was sufficient to spare some thought on what this troll was doing. That is when the words began to filter to his ears.

"All you have is your strength," the troll shouted. "You are nothing without your little boyfriend."

Jasper's shield weakened.

"I bet you go skipping down the halls of school holding hands."

"That's not true," Jasper murmured. He shook his head while his fists clenched. He looked up at the troll, wondering what happened to Colby who was there only moments before. "Colby. This is because of him."

* * *

"Colby, oh Colby," the troll laughed. The taunting echoed as the scene changed. The red cobbled street gave way to cold tiles while the buildings melted and morphed into walls. The sky dissolved into the locker filled halls at Escutcheon Academy. "You want to join him in his locker?"

Jasper turned to see his friend, Colby, desperately trying to escape the confines of his locker. Jasper's old friends standing beside him laughed at their handiwork.

"You're just a dumb brute with no brains and no future," the troll rumbled in Jasper's ear. It stood beside him now, clawed fingers reaching out to grab Jasper by the arms.

Desperate to escape the laughing faces he saw surrounding him, Jasper broke into a run before the troll's fingers could close around his arms. The jibes and harassing insults gave chase in spite of Jasper's hands covering his ears in a feeble attempt to block them out.

Jasper ran down the hall knocking people out of his way. He spared no concern as he pushed and shoved his way down the never-ending hallway extending before him. Locker doors opened with clawing hands thrusting out. Former victims of his bullying reached out from the depths of the open lockers, their tortured limbs pulling at Jasper as he ran past. All the while his troll chased behind.

At some point in his running, Jasper closed his eyes without realizing it. When at last he discovered the darkness of his aimless running he opened his eyes just before colliding into Colby. Together they tumbled to the floor and rolled several feet before Jasper scrambled away and backed himself against the wall.

"Why are you taunting me?" Jasper whimpered.

Colby reached for his friend and was surprised by his weakened mental state. "Jasper, it's me, Colby."

* * *

"You aren't real. None of this is real!"

"None of this 'is' real, just as you say.  Except me.  I am here."

Jasper flinched as Colby reached out to him. Colby shook his head and pursed his lips.  Colby reached out again for Jasper. He grabbed Jasper's arm before he could scoot away.

"Jasper! Snap out of it dude."

After pulling his arm out of Colby's grasp, Jasper backed further away. "Don't touch me. I'm not like you!"

"What are you talking about?"  But Colby knew. He was already there to hear the last few insults sent by the Shizumu troll.  "It's not like that. Just get up.  We don't have time for this right now!"

Jasper was preparing to argue further when he felt the ground beneath him shake. The tiled floor began to splinter as the earth beneath it cracked and split. While the troll lumbering toward them continued forward, two more burst through the floor to join the first in advancing on the boys.

"Jasper! Get up now; I need you."

Jasper looked at Colby with round eyes while shaking his head. "I'm not-"

Colby wasn't prepared for debate. He hoped he had enough Emassa left after his last fight, but Jasper needed a jolt of reality. While forcing a bolt of energy to his finger to write a hashtag spell useful in slowing their pursuers, Colby split his concentration to send a motivating jolt into Jasper's backside.

* * *

"We don't have time to pontificate on the misconceptions of what your addled mind has misconstrued." Colby knew Jasper would not understand —that was the point— he wanted him distracted from his other thoughts.

Jasper scrunched his face. "What?"

Colby, having finished his hashtag spell, exhaled a humorless laughing breath. "Get up and stand beside me. I need to borrow your strength to get rid of these trolls." Colby held out his hand and shook it at Jasper impatiently.

Reluctantly, Jasper took Colby's offered hand and stood. He saw the spell Colby had prepared, **#Truth**, and began to pull away.

Colby yanked Jasper closer using more strength than he assumed he had left. He released the spell and allowed it to swirl around himself and his friend. Within a few moments, they were each encased in a glowing field of energy that fit like a suit.

"What is this?" Jasper asked.

"A defense against trolling."

Jasper shook his head. "How is the truth gonna help us against those things."

Colby smiled at Jasper. "Because when you are dealing with trolls, you can choose to ignore them, or give them something they can't defend against."

"Truth?"

Again Colby smiled at Jasper before turning toward the trolls as they took their last steps toward the boys. "A weapon that uses ignorance for ammunition will always fail against an armored truth."

Jasper raised a brow and shook his head, but didn't admit to not understanding.  It was far easier to trust that Colby knew what he was talking about, so he gave Colby's hand a reassuring squeeze. When he allowed himself just to be there to help his friend, a clarity of mind occurred that Jasper never felt before now. It wasn't like when his mind would go completely blank, which happened more often than he'd admit. Jasper knew in that instant that he was connected to Colby in some way. And he was okay with that. He opened up his core of power to Colby, and they joined their magic.

Colby felt the rush in more ways than expected and he fueled the spell he prepared. **#Truth** burst from them in all directions.

The trolls covered their eyes against the rainbow of colored light emitting from the boys. The landscape around them pulsed as the fiery red hues became saturated with every other color imaginable. The lockers melted away to reveal the lush landscape of a meadow in a small grove. The trolls began to crack; red light escaped from the separating flesh. As their skin cracked and fell away in tiny pixels, a gust of unnatural wind came down from the artificial sky and blew the trolls to pieces.

Colby and Jasper were knocked backward and onto their butts. As they let go of each other's hand, the world around them faded back to the red hues that they were accustomed to from their first moment outside the entry portal to the Shiznet. They brushed the troll-dust off themselves in disgust and helped each other to their feet.

Colby looked around and saw what he thought was movement near some distant trees. Perhaps it was just the shadows, but he imagined a woman was watching them. He turned to Jasper.

"Do you see that woman?"

* * *

"Where?"

Colby turned to point her out, but there was no one there.

"I guess it was nothing." Colby looked back at Jasper who looked away but held a slight smile. "We should go look for the girls."

# Chapter 23

**#FindTheGirls**

After heading back the way they first ran from the angry birds, Colby and Jasper found the landscape different and the cave was gone. Where the entrance to their refuge from the attacking flock once stood, now rested a few boulders and stones.

Jasper kicked the largest of the rocks and swore before turning back to Colby. He searched his friend's face for an answer or suggestion but sat down on the large boulder. His shoulders slumped as he lowered his head.

"What now? The girls could be anywhere, and we have no idea what that twit Gary is playing at."

"What do you think Gary is up to?" Colby said.

Jasper huffed and pushed himself up from the rock. His face tightened as a flash of energy coursed through his arms and passed into the stone. The backlash that resulted from the boulder bursting apart pushed him the rest of the way to his feet. Jasper fell toward Colby, knocking him to the ground before landing on top of him.

An awkward moment passed before Colby pushed Jasper and rolled to the side from under him. He dusted himself off more from nervous reaction and habit being as though the virtual rock burst into pixels and no dust was present. But tiny bits of the former stone fell from the folds of his clothing and dispersed into the ground upon landing. Colby noticed how they seemed to be pulled back into the Shiznet matrix as though being recycled.

Jasper started to break the silence when Colby stared at the ground.

Colby did not look up, thankful for a valid distraction. "Did you see how the pixels got absorbed into the ground?"

Shuffling closer, Jasper looked from Colby to the ground. "So? The Shiznet has a recycling program." Jasper paused a moment, looking back at Colby. "Look, I don't want you to get the wrong idea."

Colby looked up at Jasper and breathed out hard. "This is all weird and confusing. Best not to think about it now."

"It's just that I'm not sure what it means. I'm drawn to you for some reason but not like . . . You know what I mean, right?"

"Jasper, I don't know what it is either, but I'm not looking for you to be my boyfriend or anything like that."

Colby wasn't sure he believed his words, but there was no explaining what the connection he felt to Jasper was. His confusion only clouded the situation they faced in the Shiznet, and he needed to focus. His throat tensed as he searched for more clarifying words, but didn't have a chance to say them.

The ground below them shook as two trolls pushed themselves up from the splitting red soil.

"You boys gonna start hugging it out?" a troll said as it pushed its way up, torso now fully formed and growing taller. "Time is ticking on your slo-mance. Best get on with it before we end you."

Taking defensive stances, the boys prepared to fight. Jasper looked at Colby. "What is that supposed to mean? They make no sense."

"They're trolls, Jasper. They don't have to make sense; they just have to distract us from our purpose." Colby readied a spell. **#Truth**.

The spell hit the troll, but it was weak and only caused the side of the creature to melt. It soon began to reform. The boys stepped back as they prepared another spell, this time joining their power.

Two more attacks finished off the trolls, and the boys took only a little time to watch the recycling of the bits of leftover pixel-dust. Jasper led the dash past the outcropping of rocks as Colby followed. They needed to find the girls and Gary so they could locate Aria's soul and find a way out.

Colby caught up to Jasper and waved for a slowdown in their pace. That last encounter with the trolls used more power than expected, and he needed to try and build up his reserves. They were far enough away to stop for a moment, and Colby sensed something different in their new surroundings.

The grasses and hills gave way to upward sloping cliffs that closed around them as they proceeded. The land funneled them toward a gap in the cliffs where shadows obscured what lay beyond. Just outside the opening, Colby felt the stirring of power and stopped.

"I need to rest a minute."

As he bent at the waist and rested his hands on his buckling knees, Colby looked from side to side. He could feel an odd pulse of Emassa, faint and wavering, but there was something there.

* * *

"Do you feel that?" Colby stood and turned around slowly. "There is some kind of energy flux here somewhere."

Jasper shook his head. "I don't feel anything but annoyed and hungry."

Colby reached out with his magic and felt the connection to a flow of Emassa. He pulled on the magic and allowed it to begin trickling into his core. As he began to feel stronger, Colby reached for Jasper.

Though he pulled away at first, Colby's reassuring look gave Jasper the comfort to move closer. When Colby grabbed his hand, Jasper felt the flow of power and began drinking it in. The energy they gathered was slow but stronger than previous attempts. Somehow Colby was able to connect to the Emassa and allow Jasper access by proxy.

Not nearly half energized, the flow fluttered and shifted as though something passed through, disturbing the gathering of power. Colby broke the connection as a hand raked across his arm. It was light and familiar.

"Colby, you must not linger." It was Aria's split soul in diluted form wavering before him.

Colby reached for her, but his hands passed through the apparition.

She lowered her head and waved Colby off. "I am but a projection in this degraded area. Your affect on the realm is causing destruction. You can not free me from here yet and require your friends' assistance."

Colby reached for Jasper, but Aria stopped him.

"All your friends, not just the borrowed strength of Jasper."

As she began to flicker and fade further, the spirit of his mother's other half pointed toward the entrance to the canyon. "Use your connection to them and find the way."

Colby frowned at the thought of entering the canyon. It was narrow and closed off. The hair on his arm raised as the chill shot through him thinking of past times stuffed into his locker. Colby glared at Jasper before turning back to the last remnants of Aria's soul.

"I don't understand. What connection?"

"You must figure that out for yourself child." Then she was gone.

The silence hung around them as the boys looked toward the murky entrance. The gloom pulled at them both, though it was Jasper who shrugged it off and began walking toward the unknown.

"Well, you heard the lady. Let's get moving."

Colby set his shoulders and took a deep breath. "Let's get a bit more juice stored in our magical batteries before we hike off into the canyon of doom."

Reaching into the flow of magic from the dying vortex he now saw, Colby pulled again on the Emassa. This time, it did not relent to his demand. Instead, he was met by a hand reaching out from the void. It created a barrier that surrounded the vortex and began swallowing it up. Beyond the disappearing spring of energy, more trolls lumbered toward their position.

"No time pal," Jasper said. He grabbed Colby by the shirt. "Let's go."

Side-by-side, the boys ran for the entrance in the rock wall that rose before them. Their feet met with hard packed ground covered in a layer of pebbles. The crunching of their footfalls echoed off the approaching walls and set the undertone to the loud calls from the pursuing trolls.

* * *

The material shifting with their movement gave Colby an idea. He focused his mind on the pebbles and thought of a hashtag spell. The spell formed before him without the need to write it out with his enchanted finger. **#RollingBoulders**.

Colby sent the spell downward with a shift of his eyes. The spell flashed to life with brilliant red energy and soaked into the ground as the boys continued to run. Behind them, massive boulders began to coalesce and roll toward the trolls giving chase. The boys spared little time watching Colby's handiwork, but the resulting angry howls confirmed success.

"I'm not gonna ask how you did that." Jasper kept running, but his eyes flicked back to Colby every few paces.

The bellowing grew louder and more menacing as the spell continued in the wake of the boys escape. Colby felt no pull of magic that would be required to maintain the spell. When at last they reached the path between the cliffs, the boys paused to look behind and smiled.

The trolls were prevented from gaining ground as the boulders continued to form and vex them. Those that were destroyed melted back into the ground and fueled a replacement. Their pursuers were busy just trying to remain standing.

"How did you manage that?" Jasper said.

"I'm not sure. I focused on the spell, but I was distracted. I thought about what you said regarding recycling."

Understanding made Jasper smile wider. "You set the spell to keep reusing the initial energy." Then his face relaxed. "What about the red Emassa?"

Colby guessed at an answer. "I suppose I tapped into the Shizumu side of magic." He wasn't certain, but Colby felt Jasper wanted some plausible explanation. "You already know I've got both magic abilities inside me. I just never purposely accessed the Shizumu side before."

Jasper only nodded and turned to walk further into the canyon, leaving Colby to catch up.

"Wait up," Colby said as he caught up to Jasper. "Look, I don't know exactly what or how with all this magic stuff sometimes."

"It's cool dude."

Colby accepted the response for what it was, Jasper's way of saying he didn't want to talk. So Colby walked alongside his friend in silence until he noticed something new. As Colby dragged his fingers over the stone of the canyon they traversed, sparks of energy jumped from the surface and sank into his hand. The feeling was much like a static discharge, except reversed as though he was absorbing the sparks. Colby stopped to investigate while Jasper ignored him and continued a few steps.

"Come on Colby. We don't have time to mess around."

Colby held up his free hand to silence his friend while pushing his other onto the rocks, sinking his fingers deep into the virtual wall of stone. Power flowed from the surrounding material and coursed into Colby as the walls crumbled away and turned to pixels before they disintegrated.

Jasper stepped nearer but refrained from getting too close. "Colby, you don't know what their magic will do to you."

Colby smiled as he turned his head. "Is that what's had you freaked out? It isn't their magic, just what they do with it." Colby could see that Jasper had no idea what he meant based on the sour look on his friend's face. "Give me your hand."

* * *

Jasper relented after a bit of coaxing. When his hand made contact with Colby's, he felt instantly the flow of Emassa passing through Colby and into his core.

"Whoa!"

Colby smiled. "I know, right?"

"But how? I mean this is the Shiznet and their magic, how can I juice-up on Shiz magic?"

"Shiz magic? Really?" Colby smirked as Jasper shrugged and smiled. "It's just Emassa. How it's channeled and used makes it what it seems, but in essence, it is all Emassa. And this place has access to it from outside, therefore-"

"So do you!" Jasper was finally getting it. "Then you're still connected to the outside world?"

"In a way I guess." Colby felt the energy for magic was coming from the outside, but he was not directly connected to it yet. He needed time to figure that part out. For now, he explained that he was happily able to recharge.

The walls around them crumbled away into dust, but Colby and Jasper remained transfixed on the pulse of energy flowing between them. Eyes locked on one another; they allowed themselves to relish in the connection they shared without thinking too deeply about what it meant. Jasper was the first to pull away in a sudden jerking motion.

"I'm sorry, I just can't get used to how that feels."

"Yeah, it's a bit intense having that much power flow into your core so quickly," Colby said. He knew that wasn't what Jasper was talking about.

* * *

"You know what I mean. The other feeling —or feelings— it's a bit confusing."

Colby looked at Jasper for a minute before offering any support. "It's because we're connected somehow, nothing like…nothing more."

A deep sigh and roll of the eyes proceeded Jasper's words. "Dude, I get that it's weird. And since it's just us right now, I can admit I don't necessarily dislike the way it makes me feel when we 'connect'. It's just that I'm not…you know."

"Jasper, I don't know that I'm gay either. Honestly, I've never really given it much thought with all the hocus-pocus in my life right now." Colby stepped up to Jasper and stood to leave mere inches between their bodies.

A static charge began to build up between them and eventually magical sparks began to fly. Stepping back, Colby laughed along with Jasper.

"That is the manifestation of a magic based attraction," Colby said. "This is something connected to the Emassa so let's not get too hung up on obnoxious standards of unenlightened morons and other such trumpery."

Jasper laughed and snorted. "You mean like I was before-"

Voice drowned out by a deafening roar; Jasper turned his attention behind him where Colby was already staring. The spite and hatred roiled over their skin as the trolls appeared, noticing the dissolution of the canyon walls. The boys knew that the trolls sensed what happened because of the abhorrence felt from the monsters' narrowed gazes.

Colby grabbed Jasper's arm with one hand while slapping the other, open-palmed, onto the illusionary wall to absorb more energy. "Let's end this now."

* * *

Ready to exact some Shiznet justice, Jasper prepared to funnel his strength into an attack when the flow of energy from Colby abruptly halted. Jasper turned to witness Colby looking the opposite direction and his face drain of color. Jasper's reaction was to gasp at the apparition silently pleading them away.

"You must not engage the trolls," Aria said. "You need to halt your actions against the constructs here and find your friends."

"Mom?"

"Focus on your friends, and you will have all you need to find me and leave this place." Aria's last words faded as did her presence.

Colby took a tentative step toward the area where his mother's spirit vanished. "What do we do?"

"I don't know, but you better decide quick," Jasper said pointing back toward the approaching trolls. "Focus on the girls. Where are they?"

Colby closed his eyes and concentrated on the girls. His finger began to trace the hashtag in the air, **#GirlsLocation**. His spell was vague, but the desire was evident in his mind as he pulled upon the Emassa around him. Magic surged into his intention to fuel the spell.

Jasper watched, eyes wide and grinning with pride, as Colby began to glow. When he sensed Colby required his strength, Jasper grabbed his friend and allowed the connection to join their magic. Before closing his eyes to the approaching monsters, Jasper allowed a single thought to pass to Colby without knowing. 'We'd be more powerful in real bodies.'

The creatures moved slow but deliberate at first. Their steps held caution in their ambling, but they weren't allowing the fear of Colby's gain in power to dissuade them completing the task of stopping the children.

Their pace quickened when the distant, angry voice of a woman ordered them on.

Daphne stood atop the cliffs near the entrance watching and waiting, but after seeing Aria appear to warn off her son, the field of play changed. Aria was gaining strength to contact Colby, which meant his tapping into the Shiznet power was weakening the realm. Somehow that boy was able to use this vile red magic when Daphne was incapable. Her leader was equally restricted from its use but had an obsession with the boy's magic. She was precluded from killing or fatally wounding Colby, but she could send her lackeys in to take care of him. A grin spread to frame the wickedness of her glowering eyes until the flash of light and the rolling wave of power knocked her back.

Colby and Jasper were surrounded by more magic than either had ever stored and expelled. When Colby registered Jasper's thought about having their corporeal forms, it added to his desire to locate the girls. As the magic built to a breaking point, the boys' last image was of the energy radiating from them and melting away the façade of troll form to reveal the Seekers beneath. Then they saw the woman screaming on top of the cliffs before they disappeared in a final burst of magic-filled light.

# <u>Chapter 24</u>

## **#Reunited**

Light filled the first floor of the Stevens' home as magic spilled from the portal and surrounded the six young adults laying helpless on the floor. The device that allowed the kids to manipulate its initial purpose and project themselves into the Shizumu realm was now emitting feedback in the form of arcs or plasma. The angry purple energy flows danced in chaotic jolts around the room, striking Colby and his friends more often than anything else in the space. The power was attracted to them and seemed to be absorbing their bodies.

Nana stopped at the threshold of entering the room from the kitchen when a lashing energy-strike hit near her feet. She felt the magic in the air and recognized its signature as that belonging to her grandson. Colby was enacting a spell powerful enough to reach out from the Shizumu prison realm; a spell he was casting while non-corporeal in a virtual world of negative energy. Nana couldn't stop the proud smile that formed in spite of the maelstrom of uncontrolled magic swirling about the living room. The smile disappeared beneath the wrinkled folds of her sagging frown when she saw a familiar face in the swirling vortex. That face now wore Nana's stolen grin.

The shrilling laughter that sang from the vibrant redhead in the center of swirling magic was a siren song of triumph. Daphne's vengeance-filled cackles rose with the fervor of lashing Emassa snapping and latching onto each of the six youths. A knowing glance left her face as Daphne backed away from the portal's view. In concert with the fiery red-haired woman's disappearance, the magic took firm hold of the kids and encased them in power.

Nana was helpless to stop such a perfervid spell. It was wild magic born of impassioned desperation and single purpose emotional drive. Colby excelled in powerfully intense magic born of his unbridled emotional baggage. Mostly cast out of instinct, His spells were dangerous and had not yet caused significant damage purely by dumb luck. A final flash of purple light, the spell collapsed into the vortex beginning to absorb the children and device in the process. A single crack in reality remained. It pulsed red and blue in tandem as the two magics wrestled along the border of the powerful spell's remnants.

Outside the house, on the parameter of the concealment shield, another —less lustrous— Daphne stood watching the house. She could see through the magic and knew what transpired inside the Stevens' home. The moment she waited for arrived along with a large contingent of Dreggs. Conrad was among them, but Daphne could see he was unable to staunch his ranks' desire to cancel out the magic; it was why they were created. Daphne held her hands to the shield, pouring magic onto its surface and watched the increasing fervor of the creatures.

"It's time you oversized goblins do what you're built for," Daphne said aloud. "A little taste is all it will take to drive you beasts into the house and do what I need done." She pushed the last bit of power onto the shield and stepped back as it spread around the parameter. It was the last enticement required to set the Dreggs in motion. When they hurled toward the barrier, Daphne cackled without care to who might hear.

Nana had sensed the strange magic on the concealment shield before the attack came. She stood on the back porch watching the same woman she only moments ago saw in the vortex. This woman was one of the others.

One of the three to be precise. Her attention was so set on the fact that Daphne was free and causing havoc again, Nana failed to realize the Dreggs dismantled her shield and headed directly toward her. Before she could raise power to stop them, several Dreggs rushed past. Although Nana held back the bulk of the creatures, the few who slipped by where enough to accomplish the task they were stirred up to complete.

A new shield pushed back the Dreggs that remained outside. The concealment was replaced. Daphne was nowhere to be seen. And there were Dreggs in her house. Nana ran as fast as her wobbly old legs would carry her, which for Nana's apparent age was quite fast. The return of her fractured soul with the power and knowledge that included allowed her to begin rejuvenation of her present body. What little she gained in power was not enough to prevent the Dreggs in her living room from doing the unthinkable.

The magic emanating from the vortex finished dissolving the children. As each was taken, the whip of energy shot back to the vortex, and it grew smaller until at last, the final body was taken and the vortex shrunk down to a fist-sized pulsing sphere. Colby was last to enter the portal, and with his departure, the Dreggs were able to pounce upon the sphere and cancel its magic. They sealed the entrance and way back for the kids.

Nana raised her hands and lashed out with a spell, vocalizing its words from an ancient tongue and dark place of her soul. The Emassa flowed all around her and along her arms up to the palms of her hands. There, the magic gathered and lashed out at the Dreggs. They looked surprised when the magic hit them and did not cancel out. A dim memory came to them as they realized what they had done. This magic wielder was the witch mother that created them, and her magic was beyond their ability to stop. Now they were being punished.

When her spell melted away, Nana fell to the floor from exertion. It was millennia since she channeled such a work of magic when first she created the Dreggs. Their purpose was to find and neutralize the

Shizumu and their sympathizers. Any magic not her own, and apparently that of her kin, was subject to the power of the Dreggs. There were five less of them now. Where once stood the imposing beasts who dared meddle in her grandson's quest, now whimpered five of Fizzlewink's kin. The first of his kind to return from their service to the witch who mothered them and later transformed them for a higher purpose.

Still fuming, Nana led the newly remade Nefsmari from her living room and into the kitchen. Without a word or signal, the little creatures took seats at the table and waited obediently for their mistress to address them. They waited while the old woman, the ancient witch even when they were created, bustled around the kitchen pulling things from cupboards and the refrigerator. She added these items to a pot on the stove, creating a stink in the room that raised the nerves of the Nefsmari.

After retrieving plates, Nana doled out the slop from her pot and distributed it among the not-so-eager diners. They accepted the meal with grace and reverence, though none displayed the desire to be first to taste the food.

As Nana folded her arms before them and tapped her foot, forks raised, and the creatures took the plunge into their meal. Satisfied, Nana turned back to the stove and began cleaning up the mess she made. She was unaware of the blue creatures reactions to her cooking. Their little blue features seemed to become green. They continued to eat, however, for fear of upsetting the great witch.

Nana stopped cleaning at the persistent pounding on the back door. Huffing and throwing down her towel, Nana waddled to the door and opened it for the great Dregg. She stepped to the side, allowing Conrad into the kitchen as though expecting him.

"What have you done?" Conrad said. "We are not ready for this."

"Ready?" Nana said. "Who is to say when you are ready or not, better than me?" Nana stared Conrad down. Though her memories as Bellatrix were scattered and seemed to return as needed rather than when desired, Nana continued to feel something familiar about Conrad. She did not know him through her current life experience beyond the few encounters since Colby's awakening to magic. But there was a deeper sense that their paths crossed many times over her disjointed existence. "Did you know?" She asked him.

Conrad turned to the old woman he knew better than she knew herself. "I always find you even though you never quite found yourself until now." What might have passed as a smile threatened to cross his otherwise unreadable face?

"Careful Goblin, one might think you were happy to see me."

Conrad laughed. "You have no idea Great Mother. We've waited millennia for this time to arrive."

Standing straight and confident, Nana tilted her head and gazed deep into Conrad's yellow eyes. "Then why do I sense fear from you?"

The stoic stance fell from Conrad as his shoulders sagged and his head lowered. "It has been long since I have felt the pull of the Mother and the power she has over my kind. I sense a change since last you were at one with yourself."

Bellatrix ran her hand across her wrinkled old face. She was warring internally with the life and experience of Nana. Knowing what must transpire soon, she was at odds with the different attachment to her modern family. The attachment to the boy ran deep and would ultimately present her greatest challenge. No option she could imagine was optimal, but it was of little use dwelling upon that at the moment.

"You seem conflicted, Great Mother."

* * *

"Don't call me that," Nana said. Bellatrix faded into the back of her conflicted mind. "I have work to do. Go back outside and watch the house. It's too crowded in here."

Conrad left but not before turning back and watching the old woman begin rubbing her temples and stomping off in a fit of curses. He shuddered at the sense he felt of the battling magic radiating from his maker.

One of the former Dreggs attempted to follow him outside.

"You stay inside where it's safe little one. You are of no help out here any longer." Conrad allowed only the slightest of kindness to pass over his otherwise neutral face. He lost a fighter but was not unhappy to see one of his comrades return to his natural form.

Looking back at the scorched carpet where the void evaporated, Conrad wondered how the human children were fairing. He could feel the Emassa still penetrating the earthly realm through the vortex though it was closed. This thought alone renewed his dutiful stance as he turned and exited the house.

### 

Colby and Jasper both gasped for air as they emerged from a blast of desperation-charged Emassa. The light filled the space where they reappeared, blinding them momentarily as they filled their lungs. The panting echoed off the walls as the boys' caught their breath and their vision began to clear. They saw they were back in the cavern; only now it was much different.

The portal snapped shut with a discharge of energy that thundered. The echoing through the alcoves of the small cave woke Colby. He pushed himself up to recline onto his elbows as he took in his surroundings.

Colby was back in the cave they used to shelter from the angry birds. The place was different this time as the rocky surface of the interior was pocked with missing sections. Deep gashes of nothingness spread around the chamber as though it were being eaten up by some foreign parasite. As he looked around, he found Jasper and the rest of his party of friends and family that joined his quest to find Aria's soul. He vaguely recalled the spell he and Jasper cast and the vast amount of energy they siphoned out of the Shiznet to fuel it.

The walls no longer held the look of weathered and moss-covered walls. Instead, they flickered akin to an un-rendered 3D graphic while falling away from the underlying mesh. The walls crumbled into pixelated dust just as the trolls when Colby used the Shiznet magic he absorbed. Only it wasn't just the Shizumu magic, but a combination of Nefslama as well. Fused with his signature power, Colby was affecting the Shiznet when he performed spells.

The realization that his magic could be so unintentionally destructive was troubling. He held no love for the Shizumu or their deeds but was he prepared to destroy their home, their prison, their realm. If this destruction continued, everything inside would likely perish as well. This included himself, his mother, and his friends.

Thinking solely about the safety of his family and friends, Colby decided that it mattered little what happened to the Shizumu. He needed to get the others out of this place and to accomplish that; he needed to find his mother, the girls and find a way out. As it turned out, upon further investigation of the cavern, the girls were easier to locate than he imagined. They were nestled in alcoves, attached to the vortex machine and still locked in a virtual dream state.

"We have to get them out of these," Colby said as he ran to Shelly's side.

"You've outdone yourself, young man."

* * *

Colby jumped up at the familiar voice. He heard that voice once before in a vision. It sounded much like his… "Mom? It can't be."

# <u>Chapter 25</u>

## #CaveCollapse

"I'm not your mommy, whelp. But I'd be proud if I were if only you weren't magically polluted. You have managed what none before have been capable." The Daphne doppelgänger looked him up and down with a mixture of contempt and a small bit of envy. "Take it all in while you are able. No telling how long until this realm collapses with you and your friends along with it."

"You were there in the room with the others," Colby managed. "You were with some others and talking about Gary and me."

Daphne cocked her head and raised a brow. "You were the one they sensed spying on us last year?"

"Just a waking vision, but I know your voice."

"It matters little, mutt. Your mixed magic cross breeding won't save you from the fall of this prison, and those who languished within for so long are now free thanks to you." Daphne turned and headed for a portal that formed at the exit from the cavern. "Ta-ta!"

Colby rose to give chase, but she was gone before he reached the closing portal. He turned to watch the spread of nothingness on the walls of the cave and looked outside on the landscape to see the same blight spreading more quickly.

"Colby? Who was that crazy bitch?" Jasper called to Colby who stood staring blankly at the spot where the strange woman disappeared. "She looked just like your mom, except crazier."

Colby turned to stare at Jasper's remark.

"No offense dude, but your mom is a little scattered sometimes."

Colby loosened up and laughed. "Mostly drunk, but even sober her brain skips like a buffering music stream."

"A playlist that has no theme."

Colby patted Jasper on the shoulder as he laughed and moved toward the alcoves containing the girls.

Jasper joined him and together, he and Colby began disrupting the energy beams that pulsed and streamed energy between the girls and the device. One-by-one the boys freed the girls from their alcoves and the influence of the apparatus. As each was let out, the device sounded a protest that reverberated off the walls, causing the deterioration of the cavern to increase in speed.

Reviving the girls was slower than they'd like, but Colby and Jasper didn't know how each girl would be affected by their time in the dream. They too were physically present in the realm, so getting hurt was for keeps. As the last of the ladies was gathering her wits, Colby ushered them close and began heading toward the cavern exit.

"We have to get out of here now," he said.

"No shit professor obvious," Shelly said.

208

* * *

Colby felt the urge to snap back at his sister but resisted. "I mean this realm, not just the cave."

"The whole place is disintegrating," Jasper said.

Colby explained as the group exited the cave and headed toward the stone circle they saw when first they arrived in the Shiznet. He told the girls how the trolls attacked and were revealed as Shizumu when Colby used the magic of the realm against them. The unseen result of siphoning energy off the virtual reality was the breaking down of the whole construct.

"So you were able to repel them with their magic force," Darla said. "But how did you create the spells without your phWatch?"

"It seems that even though our tech didn't make the physical trip to this realm, we know the Hashtag Magic did." Colby demonstrated by using his finger to draw out a hashtag spell.

Colby spoke with a mix of relief and concern as he explained how to use their fingers as a stylus. It was great being able to access the hashtag network, but that meant it was in the Shiznet and potentially exposed to the enemy.

"Where are we heading next. I hope you haven't forgotten mom's soul is still here somewhere."

Colby hadn't forgotten, nor had he lost the uncanny resemblance that crazed woman had to his mother. "We need to head-"

Colby's words cut short when a stalactite broke from the ceiling and crashed to the ground just behind the kids.

The device in the center of the space began to hum and vibrate. Emassa began to coalesce around the mechanics, sparking and sending pulses out toward Colby. As he moved closer, he felt a deeper connection to the real world. This connection was direct and not piggy-backing the Shizumu magic.

Rumbling and shaking of the ground beneath their feet signaled the kids into action. Grabbing one another by hand or arm, they all scrambled for the artificial daylight and relative safety offered by the exit in the distance. That distance seemed closer before their sprint began, but as they ran, the path appeared to stretch before them.

The environment somehow acted against them; the exit moved further away as they headed toward their destination. Looking back, The kids realized they had not moved an inch from the center of the cave.

The walls shook and wavered under an undulating rhythm, beating such as a bass speaker at a loud and frantic concert. With every thunderous reverberation, tenuous faults appeared and spiderwebbed along the cavern walls, ceiling, and floor. More pieces of the roof broke away, small at first, and began crashing to the floor.

Colby nodded to Jasper when his friend turned and took Colby's wrist. Sharing single purpose and thought, Colby backed-to-back with Jasper as they each drew a hashtag with their glowing fingertip. Magic surged around them and danced along their bodies as the girls watched awe-stricken.

The Shizumu magic each boy stored, raged against the rally to fuel their shared spell. Just as it felt their sorcery would fail against all effort, the device of their capture gave way to the effects of whatever assaulted their safety. As it faltered, a beam of blue radiant energy burst out from its center and hit Colby in the middle of his chest.

With barely a hint of effect, Colby took the Emassa and added its energy to that which he siphoned off the Shiznet. The reinforced spell for shielding grew and wrapped itself among the kids as the world around them exploded. The device collapsed inward, taking a flow of twisted blue and red magic into a swirling vortex before it disappeared.

Magic ripped through the air and crackled as it broke against the boys' shield. Crouched within the sphere of Emassa powered safety, the girls stared at Colby and Jasper as energy flowed around them, through them, between them.

The shared spell-work was beyond magical and inspiring, Shelly thought. It was beautiful. Two people sharing a single purposeful idea, joined in perfection to create a spell that looked as though it would stand against anything for all time. She could more than see the bond her brother Colby shared with Jasper. Anyone could see that if they chose to look. But she could also feel it in the pulsing flow of magic they radiated. Their magic flowed in harmonious ebbs without hesitation. It was perfection until the last moment when the boys broke contact and stopped sharing one another's magic. The shield fell as it was no longer needed.

Blue magically-charged Emassa sparked and scattered across the face of everything in the Shiznet. In its wake, the illusions of a realistic world crumbled in a pixelated dust storm. The red magic of the Shizumu realm coalesced with the blue hued Hashtag Magic powered by Colby. A vibrant and glowing purple settled over everything as the dust dissipated. The kids stood within a crater where what was once a cavern and outcropping of rock, was reduced to a fine sand. They were outside as though their former location never existed and the Shiznet was reforming a forest around them.

"What was that?" Darla asked. "And where did it come from?" She looked at Jasper and Colby impressed.

Colby reddened, still feeling the intoxicating effect of joining his magic with Jasper. "Something we discovered by accident."

* * *

"Which is?" She pressed.

"We can use the Shizumu magic if I take it in and…share it. I also have a connection to the outside Emassa. When combined, our magic and energy become-"

"Wonderful!" Rhea said.

"It's pretty awesome," Jasper admitted. "But it has side effects." He shifted a bit but remained stalwart at least in appearance.

Shelly wasn't buying it, however, and watched both of the boys carefully.

Colby withdrew from Jasper. Just being near him after the mass of power they shared made his head swim with…ideas.

Shelly took notice of Colby's uncomfortable shift in behavior. "You ok little brother?"

"I'll be fine." Colby's eyes shifted around taking in the rapid growth of virtual trees and forest around them. "I think we have other things to be more concerned about right now."

A single twitter in a nearby tree alerted Colby that they were not alone. When he looked up to confirm his fear, Colby saw the enraged birds gathering in the trees. Black as pitch and each easily the size of a crow on steroids, this murder of birds also held murder in their red glowing eyes.

# **Chapter 26**

## **#TransformTheDregg**

The living room of the Stevens' family home was buzzing. Not because there was a host of little blue halfbreed Nefsmari wandering about undirected. There was a real buzz as the air began to raise with a static charge. The unmistakeable signature of Emassa was growing more recognizable with each raising hair on their little bodies.

"Take cover!" Fizzlewink said. "Get out of there."

He ran from the kitchen toward the threshold of the living room when the vortex reopened. A tidal wave of energy emerged from the expanding hole in time and space, knocking about anything that stood against the flow of power.

Conrad pushed past Fizz, attempting to approach the vortex and use his power of negation to stem the flow. As he struggled against the onslaught, his Dregg features fluxed and altered as though standing in a wind tunnel. There was strange magic at play. The magical energies were altering his being in such a way they ought not. Conrad stopped inches away from the portal while the power faded as quickly as it began.

The vortex eased closed, but not entirely. Conrad reached to seal the breach, but his magical gift had no effect. The portal remained as a rippling tear in the fabric of reality. And Conrad remained transfixed. His features fell back into their regular place, but his being somehow altered.

Fizzlewink stood twirling his brow with his fingers and staring between the portal and the towering member of his mutated race. He too felt there was something changed in his new friend, but he was unsure how to broach the subject. In true Fizzlewink form, he decided to break the tension first.

"Well your face is back to a less scary resemblance to Donatella Versace, but your energy feels…off!"

Conrad grunted. "I do not know who this Donatella creature is, but if she looks worse than myself, I would not relish waking up next to her." He returned his gaze to the portal.

"What do you make of this?" Fizzlewink asked.

"I am perplexed. It should have collapsed when I touched it, yet it remains." Conrad shook his head. "I have lost my magic."

Typically, Fizzlewink would take this opportunity to gloat or reprimand. Only a short time ago, a fellow Nefsmari was left to feel useless and beneath the need of Conrad. Now Conrad was feeling incapable of performing the one thing for which the Dreggs were designed.

"Irony," Fizzlewink said under his breath. He turned to Conrad and kicked him in the back of the leg.

"Listen to me, and listen good." Fizzlewink began circling the downtrodden creature that dressed in army surplus clothing and looked every bit the soldier. "You are not bootless in any sense of the term. Just because you have lost what you believe your only asset, does not mean you've lost an edge over the enemy."

* * *

"But-"

Another kick in the shins. "Don't interrupt!" Fizzlewink jumped to the top of a nearby chair so he could stare Conrad in the eyes. "You need to use what you know as well as any magical gifts you possess."

"Without my magic-"

"You still have magic, Dregg. It's just…changed."

"How can you tell?"

Fizzlewink huffed. "Did your brain get altered as well as your abilities?" He was losing patience with this thick-headed mutated kin. "You feel magic when it's used and can track it, or at least that was part of your gift. Have you ever tried to simply feel for it while it is in a resting state?"

"Yes, but I've never felt my own magic? How would I even do something such as this?"

"How? What do you feel from this vortex and how do you know it?"

Conrad approached the portal and prepared to examine it in the manner which he was accustomed. He opened his mind and spirit, inviting the magic to touch his core. It did not work. The magic was there. He could sense it buzzing like a pair of hair clippers. Blades that move too quickly for the eye to observe, but you can feel the vibration. Conrad could feel the magic on that instinctual and subconscious level. He could not, however, take it's measure or acknowledge it's signature. Except there was something there. Something familiar yet chaotic. Conrad pulled his face, creases folding up his brow.

"Annoying, am I correct?" Fizzlewink folded his arms and looked on with a smug and all-knowing face.

* * *

Conrad turned to Fizzlewink and snorted. "You know for such a little man, you are full to the brow with a jackasses' disposition."

Fizz tried his best to look affronted, but he was far too proud of himself for besting the keen magic-sniffing ability of a Dregg. "The point is, the magic is different from that portal. Just as it changed, you seem to have changed along with it. Any guesses as to how that happened?"

After a moment of hanging with the uninvited guest of silence, Conrad came to the inevitable conclusion. "The boy."

"Indeed. Colby has somehow managed another transformation of Emassa never in my lifetime seen." Fizzlewink joined Conrad near the tear in reality. "Whatever he and his friends are facing in there, it has caused him to react in such a way that he reopened this portal."

"Worse still little man. Did you not sense the other magic flowing just beneath the signature of the boy's magic?"

Fizz squinted as he leaned closer, but not too close, to the portal. "Crap on a cracker."

Conrad raised his left brow as he looked down at Fizzlewink. "If that statement is meant to express the depth of concern I think it does, then Crap on a Cracker indeed."

Magic was flowing bidirectionally between the realms. A purple stream the had become Colby's signature of Emassa, was in actuality a thin layer of both the red magic of Shizumu and the blue of the Nefslama. The two flowed so closely together they were at first mistaken for Colby's magic alone. It wasn't his magic at all, or at least not entirely.

"Whatever is going on can't be good for this to have happened. I hope the kids are well." Fizz twirled his right eyebrow as he often does when thinking critically or worried.

* * *

"I can at the very least sense master Colby is alive and through him, I feel the others somehow," Conrad spoke flatly, but emotion began to show on his creasing face. He was concerned. "This is peculiar. I have not once in my overly-long existence felt a connection to an individual magical creature or person. Somehow I sense the boy as though-"

"You're connected to him now Conrad. The blast of power coming from the portal was from his core, and it changed you in more ways than one." Nana stood in the doorway between the kitchen and the living room. "I won't be able to reverse your Dregg mutation now. My grandson's magic has altered you more than you know."

Conrad nodded, then turned to the vortex that separated him from his new master. "I felt it, but not until I heard it out loud had I put a description to what had changed in me."

"That red magic coming out of the portal can't be good either," Nana said as she approached the creatures.

"You can see that?" Fizz asked.

"At my age and experience, there isn't much I haven't seen or learned to take notice of. For that matter, there isn't much I haven't learned to ignore as well."

"What do you mean?" Conrad asked.

"Well, for one thing, I've let my house get out of order over and over through the eons. I've always had a connection to each life I lived while the rest of my spirit remained in that dusty old house in the Yucatán. I held a small bit of influence as I observed from a distance. After a while, though, I became tired and rather bored of it all.

"I let things happen as they might without my involvement. I think, had I remained vigilant, things might not have traveled the path that leads to where we find ourselves today."

"You think highly of yourself that you might alone have changed what has transpired," Rigel said.

Startled and annoyed she had missed his return, Nana spun around to face the Professor. "A single act has the potential to change a great many things, Professor. Did you find the old man?"

"I did. He is on his way I think."

"You think?" Nana was getting more annoyed with Rigel. She narrowed her eyes at him, choosing not to ignore things any longer. "Either you passed on my invitation, or you didn't."

"We spoke, He became upset over the mention of you and something else. Something pertaining to the Daphne statues." Rigel waited to read Nana's reaction, but it was Bellatrix who maintained a passionless face. "He left abruptly, but I doubt it long before he makes an appearance."

"And what leads you to believe he will come?" Fizzlewink asked.

"I've seen the look in his eyes at the mention of Bellatrix. Many things can light such a fire. I care little for what the connection is between you two, but the flames rose at your mention. Such a burning will not go unattended."

Nana passed Rigel and headed back into the kitchen. "I need to be prepared when he decides to present himself."

"Present himself?" Rigel said under his breath. "The mighty queen awaits."

"What did you say?" Fizzlewink asked.

* * *

"Nothing." Rigel walked toward the vortex. "What happened here?" Changing the subject was his primary objective. However, further investigation of the tear in reality peaked his interest. "This is new."

"Is that all you've noticed? The vortex is changed?" Fizzlewink's patience for Rigel was thinly veiled cordialness that covered an unexplained hostility. He had no idea why he detested this man, but Fizz never distrusted his intuition. "The children are gone!"

"Oh that, well yes, I had noticed. I assume they entered the vortex?"

"They were pulled into it more like. Something shifted in the Emassa, and all hell broke loose."

Rigel, head tilted slightly in contemplation, turned to Fizzlewink and began to walk away. "I'm sure the children are fairing well enough."

"How would you know such a thing for certain?" Fizzlewink said.

"Call it a feeling?"

"I've got a feeling too, Professor, but it has nothing to do with the kids in that realm."

"Then call it an educated guess. A guess from an educated Professor." Rigel exited the room and then the house.

"Educated my furry ass." Fizzlewink moved to a chair and took a seat. "Well, I think I'll just sit here and wait."

"Wait for what?" Conrad finally spoke up. He shrank back when Bellatrix entered the room but now emerged from the background as it was just him and Fizzlewink remaining.

* * *

Fizz shook his head and began twirling his eyebrow. "I don't pretend to know, but something is bound to happen sooner or later. It's one thing for certain in this house, if you don't like the way things are going, just wait a short while, and something exciting will transpire."

"I believe that as truth little man. I shall wait to see what happens next with the children as this portal is just the beginning I feel."

# Chapter 27

## #SpellsInterrupted

The Angry Birds hovered in the trees, clicking and chattering. Waiting.

Colby looked around at the menacing birds that waited for something. Were they waiting for him and the others to move? Colby only wondered a short time before a movement to his left split his attention between what happened and what now attacked from above.

"Watch out!" Colby grabbed Rhea as he dove for the ground. It was her movement that set the birds into motion. "What were you doing?"

"I had an itch," Rhea said. "I could stand it no longer. You know how when you can't do something and try to focus on it, but it just makes it worse? Well that was my itch and-"

"Forget I asked." Turning his head toward the others. Colby waved off the diving birds and shouted. "Try to use the Hashtag Magic like I showed you."

Colby formed his spell as he pushed away from Rhea, freeing her to assist in fighting off the pissed off fowl. No sooner had he released the spell and pushed it forward to dispatch a particularly feisty attacker, the bird swooped toward the enchantment.

* * *

Beak open and wings spread, the bird swept down from above and took the spell into its mouth. Colby would have laughed at the thought of something eating words, except that his spell failed. As he scanned his friends, Colby saw their attempts were meeting with the same results.

Hashtag spells ignited into reality from the tips of each kids finger as they fought to hold off the birds' attack. Each spell was devoured by a passing bird, fattening them up with each fly-by. The more spells Colby and his companions created was more fuel for the power hungry birds.

Colby was first to realize what was happening. He felt the build-up of Emassa in an exceptionally daring crow that swooped and dipped just above his head. Colby realized their magic was doing nothing more than giving the Shiznet creatures ammunition.

"Stop!" Colby yelled. "They are collecting our spells and feeding off the Emassa."

"What do you mean feeding?" Shelly asked. She moved closer to Colby and the others followed suit.

The birds took back to the trees and landed among the branches. Branches that now barely held the increased weight of eaten words.

"Have you not noticed how much bigger they've gotten since they began eating our hashtags right out of the air?" Colby said. "We have to assume that since not one spell actually did anything, that they are immune to our magic somehow."

"How can a Shiznet virtual bird be unaffected by our hashtag magic?" Jasper asked. "Hardly seems fair."

"Fair or not, look how round they've gotten. They look like they'll all burst any second."

* * *

While he looked up and pointed, one of the birds let loose a stream of waste that landed on his hand.

"Gross!"

Shelly started laughing uncontrollably. Soon followed by the others. Except of course Jasper who wiped his hand on the grass and ground cover. The stuff would not entirely clear away from his skin.

"You just got bird 'shiz' all over you. In some cultures, that's a sign of good luck." Rhea's comment renewed the laughter. Even Jasper chuckled a little then stopped suddenly.

"The Shizumu-pooh is burning through my shirt!"

Jasper rolled around on the ground in a failed attempt to rid himself of the noxious substance. It began to reach his skin before long, forcing him to remove the garment. Had the birds not started to circle above them, dropping more waste, Jasper would have noticed the transfixed stares at his shirtless body.

Colby turned away from staring at Jasper before the girls saw and misinterpreted the meaning. He was confused still about the connection that drew him to Jasper and what he actually felt. Perhaps not precisely luck but something allowed him distraction when he noticed the birds above beginning to rain down more waste.

"Take cover!"

Everyone turned to Colby, then followed his stare into the sky. A downpour of magic infused bird droppings was nearly upon them. They each erected hasty shields above themselves and huddled close.

"We need to get away from these 'flocking' birds!" Shelly said.

* * *

"Head back the way we first came into this place. Maybe there are other realities to search." Jasper led the way, running and dodging the acidic assaults from the birds now dive-bombing them as the kids retreated.

Jasper was getting annoyed at the birds in combination with having his shirt ruined and removed. Wanting to repair his shirt and focus on more offense than defense, Jasper came up with an idea to fix his first issue. He needed to repair his tattered shirt.

Using his finger as a stylus, Jasper spelled a hashtag to remove the bird droppings from both himself and what remained of his tattered top. **#NoMoreBirdShiz**. Once he released the spell, A bird swooped down from above and grabbed the spell in its beak. Once it headed back toward the flock, the bird swallowed the spell and promptly exploded, taking out several nearby fellow birds.

Tiny pixels of Shizumu bird remains rained down on the kids below. It took only a few moments to comprehend what happened before they all copied Jaspers accidental offense and launched them toward the overeager fowl.

"Attack!" Darla yelled. Her face twisted in vengeance; she thrust her fiery red-headed fury into the fray.

The offense was working well. Too well as far as Colby thought. Though he joined the others in dispatching the seemingly stupid birds, Colby knew not everything was always as it presented itself. Soon enough, his dread was realized when the birds stopped taking the bait.

"It's not working anymore. They've caught on." Colby said.

"Either that or they have us where they want us now," Shelly said. "The doorway we came here through…it's gone."

* * *

"Shiz!" Jasper said. "Now what? We're sitting ducks out here."

Colby began to run, waving the others to follow. "Come on! There were some stone structures over this way I remember seeing when we got here."

The five kids ran for the stones Colby pointed out over the horizon. The shields they all constructed over their heads held off the dive bombing birds enough to make the journey. On more than one occasion Rhea fell, and Jasper or Shelly had to help her up and run faster to catch the others. The overlapping of all their personal shields provided the best cover.

When they approached the stone outcropping, Colby realized that there was something uniform and purposeful in their placement. These were not randomly constructed stones in the Shizumu realm. They were laid out in a formation that once he got close enough, Colby realized what they resembled.

"It's Stonehenge!" Colby darted in between the stones of the outer circle and ushered the others inside.

Passing Colby and looking up, Shelly saw the open air above and noted the lack of cover from the birds. Indeed it looked very much like an undisturbed and fully formed version of Stonehenge and what it might look like restored. Each set of trilithon were intact with two upright stones, topped by a lintel. Short of standing below the lintels, they would still be an easy target for the birds.

The crows began to fly in formation, circling the henge. They did not pass over or drop waste; they just flew in formation around the structure as though preparing something.

"As much as I hate agreeing with your sister," Jasper said while leaning against the stones, "I think those birds are up to something, and this place is not providing any real protection. What we need is to find your mom's spirit and get the hell out of here."

"And how do you suggest we proceed then?" Colby asked. He leaned against an upright and felt a sudden drain on his energy. "What the…"

Colby felt a pull on his magic. The force of it made him dizzy for a few moments. He stumbled back from the monolithic structure and took Jasper's ready shoulder. He recovered in a few minutes and let go of his friend.

"What happened?" Jasper asked. "Did you get zapped or something?"

"Not exactly. It was more of a drain on my magic reserve."

Jasper scrunched his face. "That's weird because I was leaning on these other stones and nothing happened." Jasper reached out and touched the surface of the upright Colby retreated from just moments before. Nothing happened. "Are you sure that it wasn't something else causing the drain?"

Colby shook his head and approached the stone, careful not to touch it again. Yet. If what he was beginning to formulate was correct, then Jasper wouldn't be affected. Only Colby's unique mix of magic would react with these stones.

"I think it's my blended magic that the stones react with. I want to try something."

Colby reached out to touch his palm to the upright, but Darla's shouts of warning interrupted him.

"Shields up guys! The stupid birds are making a run for us!"

Everyone raised their shields above their heads to protect themselves from the dive bomber runs of the angry birds. Much to their relief, it was much easier to defend against the attacks while not running for shelter. Their illusion of safety was short lived, however when a bird puffed itself up and made a kamikaze dive for Colby.

The bird came in at an awkward angle passing through the gap between two stones. There was no time to react. Colby raised his shield and moved closer to the others. When he brushed up against Jasper, a surge in magic made his shield stronger, and it expanded.

"Colby," Jasper said. "Do you think that joining all of our magic it could work the way our combined magic works?"

Colby nodded in motion for everyone to take hands. One after the other as they joined hands, the shield grew in strength connecting with one another's and expanding to encompass the stone structure. As it expanded, the kamikaze birds exploded upon impact with the barrier.

"What is happening?" Shelly asked.

"Our magic is combining to make the shield spell that much stronger," Jasper answered before Colby had the chance. His enthusiasm made his friend uncomfortable, and Jasper composed himself when he saw the look on Colby's face. The tinge of embarrassment rippled through the magical bond.

Darla wasn't the only one to pick up on the emotional bond that rippled through their shared magic. Being an empath, Darla had the ability to sense people's emotions. This, however, was altogether different. Everyone involved in the shared magic could feel the tension between Colby and Jasper.

Shelly cleared her throat. "So can we all share magic like this?"

"I'm not entirely sure," Colby said. "I can't imagine why not."

* * *

"But you have done this before…with Jasper." Shelly stated rather than asked.

"Um…yeah, by accident."

The moments that followed were a bit uncomfortable for everyone, most of all Colby. Though the shield was holding, the birds kept bombarding in an attempt to breach their defenses. There were far too many birds and their strength would eventually fail. He had to find a way out of this.

"I need to get to those stones and try to activate them," Colby said.

"What do you mean, activate them?" Darla asked.

Colby explained that when he touched the stones, he felt more than just a drain on both his magics. For the briefest of moments, he felt something…from outside the Shizumu realm. He wasn't sure what it was, but it was real.

Once everyone agreed that Colby should try to see what would happen, he let go of the others and stepped toward the stones. Their shield fell.

Colby ran back to the others and rejoined their ranks as they all recast the shield enchantment. As soon as the spells were formed, the barrier reenergized, but not before a couple of birds breached the forcefield and exploded on nearby rocks. Colby noticed how the grass was scorched, but the stones remained untouched after the explosion. This reinforced his notion about these rocks. They existed beyond the realm. Or more likely in multiple domains at once.

"Well, that didn't work," Shelly said. "Any other bright ideas?"

Jasper leaned into Colby and whispered in his ear. When Colby nodded, Jasper closed his eyes as did Colby a moment afterward. When a shudder ran through them both, it also sent another ripple of feeling through the shared magic to everyone holding hands.

"Whoa," Darla said. "The first time that happened I wasn't sure what to think of it, but I know that emotion."

"What is it?" Shelly asked. "Never-mind, not my business."

"No," Darla sniggered. "It's a deep bond of like…brotherly love I guess would best describe it. I feel it all the time when my uncle comes to visit. He and my dad are like totally connected like that."

Hearing this feeling put to words in such a way comforted and eased both Colby and Jasper. The tension of the magical bond, slipped free and connecting became effortless.

Colby took this as a cue to let go of the others physically, while he maintained the emotional connection to Jasper. He used that bond to continue feeding his strength to the combined magics of the others.

Colby moved to the nearest stone trilithon and placed a hand on the stone. The first reaction was a series of sparks that formed around the edges of his skin that connected with the rocky surface. After a few deep breaths and a calming feeling of reassurance sent from Jasper, Colby delved his magical essence into the structure.

The entire formation began to glow a brilliant purple, the same color as Colby's magic. Between each gap of the outer ring, images appeared and shifted of various places. Some scenes were familiar, while others were completely foreign. Colby focused his attention on one image in particular; one that looked like Gary sitting in a basement with pipes and electric workings. The image focused and then flickered as he tried to push more energy into the view, but his power was waning.

Pulling harder on his surroundings, Colby funneled as much magic as he could into crystallizing the image before him. Each time it began to focus, it would shimmer and shift, altering the view slightly. He saw someone, a little boy, then…no, it's a teenage boy, no it was a young man. The confusion stirred as Colby could not make out what was happening. There were two things he was certain of; first, this Stonehenge was a gateway, and second, the figure in the image was Gary. And something was wrong with him.

The images all vanished, and the stones went dim. A light glow remained as Colby released his hand from the upright. He took a moment to clear his head before explaining what happened to the others. While he explained what he felt and saw, Colby noticed something had changed. The birds were gone, and the shield was down.

"What happened?"

"Dude, you totally yanked the Shiz right out of these birds, and they swirled into you like a draining tub or something." Jasper was jumping around like he just watched a winning point scored in his favorite sport. "Oh, and you kinda drained a lot of our stored Emassa in the process."

Jasper was so matter-of-fact that the girls pulled incredulous faces, but as soon as he took their hands and began pushing magical power back into them, they relaxed. They could feel that he was using his bond with Colby to relay magic through him and into the girls.

"This guy is like a never ending spare battery," Jasper said. "Now that he can tap the magic of the outside world and in here, then we found a gateway to probably lead us home…we got this!"

"Ease up on the testosterone 'dude'," Shelly said. "There's still the little matter of finding my mother."

"And the fact that Gary is in trouble," Rhea reminded everyone.

"He may be in trouble, but that's not what I said exactly. I don't know what, but something is 'wrong' with him."

# **<u>Chapter 28</u>**

## **#Golem**

Gary felt himself being pulled apart. The failed illusion Daphne weaved cast the first doubts of his real purpose. Now his own battle was beginning. While he somehow felt the truth of Daphne's words, the sudden return of a corporeal feeling added more confusion to what came next.

Gary's own existence, if Daphne was to be believed, hung in the balance. If he continued to go against Colby and the others, Gary would lose his friends. Yet he would preserve his own existence. If he returned to his friends…well, the outcome was unclear.

Was he real or just a functional extension of Colby, a golem of sorts as Daphne revealed? If this was true, Colby held the power to end him at will. If Gary continued to go against his only real friend, he deserved nothing less. Helping the Shizumu and this Daphne woman felt dirty, but it could mean Gary could become a real person for good, and the Shizumu would give him real parents like the ones in his fabricated memories.

How bad could it actually get if these creatures were allowed their freedom? They could take sick and dying people to inhabit after all. People that would have otherwise ceased to exist. Maybe it could work.

Given the choice of a slow painful decaying death or an extended healthy coexistence hosting a magical entity, many would choose the latter. Gary had to believe that.

"You still doubt your path, my boy?"

Gary jumped at the familiar voice. He turned as he fell backward to see his father standing there. His mother nearby. Gary rubbed his eyes at the sight of them. He thought he knew his parents, but it felt as though this were the first time he'd actually seen them.

"You have a task ahead of you child," his mother said. "You must decide what is more important, you, or your friend's self-interest."

"What do you mean?"

Gary's Father moved toward him and leaned forward. "Your friend Colby is bound and determined to destroy an entire race of beings with his recklessness. If he succeeds in finishing his little quest, it'll be your end."

"He wouldn't destroy me…would he?"

"He'd have no choice, my boy. There is only one way to bring about his ultimate goal. That involves putting all the pieces together, or back together I imagine."

Gary watched his mother nodding agreement with everything his father spoke. "It's true dear. His success means you're no longer needed. Is that what you want?"

Gary wasn't sure what he wanted anymore. The Daphne woman messed with his mind and made him think he was a servant creature of Colby's. She convinced him to delay them so she might thwart Colby's plans, but she never explained why.

* * *

"What is so wrong about what Colby wants to accomplish, besides my alleged ceasing to exist?"

"There is nothing alleged about your demise boy," Gary's father scolded. "If his father returns, it will only mean the end of Colby's golems and all the Shizumu. This place will be sealed off forever or destroyed and us along with it."

"Wha-what are you doing here anyway?" Gary asked before getting up and running to his mother's waiting embrace. "I thought you were just voices just in my head."

In the silence that hung on Gary's last words, a wicked little laugh began to echo. Gary backed away as his mother and father began to fade from his vision.

"Because 'they were' just voices in your empty little head." Daphne laughed as she made a pouty face and reached for another hug from Gary. "What, no more hugs for mommy?"

Daphne laughed again and stood straight, leering down at Gary. "Have no doubt, boy, you will find yourself at an end if that master of yours succeeds here and ultimately in his search for his daddy!"

"Why should I believe you? How do you know any of this?"

"Oh dear thing, it's remarkable what one can learn when their spirit is free to roam the world for centuries while bodily trapped in a statue. Even better is when a desperate man comes to free you in seek of favors."

Daphne was once an accomplished enchantress. She apprenticed to the most powerful witch in the Earthly realm until she was turned away for showing more ability with ancient spells than even her teacher. She performed a spell to release herself for the restraints of the physical world much as the Shizumu did millennia before her. Only Daphne altered the spell, allowing her to multiply her power by splitting into multiple physical entities. She magically split herself in two. Then again. And again. Four versions of herself, each a little more powerful. Except for the original who lost much of her abilities for some reason.

She was without few to equal in magic and completely free to do anything she could imagine. That is until she was tricked and ended up trapped inside statues. She and two other clones were encased in lead and silver then left to rot while the world changed around her. She watched as the Shizumu were imprisoned and the world forgot about magic and her. But then a boy with more magic than anyone should have caused a stir, and his daddy came to Daphne, freeing her in return for her assistance.

"You see Jarrod Stevens, although a powerful mage in his own right, didn't know a spell to protect his son. My magics were banned and erased from history. I can't even remember most of them except for a few and especially a couple in particular. The spells that blocked magic for ten years and created you, little mud boy!"

"I'm not sure if I should take offense to that remark."

"Take whatever you like from it, but mark my words. My magic can only be reversed with the original spell. Any written record of it destroyed long ago. You'd have to be able to control time to go back and find it." Daphne laughed at the thought. "Without that spell, the only hope of getting Colby's father back is by destroying you and the other focus objects used."

Daphne stopped talking as she realized she had said too much. She stared at Gary looking for any indication he caught on to her over-share of details but saw only confused glassy eyes staring back.

"Wipe your eyes little mud boy. I shall use my enchantments to force you again like before if I must."

* * *

"Force me how. What did you make me do?"

She laughed at him. "You think it was all your own free will to manipulate that device and trap your friends in their dreams? You are clay to be molded."

"I do what I want when I want." Daphne was striking a nerve with him. Gary stood to face her.

"You keep telling yourself that."

They stood staring at each other for several seconds before Daphne relaxed her approach.

"Look, your independent thinking and will to continue this farce of an existence should be enough to persuade you. See things like this. If you want your mommy and daddy to become real. If you want to be real yourself. I can make that happen. But Colby must not leave here until all the Shizumu are free."

"But they'll take people. That isn't right."

"Says who?" Daphne huffed. "They will take people who would otherwise have died or been too sick to continue a real life. They will be doing a service to these people."

Gary had his doubts, but Daphne somehow began making some sense. "How long?"

"Huh?" What's that dear?"

"How long do I have to delay Colby and the others?"

A smile crept along Daphne's face, and her eyes sparkled. "Oh not much longer actually. You'll know when the time is right. This place will all but fall in upon itself when the last of the Shizumu has escaped."

"I'll do what you ask, but I won't hurt them." Gary sounded reluctant, but he was more reluctant to see himself come to an end if he actually was just a golem.

"Good mud…I mean good, boy!" Daphne shooed him along. "Now run along and find your friend. I'll send a few of my friends along to…well to help you if needed."

As several Shizumu trolls appeared around him, Gary felt he had just made a deal with the devil or his concubine at least. As he watched Daphne disappear through a swirling vortex that opened, he heard her voice trail off.

"I've already sent a few friends ahead of you to get the party started. Tootles!"

"That bitch is cra-cra!" Gary mumbled to himself. He heard a few sniggering agreements from the trolls now herding him along.

Either choice he had, Gary was going to lose. He had little time to decide his path as he felt the magic around him growing. A familiar power that pulsed and swirled like his best friend's energy. Hashtag Magic was coursing through the Shiznet, twisting around the red menaces that guarded him.

Gary wasted no time with forming a decision other than making his escape from the monsters. He ran.

# Chapter 29

**#LetItGo**

"Why did we choose this direction to go looking for Gary?" Jasper complained. "We already know the doorway we came through is gone."

"Yes well he may not know that'" Colby said. "And even if he made it there to discover it gone, he might have stuck around to wait for us to show up."

Jasper huffed in response but kept going. "I'm hungry."

"We all are. Best not to think about it. We can find Gary and, hopefully with all our magic, find mom's spirit and get the hell out of here."

A rumbling sound broke the silent march that followed. Shortly after it began, a vibration could be felt from the ground.

"I sure hope that is your stomach grumbling for food," Darla said though she suspected differently. "What the Shiz is that?" Darla pointed to the horizon.

"Quick, Everyone back to the stones." Colby waved everyone on while he prepared a delay-spell.

* * *

He needed more magic. Nefslama blue magic he had, having been slowly storing it since he last used it up on the gateway. What he needed was some Shizumu red magic. He chuckled to himself about the two colors knowing that they were both forms of Emassa and the color was just the way it manifested. He began to wonder as to why there was even a difference but had to cut it short to concentrate. The trolls were coming fast.

"That's it, come and get it," Colby said. He pointed out with his finger and drew a hashtag in the air. **#DrainTrolls**.

The spell took to the sky and sped off toward the oncoming horde. When the magic burst out to grab them, many trolls fell to the trap while some were able to deflect it. Parts of the hashtag magic flew over and past the approaching mass of Shizumu monsters. Where it went, Colby was not sure, but he felt it grab something Shiz-born and start sapping magic away from them.

Colby gathered and stored more than enough red magic before he finally moved to join his friends at the henge. The trolls paused to assess what Colby did to their comrades, then renewed their pursuit. They saw where he and the others were headed and increased their pace.

Colby made it past the stones and joined his friends in the center of the henge.  They quickly joined their magic and threw up a force field that encompassed the entire stone structure.  When the trolls made their arrival felt, it was punishing.

The barrier resonated with every attack thrown by the relentless monsters. If not for the fact they were under attack, the kids would otherwise have been able to relish in the high tones to deep vibrating thrums that sounded with every hit upon the shield surface. As the onslaught continued, each of them began to sense the difference in the attack from that of the angry pecker-faced incarnations they faced the first time at the stones.

* * *

The trolls were employing a new tactic, or rather a new magical offense. Colby was first to sense the change.

"They're using Hashtag Magic!"

"What?" Shelly asked. "How the hell are they doing that?"

"Because it's been released into this virtual realm. It makes sense that our VR in the real world would-" Rhea started.

"Never mind the how for Shiz sake!" Darla screamed. "Just figure out a way to blast these ugly mothers out of existence."

Colby would have laughed at Darla's sudden break from prissy-dom, except the increasing strain on the shield was more important. He took a moment to steady his thoughts and mentally reached out for Jasper who accepted him without question.

Their bond brought a shiver of joy from the combined strength and resolve. Colby let physically go of Jasper while tightening his grip on him mentally.

"Ouch!" Jasper grunted. "Ease up dude. I'm here for you."

"Sorry," Colby said. "Hold down the fort so to speak. I'm going to try and weaken their attacks a bit."

"What do you have in mind?" Jasper asked, but didn't press when Colby gave him a mental push. "Oh! Sick!"

Before he needed to explain to the others, Colby rested a hand on the energy flow from the interior of their protective barrier. He concentrated on both maintaining his connection to Jasper and what he intended for the attacking trolls. After a moment he opened up his core to receive as much magic as he could take.

"Bring it on bitches," Colby shouted.

He ignored his sister laughing at his battle cry and his urge to laugh at himself. A barely visible sheen of purple haze spread from his hand and began to line the interior of the shield. As the attacks of Shiz powered hashtag spells hit the energy field, they melted into the purple layer and sent ripples of energy toward Colby's awaiting hand.

The buffer from the bone-jarring hits on their shield was a welcome relief. That brief reprieve that Colby afforded with his absorption of the magic was replaced by a new sensation. A burning. A burning that started first as an itch that you couldn't quite reach on your nose because your hands are full.

Colby did not precisely know what to expect once his magical limit for Shizumu red Emassa was reached, but he was finding out as he let it overflow into the bond with his friends. He took in as much as he felt he was capable, his hope was that his friends could take what spilled over.

Jasper was confused at first by the foreign feeling of the magic, but he soon funneled it into his core. It didn't agree with him. It felt like he ate a sandwich that sat out in the sun all day and went wrong. He felt like he was about to heave magic. And he did.

The burn the girls first felt was nothing compared to what proceeded. Scorched by magical overflow, the girls screamed as it pushed into them without restraint. Through all the pain-filled shouts, Colby latched on to them all and held them together. He needed them to hang on as long as possible.

The Shizumu were relentless. Their persistence paid off as a breach formed in the humans' barrier. Rather than continue bombarding as a group, some of the creatures broke away from the assault and dropped their façade. The trolls melted into the plasma shapes of their actual Shizumu form and squeezed past the shield. With the humans engaged in maintaining their weakening defense, they were free to escape their long-time prison. Colby made that possible when he activated the gateway.

"COLBY!"

Colby was unable to identify who shouted his name or whether it was just in his head, but he saw what must have been the cause of the alert. He turned to watch as several entities escaped through an open portal between the gateway stones.

"Oh, Shiz!" Colby said before pulling his hand free and rushing the gate. "It's a trick!"

Colby worked at the breach to seal it before more could get past and exit into the real world. He was able to fix the hole, but not before another opened on the opposite side of the shield. More Shizumu entered and headed to a portal that opened to the human reality. Colby ran to the new breach.

"I can't keep them from getting out." Colby was shouting in a mixture of anger and self-blaming disgust. How could he have fallen for this? From the beginning, this was an elaborately planned foray into their realm to trick him into giving the monsters inside a new way out.

"Focus Colby!" Shelly yelled. "There's no time for pity parties little brother. Let loose the monster inside, on those outside!"

He understood. Finally, he could live up to the nickname Shelly gave him long ago, 'Colby Monster'. He reached inside to that place he hid his anger. The place where all the years of tormenting from bullies, the feelings of self-loathing, the self-hate and hate for everything that hurt him was buried. Colby grabbed hold and pulled it forward, mindless of his connection to the others. They felt his pain, shared his hurt, chewed on his anger and spat it out.

All the Shizumu magic his friends and sister held was let loose in a single unified cry for vengeance. They had no particular target for their combined fury, only the unrestrained need to lash out with every hate-coated ounce of their beings. Spite oozed from every pore as the Shizumu magic spread across their bodies and coated them in Colby's rage.

The pressure built-and-built beneath the restraint the Colby exerted on everyone. He wasn't yet ready to let it go. Colby watched through eyes that shifted to an angry red that covered his entire iris and the whites pulsed with bulging red veins. When the kettle of vengeance boiled over he freed himself of the pain, the years of pent up anguish and the need to get back. Colby felt a hint of guilt in the back of his mind coming from somewhere near. He turned to look at Jasper who wept and looked back with sorrow-filled remorse. Colby set his magic free.

Jasper was already prepared for this moment. Jasper knew for some time now that he would not get away with what he put Colby through for so long. He liked to pretend that Colby would forgive and forget, but the emotional onslaught he just experienced proved him more wrong than he could have imagined. When Jasper not only felt, but then saw the backlash coming, he opened himself up to accept it, willing himself to take away the pain. He got more than he expected.

The magic slammed into Jasper with enough force to break his connection to all the others and sent him flying into a stone upright some distance behind. Though his physical connection was lost in the backlash, his magical bond remained under the vice-like grip of another, holding everyone together for a final act of retaliation, and Jasper was to serve as the fulcrum.

Colby stared at an reflection of himself replaced in the swirling image between one of the sets of trilithons. A vision of himself whispered words only he could hear. He tried to shake the illusion free, but he understood everything his image shared with him.

Colby turned and raised his arms up and opened his hands. Palms against the shield, Colby tilted his head as though issuing a silent command. The shield dropped just as the red glaze coating his companions dissolved. The magic he forced into them was released in a single glorious moment of unfettered, restraint-free fury.

Every Shizumu in sight was decimated. Their fake troll shells blown away like dust in the wind, their exposed plasma bodies shriveled into nothingness as their magic flowed forward and collapsed into Colby's kneeling form. When the last of them was absorbed, Colby spread his arms and sent magic into the surrounding stones. The gates activated entirely but were now coated in a protective shield of magic. The magic that he knew would not allow another, single, Shizumu an escape from what he planned for this realm.

Colby released his grip on the others, and they all fell to their hands and knees, gasping and crying with the remnants of Colby's remaining emotional onslaught. Only now did he feel what he subjected them to. Only now, he realized, did they understand his pain. He turned away without embarrassment for the tears streaming from his eyes that faded from an anger-filled red to a shining and brilliant purple.

"Mother!" Colby screamed as he painted her name rune it the air before him.

The gates shifted in response to Colby's unexpected command. Every image of the outside world dissolved into a glowing red as beams of energy flowed out and collided in the center of the henge. When the light faded, a single red glowing form of plasma remained in the center. Aria's spirit.

"You command, I come, my surprisingly powerful son."

# **Chapter 30**

## **#LashOut**

Aria woke from her fitful sleep. "Colby!"

Bellatrix, Nana, ran to her daughter's side and grabbed a rag to wipe her sweating brow. "Shush now child. Colby is fine; he'll be back very soon."

Aria pushed her mother's hand away. "Don't talk to me like I'm completely without a grain of sense in my head old woman."

Bellatrix sat back and smiled. "There's my girl. Where have you been?"

"Don't riddle with me lady; I haven't the patience. Where is my mother?"

"Oh dear. I am your mother, Aria. This fever has muddled your brain."

Aria looked at Bellatrix through squinted eyes. "Oh she's in there somewhere, but the creature before me is far older than even my overly wrinkled and haggard old mother."

Affronted, Bellatrix sat back and her disposition changed abruptly. "Haggard? Who the hell do you think you're talking to child. I'll wash your tongue with lye and sandpaper."

* * *

"Welcome back mother. Seems I'm not the only one with a split-personality anymore."

Before Nana could ask how Aria knew, she raised her hand to silence the persona of her mother of the last several decades. As she sat forward to pour herself a glass of water, she looked around the room.

"Surrounded by the tools of my present trouble," she said with disgust. "I suppose the time magic in this room is what has kept me from certain death?"

"You know about-"

"Spare me the theatrics mother. I am in my full mind, oddly, but I don't know for how long this time. Skip to the part where you tell me why my son and his friends are in the fucking Shizumu prison and that bitch Daphne is there."

Nana grimaced. It has been centuries since Bellatrix felt such a presence of mind in her daughter. This proximity sent confusion through the mind-side of Nana who only remembered forty-odd years with Aria as her daughter. It was all a bit confusing. She realized that Aria was Bellatrix's daughter and every reincarnation somehow found her again and became spelled into thinking that 'self' birthed her and lived a life as mother to the ancient sorceress before her.

"I'm not sure where to begin. It's all still a little muddled up here," Nana said as she pointed to her head.

"Then let me talk to that witch taking up camp in your head. Oh mother Bell, come forward and tell me a story."

Bellatrix reasserted herself in Nana's mind. "Hello, little one. How fair thee?"

* * *

Aria huffed and sat back. She waved her hand, and food appeared before her, and she began to eat.

Bellatrix stiffened. "You are reconnected?"

"For the moment, but only due to some extraordinarily powerful magic that comes from…my son?"

"Oh, that…well, it's a good thing your sitting down."

Bellatrix reminded Aria of the long ago spell that she attempted to prove herself capable of her mother's magical reputation. She split her soul to increase her power by augmenting an ancient and forbidden spell. The very spell by which the Shizumu themselves were created. The difference being that Aria created a cloned twin that went wild with magic and created two more copies of herself; each was more crazed than the one before.

After that, the details were unimportant for the present situation, so Bellatrix skipped to the here and now. Aria's son was in the Shizumu realm in an attempt to rescue the only piece of Aria that kept her whole, her magical spirit. This spirit form was essentially what the Shizumu were. Though Aria was capable of conjuring and displacement magic, as a split entity she was no longer the enchantress she was before the 'event'.

Aria needed no reminder of her poor attempt at impressing the great and powerful Bellatrix, so she insistently requested a skip forward. Though her memories were clouded from the point of Colby's first awakening to magic, she could infer that something else was involved that her mother either didn't know or was unwilling to reveal.

Many centuries ago, Aria was learning magic from her mother when she decided to show her power through a forbidden spell. A spell Aria felt she could master where others had once failed. It was a spell that would increase their power and allow them to accomplish great feats that their physical connections to the earthly realm restricted.

After her increasingly crazed copies had wreaked havoc on the magical ancient world, The elders decided to take action and captured, then imprisoned her creations until such a time the spell could be reversed. That time never came as the spell books Aria created, as well as those of Daphne and her spawn, were destroyed.

"It was for the greater good my dear. I hope you understand."

Aria broke a glass and pointed the sharp end toward Nana's throat. "If you don't find a way to stop that ancient harridan from dancing over your mind whenever she wishes, I'll gladly help you stop it now!"

Nana nodded and rubbed her throat as Aria retreated. "Resentful much?"

Aria grunted and dispelled the glass with a wave. "If you ever get the upper hand and delve deep enough into Bellatrix's psyche, you'll understand."

Nana shook her head. "Is that even possible?"

Aria laughed. "Why not. It's happened before. Who's body is it anyway." Not wanting to stray from the subject Aria pulled herself closer to Nana. "So what isn't that bitch telling me that you will?"

"Honestly I don't know where to begin. There does seem to be a lot of unresolved thought around the creation of the Dregg!"

Aria started to object, but a voice clearing his throat in the shadows stopped her.

"I think that's because of my presence in the boy's...I mean your son's life, my lady." Fizzlewink walked into the light of the room and revealed himself to Aria.

Aria's expression lightened. "Ah…little blue cat-man? How have you been fairing?"

Fizzlewink was surprised by the recognition. "You remember me, my lady?"

She laughed. "Bits and pieces my furry little friend. And please drop the 'My Lady' bullshit! You know me better than that."

"Better than you know yourself at times I imagine." Fizzlewink was not apologetic in his statement.

"Direct as ever. That's what Jarrod liked best about you."

"Likes my dear, let's not use the past tense in regarding your husband."

"I'm sorry Fizz, but you were not there when he sacrificed himself for our son's safety."

Fizzlewink shook his head, yet smiled at Aria. "Perhaps…but you also left before the spell ended. Jarrod did not perish as we expected. Colby has seen and spoken to him."

Aria was not reassured. Her last memory of her husband was of being trapped in a failing spell. "I thought the summoned creature took him?"

"Oh, he was taken…sort of," Fizzlewink said. "It seems, however, he planned for a betrayal and somehow preserved himself in another reality. Only after Colby managed to communicate with Jarrod a few weeks ago, did I realize what happened."

Fizz, with the unwelcome help of Bellatrix, filled in whatever blanks Aria requested filling. Im turn she advised them on whatever feelings of events she could on the kids in the Shizumu prison realm, a wasteland remnant of the former Nefslama home world.

"You mean the Nefslama world is gone?" Fizzlewink asked. He turned to Nana slash Bellatrix for confirmation.

"I'm afraid the stories are overly exaggerated and warped over time little cat-man," Bellatrix said as she reasserted herself. "Our world was already perishing when we fled for this one."

Aria interrupted an argument that brewed between her mother and the little blue man.

"So my twin, Daphne, has been freed and is what, seeking retribution through torturing my children and their friends? And my Husband's 'brother' is returned from the waste and is seeking revenge on all of humanity? Have I missed anything?"

"I don't pretend to know what that little…witch is up to, but she's aligned herself with some powerful friends." Bellatrix paused to take a glass of wine that Aria spelled. "All I know is that the children were completely pulled into that cursed place, and I believe it was a trap."

"Ya think?"

"No need to be snippy my dear," Nana said. "What we need is a strategy."

Aria sensed the change in character from the persona of her mother. "Where'd she go?"

"Never mind that old crone. What we need now is a bit o' conniving and deceitful planning, that if you'll forgive, but that battle-ax of a mother you remember is not capable of in this day and age."

252

* * *

Aria smiled despite herself. She felt herself liking this altered side of her mom. "What do you have in mind?"

Nana returned the smile. "Well if you don't mind. I'd like to involve the bastard that first cast your clones in statue?"

Aria smiled broader. "Oh, I wouldn't be expecting that."

"Precisely," Nana started. "And speaking of that, what else might we use against...yourself?"

Aria's cognitive side was gone. Despite Nana's relentless persistence, she couldn't rouse the woman who now stared back with blank eyes.

"Well, crap on a cracker!"

Fizzlewink turned to Nana, "She's gone. Something has happened in that horrid place you allowed the kids to venture."

"Me? Why you little flea-ridden sack of underused flesh. I should have-"

"What?" Fizzlewink interrupted. "You should have what? Transformed 'all' of my people? What of my wife and children still trapped in that spell of yours in Mexico?"

Bellatrix fumed. "You self-serving little...ungrateful mongrel!"

"Self-serving? That is rich coming from you. Name-call all you want. I'll not leave this room until you explain to me how my sacrifices and those of this modern incarnation of your family have served your greater goals."

The room fell silent as Bellatrix and Fizzlewink attempted to out-stare one another. Until Aria snapped back into reality, there was no argument or admissions.

"What is happening, mom? Why am I in Jarrod's study."

# <u>Chapter 31</u>

## #SpousalReunion

Fizzlewink stared daggers into Bellatrix from across the room while Aria tried to make sense of her current situation. The last thing she remembered, she was feeling ill and fell in the living room after some magical attack occurred.

Now she found herself nearly comatose, laying back on a couch she hated in the one room of her home she avoided like a cat avoided bathing. Jarrod's study, why was she in this room and how did she get there. What confused her more was watching her mother argue with that cat.

"We're all just pawns in your greater game, aren't we? Tools for you to use and throw at the Shizumu or anyone else who gets in the way of the great and powerful Bellatrix, Great Witch of the Maya and whatever titles you've had over the countless ages you've walked this Earth."

That cat is pissed off, Aria thought as she watched. It keeps hissing and raising its shackles at my mother like she threw water at him. She was no longer in a state to understand his words or see him for more than the cat he disguised himself as to normal humans. She knew who he was. She remembered more now than she has for many years, but the magic was lost to her again for some reason.

* * *

"Tell him," Aria said. "I can't take the sound of his screeching any longer."

Bellatrix sat down next to Aria as she lay back on the sofa. She knew it wouldn't be long now before Aria succumbed to the separation of her spirit and body. She witnessed it many times in the early days of the war with the Shizumu. The War of Souls.

"This is all my doing from the very start." Aria looked at Fizzlewink as he meowed back. "Please do something about your form Fizzlewink. My abilities escape me at the moment."

Fizzlewink shifted to allow the non-magical to see his true form. "Why does this keep happening to her?" he asked Bellatrix.

"It's the consequence of her spell that split her apart, cloned her," Bellatrix answered. "Have you never wondered where the second wave of Shizumu got the knowledge to cut their magical spirit from the body and both survived?"

Fizz shook his head. "I assumed they created it as a means to grow their power as they did millennia ago."

Bellatrix looked back at Aria and dabbed her sweating brow. "No. One Nefslama started something and lost control of her enchantment."

Aria was young, by Nefslama standards anyway. She was powerful and headstrong, two traits that do not mix well in a young mage. It was while attempting to impress her mother, Bellatrix, that Aria stumbled upon a brilliant and disastrous modification to a forbidden spell. The spell once used to strip magic abilities from those receiving the ultimate punishment from the council of elders. A spell created by Bellatrix, herself.

Through her experiment, Aria was able to split her magic and create a clone through combining several spells including one for creating a golem. When she succeeded, or assumed it a success, she presented her doppelgänger to her mother and teacher. Bellatrix became furious and ordered the abomination destroyed. Unfortunately, this was no ordinary mindless creature created from mud and clay. It refused to allow itself to be put down and fled, taking the spell Aria created with it.

The creature was a life all it's own, but still a copy in a sense. The problem with copies is that they lose a bit from the original with each copy made. In this case, the mind was not entirely stable. When it used the spell to make additional copies of itself, each new version was a bit more unhinged than the predecessor.

"The only saving grace was that the creature's attempts stopped after the third copy," Aria added to her mother's story. "The essence of the spell was the sharing of magic. It has its limits. Daphne must share my magic with me and her clones. It's all connected."

"You mean you are connected to this, what did you call her? Daphne?"

"Essentially, yes," Aria said. "Our magic is part of a shared connection. It is the one weakness we used to stop her the first time and imprison her in statues."

"Forgive my ignorance," Fizzlewink said, "but what has any of this to do with what happened with the ancient war and the altering of my people into the Dregg?"

Bellatrix began to fume, but Aria patted her arm. "It was Daphne who created the rebellious Shizumu. She sought to punish my mother and the elders who wanted her destroyed. She created another modification to my spell, something to create an untouchable army."

"That crazed woman split magic itself at the core of its seat in the Nefslama soul," Bellatrix spoke with disgust dripping from her every word. "The thought of such a violation to the spirit is revolting."

"And the Dregg come in where?"

Aria, with her mother's assistance, sat up on the couch. "The Shizumu were one side of magic. The other side remained in the Nefslama from where they were pulled. It's tricky business splitting magic, nearly impossible to reunite."

Bellatrix took over the explanation. She saw Fizzlewink's impatience and decided to summarize the science of magic rather than get into a full lecture of the principals and such. In short, she explained how magic is neither good nor bad; it simply is a tool, used for whatever purpose as the wielder deems fit. Magic is at its root, however, a combination of opposing forces that transcend reality and exist in a multidimensional state.

Once the magical essence of a mage or another magical creature is split, the two opposing forces try to balance themselves. This reaction makes them 'seem' whole so they will not easily reconnect to their original partner. The act of pushing them back together is disastrous.

"We found out the hard way that trying to force a Shizumu spirit back into the Nefslama body causes a sort of nuclear reaction and the host combusts." Bellatrix closed her eyes at the vision as though remembering first-hand accounts of this procedure. "The Dregg were created as a neutralizing force, something capable of coming in contact with the Shizumu so they could be captured until we could fix them."

A mature male voice came from the doorway. "But you couldn't fix them and look where we are today," Jenkins said. He entered the room unencumbered by the time barrier spell.

Fizzlewink turned and started toward the old man. "Who are you to come into this house uninvited?"

* * *

"Relax little man," Bellatrix said. "I invited him here. Though he took his time in coming."

"Hello Bell," Jenkins said. He moved over to Aria and took her hand to his lips. "And hello princess."

"Daddy!"

"Yes sweetheart, It's me." He looked back at Bellatrix, feeling the heated glare she gave him. "What mess have you gotten yourself into in this incarnation, wife."

Bellatrix stood and huffed. "I'll have you know I had nothing to do with this."

"Perhaps not directly, but I fear that an old specter has come back to haunt you." He looked back at Aria and tittered. "I assume you can feel it."

Aria closed her eyes and nodded. "I've felt it for some time now. Years actually."

"Would somebody care to tell me what this is about? I asked you here, Betelgeuse, for your assistance in protecting our family from a Shizumu threat."

"And you shall have what little help I can give, but it'll take more than your guard dogs outside and the help of your minions." Betelgeuse looked at Fizzlewink and winked.

"Wait, you are Betelgeuse. Jenkins, the old man Colby played Runes with, in the park?" Fizzlewink was confused. He never met the man in all his centuries of existence, but he heard the stories of his and Bellatrix falling out.

* * *

Betelgeuse was a pacifist. His disagreement with the elders about destroying Daphne and the Shizumu was the cause of their disbanding and the split of a once and powerful royal family of mages. Of course, they did not use royal formalities when the Nefslama came to the Earthly realm, but that did not mean they stopped being a great house.

Bellatrix forced Betelgeuse to leave when he refused to help capture and then destroy Daphne. In fact, it was Betelgeuse's theft of the Daphne statues that caused them to split their house in the first place.

"I've missed you, Princess," Betelgeuse said. "But I had to keep vigil on your sisters."

Aria twisted her lips. "I wish you wouldn't call them that."

"Well you created them, and they are just like you…well mostly."

"They're nuts," Bellatrix said, though it was more Nana then Bellatrix now. "Each one more off-the-ranch than the previous. And they are not family."

Betelgeuse huffed and turned back to Aria. "Same old argument, same old crone, no matter what incarnation." He looked back at Nana. "Though I will say there is more of the original this time than in the past. How did you manage that?"

"My seclusion has ended. I am returning in full."

"Oh. Well, that is unexpected, but not entirely without advantages."

Bellatrix moved closer to Betelgeuse and poked him in the arm with her finger. "What are you prattling on about you old coot?"

"If you'd paid any attention to the events going on around you, you'd already sense the trouble brewing." Betelgeuse shook his head. "You never could see beyond your own sphere of influence and agenda."

Bellatrix stepped back, affronted and confused. She thought back to everything that was happening around them. The return of the Shizumu, the attacks on her home and the kids, even the convergence of the Dregg never actually made sense. Colby was a draw, without doubt, but such powerful magics in the air and centered on the Stevens' household was perplexing. Realization began to settle in her shared mind when she looked back at Aria and her present condition.

"Now she's getting it," Betelgeuse said.

"Well, I'm not," Fizzlewink said as he sidled up to Betelgeuse. "What is all this about then?"

Bellatrix sat her fanny on the armchair next to the couch and looked at Aria. "Revenge."

"Oh, I'm afraid it's much deeper than that love." Betelgeuse tittered again as he stroked Aria's sweat-dampened hair. "Now that they're free, who knows what they've got planned, and they have help."

"Who would help the Shizumu?" Fizzlewink asked.

More tittering from Betelgeuse brought Nana's quipping personality forward more. "If you don't stop that tittering I'm gonna turn you into a bird and feed you to the cat. It sounds like a turkey in tap shoes."

"I don't eat birds."

Betelgeuse laughed. It was mirthless, but he was somewhat amused by the banter between Fizzlewink and this woman who was becoming more like his old wife. "I'm afraid it's the Shizumu who serve another force seeking vengeance and perhaps more. The Daphne are free and have been for some time I suspect." He turned to Aria for confirmation.

When Aria nodded, Bellatrix sat forward. "How long?"

Aria looked down as she twisted a tissue in her hands. "Ten years."

Thinking back through Nana's memories, the pieces began to fit together. It was ten years ago this trouble started, or so Nana thought, but Bellatrix began to see deeper into her history.

Ten years ago a plan was set in motion. Colby tapped into magic so strongly it caused an act of desperation to protect the boy from those who might use him as a tool.

Betelgeuse pushed his point home to Bellatrix while not looking away from Aria. "Who would seek the assistance of a powerful enchantress, someone with the knowledge to perform most anything imaginable. Who would make a deal without thought to the consequences to protect a child and family from the evils seeping through the magical community?"

Aria held a face filled with shame. "I never thought he would use the knowledge of Daphne's existence for this. When I realized what he did, it was too late."

Light of understanding fell upon Fizzlewink. "The spell Jarrod created. He got it from Daphne didn't he?"

Betelgeuse tapped his finger on his nose. "And now she has been free for ten years to exact her revenge upon my wife and family. Even I was fooled by the illusion she set on those statues when Jarrod released her."

"She must have trapped Jarrod in the spell she created for him, or worse."

"Not to worry Princess, I doubt she killed your husband. Daphne is a lot of things, but a waster of magical sources is not one of them."

"She is after Colby isn't she?" Fizzlewink asked. "If it's a source of power she is after, he's like a cosmic battery that can fuel a star."

Betelgeuse smiled. "I think she may have underestimated my grandson. I've been watching him, and there is something more to his magic I'm not yet understanding. That may prove a problem for Daphne being able to control him."

"But manipulate?" Fizz asked. "That she can do easily with that boy and his emotional needs are easily twisted."

"Yes, she can manipulate. She gets that trait from my wife."

"Oh shut up," Bellatrix said. "We need to figure out a way to get Colby and his friends back."

Betelgeuse placed a hand on Bellatrix's knee. She did not reject it. "They'll have to figure that out for themselves."

# Chapter 32

## #ActivateGateway

Colby sat on a stone in the center of the henge staring at his mother's spirit not knowing what to say. He wanted to hug her, but that would be problematic given his magical reaction with Shizumu. The entity before him wasn't Shizumu exactly, but close enough that Colby didn't want to risk coming in contact.

"You seem different my son, and I don't just mean your lovely violet eyes."

Colby looked at her as though not hearing a word she spoke. He understood what she said, but was unconcerned. Colby knew that he was somehow changed after taking in so much magic. It was more than Emassa he stole from the creatures. However, he took all of them. And though he released the magic into a shield around the gateway, something remained within. Remnants of what they were.

The knowledge of the creatures lives, their torment from imprisonment, their need for vengeance, their hopes for more than the life they knew inside the Shiznet. They were life, not physical as one might understand a living being, but the source of life, free of physical restraint. He snuffed them out without a thought, and now that weighed on him. Heavier than his pain that he freed himself of and inflicted upon his friends, the

Shizumu pain was greater, and it filled him easily where he voided himself of his own.

"I'm fine."

Though he was anything but fine, Colby wasn't about to show what now stirred within him. He would bury this deeper than he ever buried his emotions. He knew that what he now held was more dangerous than any temper-tantrum-fueled magical outburst he ever conceived.

The entity remained silent but saw through his ruse. "What now? Can we leave this place? I really must get back to my body."

"Soon," Colby said.

By now the others were sitting about, nursing cuts and bruises with the help of Rhea's healing ability and some Hashtag Magic. The hashtags were no longer twisting under Shizumu influence, so the kids had limited problems patching themselves up.

Rhea made a gesture to check Colby for wounds, but he waved her off knowing he had none. No scars were visible anyway. The damage he sustained was internal and more spiritual in nature. Rhea could not help with that. Colby would have to find his healing without help.

"What are we waiting for?" Jasper asked. "Let's get out of here while we can." He pointed out the disintegration of the Shiznet all around them. It was closing in fast.

"We need to wait for Gary."

"Oh yeah," Jasper admitted. "I forgot about him."

Shelly sat across from Colby, keeping her distance from the spirit of Aria. "How long are we gonna wait for him if he is still-"

* * *

"He is still alive," Colby interrupted. "He is on his way here, as are more Shizumu."

"Can he outrun them?" Darla asked.

Colby shook his head. "They aren't chasing him. They are escorting him."

Jasper stood and puffed his chest. "That little traitor. I knew he was no good."

Colby settled his friends. "It isn't his fault. He was tricked into helping the Shizumu and their mistress. We were all tricked."

The entire foray into the Shiznet was a trap, as Colby explained what he began to understand. Having the memories from the Shizumu he absorbed, filled in the gaps. Their mistress, Daphne, sought a faster way of freeing all the Shizumu from this prison realm. The first plan using computers and the influence over Jasper's father was foiled when Colby created the program to block the blue screen of death virus. But this woman was playing a long game.

She had backup plans, and the device that brought them to the Shizumu realm was set up to bring Colby and his friends into the realm and borrow their magic while they were kept in a dream state. That plan was dashed when Colby inadvertently broke the spell and pulled everyone physically into the Shiznet.

Daphne must have already prepared for the chance this might happen and then tricked Colby into activating the gateway. The last recourse for escape from the Shiznet. Knowing that the elders in their weakness for humane treatment would not allow the Shizumu to perish, built a failsafe into the stones.

* * *

"This was the gateway used to send the Shizumu here. Once we were brought here, the realm began to fall apart. It was not designed for corporeal beings and certainly not for Nefslama based magic." Colby stood and walked over to a trilithon. He peered into a portal that formed between stones and gazed into the shining images of places and worlds beyond. "When this realm fails, the gateway can be activated by the magic of a certain kind of Nefslama mage as I understand it now."

"Your magic is different because you have both forces in you," Darla said. "But don't we all have Nefslama blood, couldn't any one of us activate the gateway?"

"No," Aria's spirit interjected. "Colby is different because of how pure his magic is as well as the fact they coexist in a separated state somehow. This is beyond rare and also why Colby is-"

Colby turned to the spirit and cut her words off with a single look. "It is not important beyond the fact only I can open these gateways. That puts us in the most danger now. As soon as Gary gets here, we must convince him to return to us."

"What do you mean?" Rhea asked. "Surely he will see we are still alive and be happy to get out of here like the rest of us."

"As I said before there is something wrong with him. He is not thinking clearly and who knows what else he might do against us."

The kids remained silent for a few minutes, each picking around the inner circle of the henge. Then Jasper began to think out loud.

"He manipulated that map we first used I bet. And then there were the shifting paths. I bet he even helped put us in those dreams."

Colby didn't say anything. That was confirmation enough for the others. Feelings of betrayal and anger began to stir them. Colby could sense their agitation through the link he still held to the collective. Remnants of his emotional transfer remained in his companions.

Before Colby could think of a way to flush the emotional garbage from his friends, Gary and his retinue appeared over the hill approaching the henge. It became apparent though, that Gary was running ahead of the Shizumu the closer he came. Unfortunately, Colby was unable to relay this information to the others before Jasper released a spell aimed at Gary.

"I'll beat some sense into the little turd." **#AirBurst.**

Colby wasn't fast enough to react. Deep down a part of him wanted to watch Gary being knocked on his ass. He lowered his hand and let the burst of air from Jasper's spell hit his friend.

Gary was too busy running from the Shizumu to see the attack until it was too late. He slowed his run but was still moving forward when he met the oncoming blast. The force of the spell was increased when Gary collided with it and was sent flying backward. When he hit the ground, Shizumu soared past and over him toward the gateway. When the sparkles cleared from his eyes and the pain began to set in, Gary opened his eyes to see Daphne standing over him.

"I told you they were not your friends," Daphne said. "Now do you believe me?"

Gary refused to agree. "It had to be meant for the Shizumu."

Daphne laughed. "Do you see more attacks coming? No, my dear, that blast hit its intended target."

Gary looked to be sure for himself and saw that Daphne was right. His friends were not attacking the Shizumu who ran unimpeded toward their freedom. Colby and the others didn't try to stop or even slow them down as the wraith-like red masses converged on the gateway. Gary buried his head in his hands and wept. Had he continued to watch he would have seen the Shizumu slamming into the gateway portals and be slung back by a force field that barred their escape.

Daphne squatted next to Gary and tittered in his ear. "Are you going to let them get away with this? Will you let them abandon you here while they make their escape?"

Gary hesitated for only a moment. "No."

"Then do something about it." Daphne backed away from Gary and waved her hand to create a portal of exit. Nothing happened. She tried again but resulted in barely a crackle of magic that swirled and puttered before disappearing. "That abominable little shit!"

Gary looked up at Daphne who started walking toward the henge. He got to his feet and ran to catch up with her. "What should I do?"

Daphne stared straight ahead. "You need to keep them busy until I figure out how he's stopped me from leaving. Kill his friends if you must. Leave Colby to me."

"Kill them?"

Daphne spun on Gary and back-handed him across the face. "They are nothing mud-boy. They are his weakness and his strength. Without them, he is no match for me. Do as I say, or I'll end you myself."

Gary rubbed the tears from his eyes, looking at the moisture on his hands. He didn't recall ever crying before. The more he thought about it, Gary remembered nothing that didn't involve being around Colby. He was always with Colby, helping him, doing what Colby wanted. He was nothing without Colby. No more.

* * *

Gary dismissed his reluctance and doubt then prepared his attack. He approached the gateway while setting up a barrage of spells and allowed them to hover in the air around him before sending them off against his so-called friends.

He was setting up prep-spells the way he would if playing Runes, except these, were real magic and not a game. Hashtags spun and swirled around his body as Gary fueled them, and at last launched his offensive.

Spell after spell lined up and began peppering the kids thrusting up hastily constructed shields within the henge. Between Gary's spells and the attacking Shizumu, the kids became separated and unable to combine their strength into a unified barrier of protection.

Colby felt the magic being siphoned away from his core. Gary was unable to access the Emassa without Colby's connection, but Colby was unable to cut his friend off while defending himself at the same time.

All the kids were engaged in dodging spells while trying to keep the Shizumu wraiths away from the portals. Although Colby assured them his barrier that coated the stones would prevent the creatures from leaving, there was a new concern that appeared. A woman, no three women, who wanted access to the stones.

The three Daphne converged on the henge and began testing the red energy barrier that blocked egress from the Shiznet. Each one approached a different area and worked their way around looking for a weakness. They found it.

As the three women moved closer to Colby, he noticed how much like his mother they appeared.

"Mom?"

# Chapter 33

## #Trapped

"Don't trust her," Aria's spirit energy said.

Colby didn't take his eyes off the three women walking abreast toward him and the portal he stood before. He purposely left this one exit to his back because it was their way out. A small area remained unguarded by his spell so he and his companions might escape at the last moment before the realm collapsed. These doppelgängers to his mother saw his planned exit and were coming for him.

"Move aside and let us leave child," the middle one said. "This doesn't have to get ugly."

"It's already gotten ugly, Daphne," Aria's spirit answered. "What did you expect would happen by bringing me and these children here?"

Daphne laughed and her sister's followed with crazed cackles. "Exactly what has happened. The boy here did what only someone of his cross-breeding could do, open the gateway and free my army."

Colby looked through the knowledge he stole from the remnants of the Shizumu he destroyed earlier. He knew they reported to this woman, the center one with the reddest hair and clearly less crazy than the other two.

The Shizumu feared her, so they obeyed without question. Their orders were to escape the realm and wait for her next orders. They were not to harm Colby, but only him.

At that moment, Colby knew that his friends would be killed if he blocked this woman's escape. He couldn't risk them, but he also didn't wish to unleash all these Shizumu upon the world. He had only seconds to find a way out of this situation.

With no time left, Colby came up with an idea.

When Daphne and her sisters stopped inches from Colby, he stepped aside and allowed her to go. As soon as they exited, Colby shut the portal and sealed himself, his companions, and the remaining Shizumu in the collapsing prison.

"What have you done?" Shelly shouted. "That was our way out."

Colby raised a hand silencing his sister and pointing to the Shizumu now swarming together above the henge. "It was also their way out, and those crazy ladies way back in."

"So you've what, trapped us in here?" Jasper shouted. "Brah, not cool."

All this time, the kids still fought off Gary's attacks, but they suddenly ceased as Colby sat on the ground and exhaled. "Would someone go help Gary into the henge?"

"Seriously?" Jasper asked. "He's attacking us."

"Not anymore he isn't," Darla said. "He's just standing out there staring at his hands."

"I cut him off from the Emassa," Colby said. "He's harmless for now."

* * *

When no one else volunteered, Shelly stepped forward. "I'll go drag the little shit in here."

Colby grabbed Shelly's hand as she passed. "Don't let on that it's only him without magic." He turned to the others. "That goes for everyone. No magic yet, we're gonna need it soon."

"And if those things attack?" Rhea asked, looking up at the Shizumu circling overhead.

"They can't escape, and they don't seem interested in us for the moment."

Colby couldn't have been more wrong. He only had a knowledge of those Shizumu he absorbed. That information was not a complete picture of the collective goals of these creatures. Once they saw Gary entering the stone rings with Shelly, The Shizumu began circling above in a new intricate pattern.

Weaving rings with hundreds of red energy wraiths started a humming chant. The sounds of their spell began resonating and sending vibrations through the air and down to the humans. The magic was not meant for them. However, Aria was the target of their enchantment.

Aria's spirit became enraptured by the Shizumu conflagration. She turned her glowing eyes to the dwindling skies above the Stonehenge, listening intently to their call. That is what they were doing, inviting her to join them.

Aria moved away from Colby and toward the center of the henge structure. As she drifted away, Colby noticed Aria's reacting to the Shizumu spell. He felt something as well, but was not compelled as it appeared Aria's spirit became. He moved to intercept her.

"Um. Mom? Mom's spirit?" Colby asked. "How do I even address you?"

* * *

She did not respond.

"Hey, You!" Shelly called. "Casper lady?" Shelly shrugged when she also got no response. "She's not listening."

Colby moved to the center stone and climbed on top to block the spirit's progression. When she moved forward, the spirit soul of his mother moved around to pass Colby. Instinct overruled sense, and Colby reached out to grab at the energy-being floating toward inevitable disaster. The screams that came forth from both it and Colby made the other kids flinch and cover their ears.

Through the contact with her spirit, Colby could sense his mother. She pleaded with him to let her go, but he knew it was the spell talking. Even if he wanted to let her go, Colby knew he was unable to release the spirit. His soul was connecting with hers and through that connection, became enraptured by the Shizumu calling spell.

Aria, still screeching and wailing her discomfort, began rising to the welcoming Shizumu swirling mass. Unable to break free of Colby's grip, the spirit began to drag his soul along with hers.

Colby's spirit began to respond to the spell and wanted to join them. It was a disjointed feeling in his mind that alerted Colby to the threat. He began a battle of wills in his mind and body. A piece of him wanted to be released from the fleshy trap. What typically required a difficult spell and enchantment combined with lots of magic, was happening from no more than a combined calling spell from the Shizumu above.

The Shizumu focused their combined power and knowledge of the process that freed them ages ago from the fleshy confines of a body. Though they wanted nothing more than returning to vessels of their own, they sought comfort from adding to their ranks. If they couldn't leave, they would take any available souls with them.

* * *

Aria pulled harder, and Colby's soul began to slip free. As he looked at his upraised arm, he glimpsed the outline of his spiritual form rising above his skin. The full breadth of his body began to ache as he was being pulled apart from the inside. The longer he watched, the further his spirit slipped free of his body.

As he neared giving up the struggle, Colby felt a cooling relief begin to flow over him. Not realizing he had closed his eyes, Colby opened them to witness his soul beginning to retreat into his skin. Looking around for a source, Colby found Shelly grasping his other hand. He saw her lips moving in the silent command for his spirit to settle while she kept his hand in her white-knuckled grip.

Shelly, being a medium, had a connection to the spirit realm. When she saw what was happening, she ran to her brother and grabbed hold to keep him from raising into the sky. As she saw his soul-wrenching free of Colby's body, she began calling a silent demand to her past ghostly encounters to help her save her little brother.

Countless shimmering hands began running over Colby, tugging on his soul and pulling it back into his body. He knew the moment his spirit reconnected when the arguing voice stopped in his head along with the sounds of the Shizumu spell.

Somehow during the struggle, Colby let go of Aria's soul, and it now floated up and away, closer to the swirling mass of oblivion above.

"Everyone quick!" Colby shouted. "Get to a side of the outer stone ring and erect a shield while touching the stones."

Colby took only a moment to smile a thank you to Shelly, and they separated, each taking a place along the outer ring. As he touched his stone and turned, he saw Gary standing and waiting to be told what to do.

* * *

"Just sit down somewhere. You aren't needed for this."

Gary sat, both understanding and resentment wrestled in his mind. He realized that it was only he whose magic was shut down. If Colby could do that, then he truly was just a puppet, a golem tool for Colby to use, except now he wasn't even useful to his creator. Then it dawned on him. Colby would know that he created a golem servant, but never mentioned having done so. Colby didn't even know about magic when this all started. Another trick of that woman Daphne. How could Gary have been so easily fooled?

Colby saw the struggle in Gary. The boy wore his thoughts on his face like a mask. As much as Colby wanted to figure out what was happening with his longtime friend, now wasn't the time. He turned back to the task of shielding the henge and sought his connection to the others through the bond they all shared. By using the energy shield encasing the stones, Colby was able to touch the magic of each companion and combine them.

A barrier formed around and over the stone henge placing a blockade between Aria's spirit and the Shizumu mass swirling above. They were locked out, but their spell remained, and the creatures reacted with stirred up frenzy.

The Shiznet was collapsing faster now, and it was approaching the gateway henge.

Aria became agitated when she reached the shield. Unable to pass and join the song of her suitors, Aria sounded her desperation and desire for escape.

"Let me go!"

# <u>Chapter 34</u>

## #Enthralled

For the first time since the spell began, Aria looked away from the casters and down to Colby. Clarity soon began to return as she looked up and around her. She could still hear the spell chanted from the monsters outside the shield, but it no longer compelled her reckless abandon.

She allowed herself to drift back down from the barrier that now prevented the Shizumu spell from affecting her. As she made her way toward Colby, she noticed dissolution of the outside environment. The Shiznet, as the kids liked to call it, was breaking down as a result of both the corporeal presence of Colby and his friends, along with the draining of magic that created it.

Aria looked back at Colby and saw the visual trail of energy that flowed into Colby and outward toward his friends. Being an energy based entity, she existed on a different plane that allowed her to see magic, not just feel it. This added sight is also how the Shizumu and seekers were able to locate magic users as well. But when Aria observed Colby, she saw something else.

Not only was he channeling magic from the gates, but he was also siphoning it off of the realm they inhabited. And there was another thinner thread of power that led from Colby to each of his companions, including Gary. Aria saw no magic, no Emassa emanating to or from Gary, but something was connecting him to Colby.

Colby watched Aria staring at him and then Gary. Did she know, he wondered. Colby knew that something was off about Gary, that he wasn't entirely rational.

"Do you see it, child?" Aria asked.

Colby nodded but kept his eyes locked on Gary who sat slumped and looking defeated. "What is he?"

Aria's spirit giggled. It was an airy and echoing sound that brought Colby's eyes back to her. "Not the right question. The question is 'what part' is he."

"Huh?"

"Think about it child, and you'll begin to understand," Aria said before turning away and heading for Gary.

Colby watched her go and thought about what Aria said. 'What part', he wondered. When he allowed himself to focus on this new insight, his mind began to focus as did his eyes and he saw it. Colby saw the thin trail of white energy that traveled from himself to Gary. Even though he blocked Gary from the Emassa, there was still an active connection between he and the boy with whom he connected with and felt was an extension of himself. That is when it clicked. Gary was a part of him. When Colby focused on that thread connecting them and followed it back to himself, he saw the others.

Five thin wispy trails of power tethered him to his companions. The only difference between the one leading to Gary and the others were the purple lines of Emassa transmitting along that thread to the others. Colby's mind began to swim in the ocean of understanding. Shelly's link was a bit more substantial, but the other five were the same.

Gary looked up at Colby; he felt something. The gaze was unreadable. Gary saw no indication of what Colby was thinking from the expression on his face, but he could sense that Colby was assessing him. And why shouldn't he? Gary already betrayed Colby and his other friends twice since they entered this forsaken realm. Gary knew he would not be allowed a third time.

"What does this mean to you golem?" Aria asked when she began circling Gary. She hovered and swirled around him as he watched her. Trails of red energy swirled and cascaded off of her like a fine mist. "You have gone off on your own and betrayed yourself."

Gary shook his head. "I don't know what you are talking about."

"Do you not?" She stopped in front of him and peered into and past his eyes. Her gaze penetrated his exterior and delved into the heart of what he is. She found the source. A minuscule droplet of blood. "Oh, you are quite an achievement. I had no idea Jarrod was so talented."

"What are you talking about?"

Aria spun around and drifted away. "Think on it, creature." She giggled as she left, watching Gary's face twist in confusion as she moved away.

Jasper watched the entire scene play out before him. What was Aria's spirit doing, he wondered? First, she spoke with Colby, then Gary. Was she playing peacemaker, or was she now affected by that Shizumu spell and trying to stir up more trouble?

"Hey, traitor!" Jasper said in a whispered shout. He waited for Gary to turn his way. "What is she telling you? Is she in league with the spooks outside? Are you helping her to set them free?"

* * *

"Shut-up Jasper," Gary said as he stood. "You don't know anything. Just stand there and use your only skill, strength." Gary turned away and walked toward the barrier of a nearby portal. "All brawn and no brain."

Jasper glared as he stepped away from the stone, heading for Gary. "You take that back!"

The shield began to flicker and fail.

"Jasper," Colby shouted. "Get back to the stones. You're breaking the spell."

Jasper ran back to his spot and placed his hand back on the stone. The shield returned to a steady hum and pulse of magical energy. "Sorry, but I think he's up to something with your mom's ghostly self."

"He's not up to anything and neither is mom's spirit." Colby saw the jealousy in Jasper, something he spent a lot of time working on himself. "Gary made a mistake, and I'm certain he won't do it again."

"What makes you so sure?" Jasper said. "Twice already he's betrayed us. Third time's the charmer, they say."

Darla laughed. "Third time is the 'charm' you dumbass."

"Who are you calling dumb?"

"I think she was talking to you," Rhea added.

"Nobody was talking to you Rhea," Shelly said. "Let dumbass and clueless fight their own battles. Maybe you can sparkle your healing on them after they give each other fat lips."

"Hey Bride of Frankenstein, nobody needs your smart-ass remarks."

* * *

Colby was stunned silent by the outburst from his companions. The in-fighting was unexpected and escalating. At first, he thought it might be a result of the Shizumu enchantment, but he realized that this was coming from somewhere else. All the things he heard coming from their mouths were things he remembered thinking to himself over the months since they were thrown together.

All his frustration, jealousy, anger, bitterness, the negative emotions he held trying to keep his temper in check were flowing from their lips. It dawned on him then, all the emotional baggage he shoved into them was bubbling up and seeking release.

When he shared himself emotionally with them, he thought that was the end of it, that he'd finally let go. All he managed was finding a new place to hide his feelings away, but they didn't want to be hidden. Colby's emotional seed was planted in them, and now it sought the light of day.

He continued to listen, uncertain what he could say or do to stop the bickering. When the heat of their verbal battle reached a point he could listen no longer, Colby snapped.

"Shut it down!" His words echoed throughout the interior of their shielded refuge. Silence followed.

Not even the humming chant of the Shizumu spell remained. Nothing but dead quiet filled the air. It was bliss to Colby. All the voices in his head stopped. The self-doubt, loathing, hatred, jealousy and more were gone. When at long last he opened his eyes and looked at his friends, he spoke.

"I'm sorry."

"What are you sorry for? Gary is-" Jasper started.

"Gary is not to blame for anything." Colby looked at Gary. "It is my failure, not his."

Gary and Colby shared an understanding thought.

"But-"

"Jasper, that is enough. There are more important things at stake here than my pettiness. Let go of the emotions I flooded you with. All of you."

When his friends and Shelly relaxed and understood what he meant, Colby watched as they each maintained and let his feelings flow back through their individual connections, back where they belonged. They were his feelings and failings. He needed to own them.

The magical energy Colby was using began to wane as he tucked those emotions away, not as deep as before, but out of the way. He felt the ebbing tide of Emassa as the Shiznet neared an end. The Shizumu were quiet but a pleading emanated off of them that Colby could not ignore.

Who was he to condemn these creatures? They were not entirely to blame for their situation or Colby's. He knew from the knowledge he held from the spirits he absorbed, that most of these wretched souls were only seeking freedom from a place they could no longer bear. They had a longing for connection to something else. But could he free them and thus allow the possession of innocents in the human realm?

At that moment Colby made up his mind and dropped the shield.

"What are you doing?" Shelly shouted. "You're gonna get us all killed."

Colby shushed her and pointed upward. "They are not attacking."

Though the Shizumu cautiously lowered themselves within the confines of the gateway henge, only one made its way to Colby. A slow and deliberate approach, the soul of some long-dead Nefslama made a silent bargain with Colby.

"It is done," Colby said. "Prepare to go home."

Colby reached a hand around and touched the stone portal while hashtaging a spell with his other. **#OpenTheWayHome**.

As the portal swirled and created a pathway to traverse from this realm now void of anything save the gateway, Colby ushered the others near the vortex. Colby moved away and instructed the others to step through. Aria stayed behind at his request.

When his friends were gone, Colby turned to Aria. "You must not tell anyone what I am about to do."

Aria tilted her disembodied head. "Are you sure about what you intend?"

"If you know what I'm about to do, then you know I must."

"I hope you don't regret it." Aria turned and paused before going through the gateway. She saw the figure that waited behind, shifted into the spirit realm, watching. Aria nodded at Shelly and entered the pathway home.

Shelly used her new talent to find out what Colby was doing as Bellatrix instructed.

"I hope I won't either," Colby admitted to himself. Taking a deep breath, Colby expelled all the Emassa he stored inside the center of his magical core. Colby wasn't sure he could trust the image he saw of himself in that portal, but he was out of options. He felt hollow and vulnerable.

The Shizumu moved closer, but they did not attack.

* * *

"Here goes…everything."

He lifted his hand and pointed his finger toward the Shizumu mass that closed in around him.

**#IntoMe**.

# Chapter 35

## #BackToSchool

Conrad was first to feel the strong presence of ancient magic. The power of Emassa was being pulled from everywhere. It centered on a location not far from the Stevens' home. An old place, though now covered by modern structures, the magical portal reawakened.

"We must go," Conrad said. "Something is coming."

Several Dregg moved out, followed by Fizzlewink and a few of his kind. Conrad began to stop them but decided to allow the little men to find a use. Though they did not have the strength they once had as Dregg, being transformed back into Nefsmari meant they could use magic that the Dreggs could not.

"Don't even think of counting my compatriots and me out of this," Fizzlewink hissed.

"Wouldn't dream of such a thing little man," Conrad said. "But are you certain you don't wish to stay behind and-"

"And what," Fizz interrupted. "I have no desire to sit around here listening to Bellatrix and Betelgeuse fighting upstairs."

* * *

Conrad laughed. "I understand fully." He patted Fizzlewink on the back as they both walked off, looking up toward the attic and shaking their heads.

"Where are we going?" Fizzlewink asked.

"There is a very powerful disturbance of magic nearby. It is at that school the boy and his friends attend."

"The basement?" Fizzlewink asked. "There's something down there you know."

Conrad looked down at Fizzlewink as they picked up their pace. "You've been there?"

"I followed someone there once," was Fizzlewink's short answer. He remained silent as they began to run toward the Escutcheon Academy, Colby's school.

The magic was getting stronger; they could feel the thrumming of a build up of energy as though something was burrowing its way up to the surface from a deep dark forgotten place. When at last they reached the school, Conrad led the rough and motley crew into the front entrance. Someone was there waiting for them.

"You can't be here," Dean Tiddle said. "School is in session, and most of these children are completely unaware magic exists, let alone they come from supernatural bloodlines."

"Move aside old mage. These kids will see only some gruff-looking men and scrawny old cats running down their hallways." Conrad could have bored holes through Tiddle's head with his drilling stare. "Unless you wish whatever is coming through the portal in your basement to reach them instead."

* * *

Tiddle winced. "That portal was sealed long ago. It can't be…Jarrod?"

"Not likely," Fizzlewink said. "But perhaps his son?" Fizzlewink raised the question to Conrad.

"I feel it must be." Conrad pushed past the whimpering old Dean and headed for the doorway leading to the basement stairway.

"Those kids have a lot of make-up homework…" Tiddle shouted after them. "Oh bother." He shuffled after them, shooing teachers and students back into their classrooms. "Back to class…nothing to see here."

When Tiddle caught them up, he found the entourage of Dregg and cat-man mages heading down the rickety old metal stairs into the bowels of the building. He stepped onto the landing and snapped the door shut behind him before grabbing the rail.

"You know that chamber has been sealed for over a decade. And the portal hasn't been used-"

"Dean Tiddle," Fizzlewink said as he jumped up to walk along the railing beside the fidgety old mage. "I think you know better than that. Jarrod Stevens used the magic power emanating from this site many years ago to fuel a spell."

Tiddle acquiesced. "I was there. But we sealed it back up as Jarrod requested. He never came out."

Fizzlewink flicked his tail, and it settled in the shape of a question mark. "You expect to find a set of dusty old bones in there?"

"Well…"

Fizzlewink dropped down in front of the Dean and transformed back to

Nefsmari form. "He's not in there, nor is he…dead."

"How do you know?"

"Because Colby made recent contact with…well, a part of him."

"A summoning?" Tiddle asked. "I understand that the sister has the gift of spirit-walking."

"He wasn't a ghost. It was some spell Colby triggered within the ancient chamber beneath the pyramid of Chichén Itzá. They spoke, and Jarrod wouldn't let Colby touch him."

Tiddle pushed past Fizzlewink and continued their walk toward the metal doorway deep in the catacombs below the school. "Well, that says something doesn't it."

"What does it say," Fizzlewink said as he caught up to the Dean.

"It confirms at least that Jarrod is not dead. A ghost could not use that ancient temple."

"What do you know of the place? I spent ages living in those grand old cities and never heard of the hidden chamber."

Tiddle snorted a chuckle. "It wasn't always hidden. The current structure was built over the top of the old one. It was a building from long before your kind were even created. All this according to something Jarrod once told me."

"Go on," Fizz insisted when he noticed Conrad slowing to pay attention as well.

"Jarrod once told me of a series of ancient structures built from the remains of the vessel used by the first of the Nefslama who escaped into this realm. These buildings each had foundations set upon places of power. Along lei lines if you are of a mind to believe in their existence."

"They exist," Conrad assured. "They haven't been active since the time of the Druids."

Tiddle raised his brow. "Well then, this temple was once used as a means of either physically traveling between or simply sending a sort of holographic version of one's self to communicate with someone another location."

"So you're saying Jarrod was somewhere transmitting this message to the boy?" Conrad pressed. "Where are these places?"

Tiddle laughed. "Oh, my. They exist all around the planet; places buried by newer structures and forgotten to time. This was all theory you understand. The rambling of Jarrod Stevens while sharing stories of his travels and discoveries. I never really believed most of his tales…until now."

"We have to tell Colby," Fizzlewink said.

"NO!," Tiddle insisted. "You can't breathe a word of this to anyone, especially Master Stevens."

"Why?" Conrad insisted as they approached their destination.

"I was sworn not to speak of the full events from that night until released from my bond of secrecy. It's a magical binding, that if I break I…just understand I must not talk about more than I have already shared."

Fizzlewink could see the sincerity and panic in the old mage's eyes. Whatever happened, he figured the knowledge this man held might affect the outcome of Colby's quest somehow.

* * *

"The deeper we journey down this rabbit hole, the less I think it likely we will all climb our way out."

"Well said my little friend," Conrad said. He turned to the doorway and watched as the runes began to glow.

Fizzlewink recalled the day he led Colby to this place. He only knew of it when he followed Jarrod and Aria here the night Colby was hobbled of magic. Looking back to Tiddle, he wished now he had stuck around to see how that fateful night unfolded. Instead, Fizzlewink —now stuck in cat form— ran back to the Stevens' home to fulfill his promise to watch over Colby.

Perhaps now that this door seemed insistent on opening, some answers might follow. Someone or something was coming.

"We are not alone," one of the Dregg said.

Conrad turned with the other Dregg, looking down the darkened and pipelined corridors. Steam sprayed from the pipes of boilers working to stave off the first chills of fall from the building. The occasional drip of water from decades old waterworks and drains filled in the remaining silence.

The scraping sound of a desk being moved overhead spooked Fizzlewink and he hissed while his hair raised.

A red glow began to light the way down the seemingly endless catacombs that stretched out around the center space where the Dreggs, dwarf-mages, and Tiddle now stood.

"Seekers?" Fizzlewink asked.

Conrad growled. "No, their masters."

* * *

"Oh-Shiz!" Fizzlewink prepared for a fight that didn't come.

The Shizumu appeared in the blink of an eye and sped toward them. At the last moment, they scattered and disappeared among the pipes, boilers, and drain systems.

Dreggs spread out to protect the others since they were unaffected by Emassa. They waited for a fight that was not coming.

"They sense the magic being stirred up here as well. What do you think that means," Fizz asked Conrad.

"It means they are here for whatever is coming, maybe. It's hard to tell with these things; they don't follow any regular patterns anymore. I miss the old days when things were simpler."

"Oh yes, the old days when all they wanted was to kill every last Nefslama…"

# **<u>Chapter 36</u>**

## **#InBetween**

As Colby followed the others through the vortex portal from the Shiznet or the void that remained of it, he opened his senses to the energies that surrounded him. Though he could sense the others ahead, he could not see them. He couldn't see himself for that matter.

While lifting a hand before his face, Colby couldn't see it. He knew it was there. Colby felt it like a phantom limb might be experienced. He felt as though his entire body was amputated. His mind was there, along with hundreds more. The Shizumu he carried inside him. He wondered how they could still be there when his body seemed to be gone.

Colby was alone with his thoughts. Gone were the endless voices of Shizumu in his head that began the moment he took them inside himself. They swirled and bulged within his core to the point just before he felt he might explode. Compared to the limits he once reached for storing Emassa, the room the hundreds of Shizumu spirits were taking refuge in was incalculable. Colby imagined himself one of those people that were stick thin and still managed to out-eat the four-hundred-pound behemoth at a food eating contest.

Alone for the first time in months, it was pure bliss. He felt like himself again, though that thought disturbed him. He was never happy with who he was…until magic entered his life. Before then he had Jasper for a time, until he left, then came back as a complete douchebag. Gary arrived immediately after as though by, magic.

Alone with his thoughts again, Colby grabbed hold of what eluded him this entire time. Everything happened to him when it was needed. Jasper came along when he needed a friend. Then he left without explanation and suddenly Gary was there. When Colby had feelings for a tender touch that was lost when his mom closed herself off, Darla showed up. At the time he wished for his life to be different, Magic exploded into his world. Things were being laid before him as if by a response to need.

"Now you're getting it," a voice echoed through the void.

"Who said that?"

No response.

Colby felt himself going crazy. He focused now on just getting back to reality. With that singular thought —desire— his surroundings collapsed, and he fell through light into dark.

Oof!" he heard. "Get off me stupid."

Colby's senses all returned in an instant of intense pain. He screamed out.

"Hey!" Shelly yelled. "What's wrong with you?"

"Sorry," said Colby. "I didn't realize…were you in front of me the whole time?"

Shelly didn't answer. She only held out her hand to assist her brother in getting up from the floor.

* * *

Colby accepted a helping hand from the floor. He opened his eyes and allowed them to adjust from the sense of being sent from an environment full of light to one completely void of even the slightest flicker of a flame.

"Somebody create a light," Colby said. "I find myself without the strength to do so."

As if by command, the room brightened, though not a daylight or even incandescent bulb strength brilliance, there was light. The source of light came from innumerable runes etched into the walls surrounding them in the circular room they now occupied.

The kids all turned to stare at the walls and walked toward them. They ran their fingers across the runes and felt the vibration of a spell much older than their combined ages. The reverberation sent a shiver through Colby's bond to each of them that returned the moment he exited the vortex. He was overcome by his senses and spasmed.

"Hey!" Rhea said. "Are you ok?"

Colby waved her off. "I'm fine." He was better than fine. He felt like he was suddenly refreshed from an aching need to drink. He let all his senses return as he watched the others become dizzy and fall. "Yeah, that first step is a kicker."

"Where the hell are we?" Shelly said.

Colby looked around and understood. "Where this all started, at least our chapter of the story."

"What does that mean?" Darla asked.

"I'll explain later." Colby pushed himself up from the floor and began scanning the walls for the door. Once he found the door, he motioned toward it and issued a hashtag spell. **#OpenSaysMe**.

Nothing happened.

Remembering he expelled all his Emassa and now played host to more guests than even a frat party could manage, Colby asked for someone else to open the door and pointed it out. Every attempt by another failed.

Colby realized it had to be him that first opened the door. "I need to borrow some Emassa."

"What? Why can't you just tap into it," Shelly asked? "When she tested it herself she realized there was no access. The room was sealed off from outside magic. "Here, take mine." Shelly walked up to Colby and offered her hand.

"No," Colby said. "Thank you, but Gary can provide what I need."

Jasper grunted and made a move forward and insinuate himself, but one look from Colby stopped him.

Gary shuffled up to Colby and held out his hand, eyes not leaving the floor.

"You don't need to offer yourself like a sacrifice, Gary. I could take the magic as needed even without asking." Colby waited for Gary to look him in the eye. "I just thought it polite to ask a friend to offer it first."

Gary smiled and lowered his hand. He closed his eyes and expressed his approval.

Colby siphoned off the magic to fuel his hashtag spell and let it sink into the door. "Thank you."

"If you need more, I'm willing-"

* * *

"Thank you again," Colby interrupted. "But I'll be better once we leave this place."

The door opened, and the kids wasted no time piling out of the space. It wasn't from feeling claustrophobic or dank and dusty. It was the complete isolation from Emassa and anything outside. Add to this the fact they were finally away from the digital-meets-magic VR realm of the Shiznet, even the basement of the school was inviting.

Colby saw the welcome party outside and was touched, if not a bit suspicious. When they beckoned him out, he refused. "Give me a minute. There is something here I need to do." He walked up to the door and closed himself in again. Though he didn't see Shelly exit the room, he assumed she must have begun the long walk out of the basement. Before the door closed completely, it stopped, blocked by an invisible force. Colby thought he had heard a grunt before the door swung back open.

Shizumu flooded the room from the catacombs outside. As soon as they all entered the space, the door sealed shut again.

The Shizumu approached Colby and halted, shock and awe rippled through their ranks, and they backed away.

Colby looked at them and understood they sensed what was inside him. Before he could say a word, a new presence made itself known.

"Hello…me," an older looking and run down version of Colby said.

"What the-"

The shizumu began to converge on the new member of the conclave. This new Colby raised his hand, and a pulse of energy pushed the Shizumu out of his way as he approached the other version of himself. He stopped at the pedestal in the center of the room and motioned for himself to approach.

Colby, the one full of Shizumu and no magic, hesitated before moving with the draw of his curiosity.

"What is this?" Colby asked the reflection of himself. "Who are you?"

Colby, the older Colby, laughed. "I'm you, or another version of me-you…it doesn't matter. You already know me since you've done as I instructed."

Colby shook his head but remembered the images he saw in the portal. "That was you? I mean me?"

"Time, portals, all a bit confusing for you right now. For the moment just listen and do as I say. As 'you' say."

Colby wanted to believe he was being subjected to some spell, but deep within he knew he was facing himself. "What do you want from me."

The other Colby smiled and motioned his hands to the pedestal. "Place your hands here and learn."

When he approached the center of the room, Colby reached toward his doppelgänger.

"Do not touch me," his reflection said. "That would be…bad."

Colby frowned, but did what was asked without hesitation, and was immediately sent into a flurry of images and sensory overload.

Colby saw his father, standing before this same rock column protruding from the floor. His mother stood to the side and wept as Jarrod looked back with sorrow. Colby watched as his father cast items into a mortar and spoke an unheard spell.

*  *  *

Images of himself as a small child getting pricked by a pin and bleeding followed by pictures of Gary, Jasper, Darla and Rhea, filled his mind. Then he saw a vortex opening.

From the vortex, images of a Shizumu entering the room filled him with dread and familiarity. The visions shifted to his father melting and getting pulled into the same vortex while the creature pulled the skin of his father over his glowing form. The skin reformed into a new face before his father's essence vanished into the vortex that collapsed. Colby started to recognize the face on the new figure when the images abruptly halted.

Colby buckled over and tried to vomit, but having not eaten in immeasurable time while in the Shiznet he just heaved. Instead, a steady stream of Shizumu energy flowed from his mouth, eyes, nose, and ears.

"You've seen enough for now," Colby two said. "I have to see you, sometime else now. Just remember this spell, **#BanishToTheVoid**." Then he left.

Unable to make much sense of what he experienced, Colby just sat back and watched the hundreds of Shizumu swirling around him. Colby focused on the emptiness inside left behind by the evacuation of so much energy and mass from his core. There was no way to fill it.

The Shizumu became crazed with the need to escape the confines of the chamber. One of them flew up to Colby and hovered before him.

"We can't leave here. Help us."

"I can't," Colby said. "I expelled all my magical energy to store your souls."

"Use mine," the spirit said. "I will give myself to allow my brothers freedom."

* * *

At this one Shizumu's words, others came forth to offer their energy for the sake of the others. Even those among the mob that greeted his exit from the void were willing to sacrifice themselves for the benefit of the others. Colby saw the Shizumu in a new light.

"That any of you would give yourself for another speaks volumes to how I've been preconditioned to think of you as a race. I can take a small amount of you as a group without ending a single life if you will agree."

The Shizumu agreed without a moment of thought.

Colby raised his hand to pull on their collective energy to take only what power he needed and not a drop more.

The door opened without Colby having taken a trickle. He sensed another presence and heard a whispered, **#OpenSaysMe**. Thinking it was his other incarnation, Colby shrugged and nodded at the Shizumu.

No sooner had the door opened a crack, the Shizumu forced it open completely and fled from the chamber leaving Colby alone, panting in the darkness as the runes on the interior walls faded and disappeared.

Fizzlewink rushed to his young charge and looked him in the eyes, "What were you thinking?"

"Fizz." Colby exhaled and waved off Fizzlewink's breath. "Good to see you too, but have you been eating Nana's fish?"

They both laughed.

Colby stood with help from his friends. As he made his way through the doorway, he relished in the access to Emassa and let it flow without reserve.

* * *

Conrad watched the movements of the boy. His usually stoic façade shifted to surprise when he saw how much power the boy was taking in and was not nearly started replenishing his reserve. Conrad realized something extraordinary happened while he was away to allow this change. When he turned his attention to the chamber and thought back on the number of Shizumu that escaped the room compared to those who entered, he frowned.

"What have you done here boy?" Conrad said.

Colby looked up at the goblin-like man, "Started something long past due."

Conrad grunted.

"And what is that?"

"Reparations, and perhaps an alliance against our true enemy."

"And who is our true enemy?" Conrad asked.

"I don't think I know yet, but it isn't the Shizumu."

# <u>Chapter 37</u>

## **#Grandpa**

As they began their exit from the basement, Colby advised Aria's spirit to return home to his mother. When she feared the interference of the Shizumu, Colby assured her they would not bother her. Something in his answer made Aria realize Colby was more than certain she was safe to leave. After he had layered a spell upon her essence that would allow her to pass the time bubble barrier, she made her way out of the basement and out into the open skies.

The split soul of Aria sped back to the Stevens' home and wasted no time piercing the barrier that shielded the activities around the house from outside view. The energy essence did not notice the full collapse of the barrier. She headed through the side of the house and dove into the center of her natural home.

Aria sat forward and gasped as the air was driven from her lungs. As she caught her breath and sucked deeply on the air of the room, Aria felt the rejoining spread through her body. From tips of fingers to the end of her toes, the feeling returned to her body, and she soared back from the brink of death.

As the color of her skin became more pink than gray, Aria looked about the room with clear and magical eyes. She saw the shielding spell melting away from around them while she listened to the arguments and blaming-bluster sparring between her parents. Neither of them took notice of her transformation.

Betelgeuse paced the room, touching every object, twisting it around and testing it for magic. He quipped back at Bellatrix's jibes and complaints of his inadequacies. The two of them bickered back and forth about old arguments that should have been long forgotten until Bellatrix made a comment that silenced the room.

"It's your fault she even found those blasted spells to begin with."

Betelgeuse turned back from the bookshelf and dropped the volume he carefully examined moments before. As the tome slid beneath the desk without notice Betelgeuse leaned onto the desk and snarled at his estranged wife.

"How dare you blame me for your failure to explain the need for restraint to any of your apprentices, let alone our daughter. Had you followed the original agreement centuries ago, we wouldn't be in the position we face now."

"Oh! And what position have you been it beside cowering and hiding?"

Betelgeuse fumed, and his face turned red. "I have not hidden you old harpy. I've been keeping watch on your mistake and following a plan set forth by someone who knows better what might happen."

"Ha! Who knows better than me how things will turn out. I plan on sticking to the original design if necessary, but I would welcome any idea that would provide an alternate sacrifice."

"There is an alternative, but you will only muck it up if you were allowed to know the full details."

* * *

Now Bellatrix became red-faced and shook her fists at the old man. "Just like you. Still an elder through-and-through."

"What's that supposed to mean, woman."

"Sexism is older than recorded history is what I mean. You men of the council never took the word of a woman over your own ideas."

"It has nothing to do with your sex, witch. You've always failed to see the bigger picture. Your self-imposed exile was the best thing you ever did."

Bellatrix had nothing to say for a change. She withdrew, leaving Nana's personality in prominence. "Have you always been such a horses prick?" Nana asked.

Betelgeuse shook his head and leaned back. "I beg your pardon?"

"No need to beg Mr. Beetle gist. Or whatever your name is."

Betelgeuse realized his wife retreated within her host. "Typical. Run and hide from the truth."

"Ha! Truth?" Nana said. "You wouldn't know the truth if it kicked you in those shriveled old raisins you call nuts."

Betelgeuse laughed despite himself. "Oh, I can see so much of her in you old woman."

Nana stiffened as the insult slapped her face. "Who are you calling old?" She ran after the man, who just laughed and strode away. The two of them chased one another around the desk. Aria's laughter broke their race for dominance.

"Arialia?" Bellatrix said as she resurfaced. "You're…you again."

* * *

Aria laughed. "I haven't heard my full name in…well, a very long tie mother. But yes, I'm mostly whole again thanks to my son, daughter, and their…friends"

"What do you mean by mostly dear?" Bellatrix asked. "You look complete." Then she looked closer. "Oh, I see."

Aria smiled. That smile that says yes there is something wrong, but it could be worse. "A minor issue for another time."

Aria accepted the hugs her parents pushed on her for a few minutes before she pushed back. "Ok…Okay. We need to prepare for my son and daughter returning, and you explaining your presence to them daddy."

Betelgeuse grunted. "I suspect that will be easier accepted by the girl than Colby, especially after my having played Runes with him. Then there was the fact I allowed him to instruct me to…well, that is between him and me."

Cheerful voices and the slamming of the door downstairs made them aware of the kids' arrival. Without further thought to their arguments, the three began their way downstairs until Bellatrix noted the missing barrier.

"What happened to the spell around the room?" Bellatrix extended her awareness outward. "The entire house is no longer protected."

Aria cleared her throat. "Side effect of Colby sending my spirit home perhaps. He had to attach a spell that would allow me past the time barrier."

Bellatrix thought it odd that the same enchantment would dispel her work to surround the property, but she didn't think too deeply and shrugged. She waddled along and caught up with her husband and daughter as they descended the stairs.

* * *

Nana's persona emerged as she pushed her way past Aria and Betelgeuse and hurried down the stairs calling out for the kids. When she arrived downstairs, she encountered the Dreggs and Fizzlewink with his new followers crowding the living room. She weaved her way through the collective of creatures to find the kids raiding the kitchen.

"Oh my heaven you must all be starved half to death," Nana said. "Let me cook you all up a feast."

"NO!" the kids said in unison.

"It's fine Nana," Colby said. "There's plenty to get us started here, and Jasper's dad is headed over with some to-go from the diner."

"Oh pish," Nana said. "I am quite capable of cooking you something tasty and filling. I have a little more help up here these days." Nana tapped the side of her head with a finger and winked at Colby.

Nana pulled Colby into a hug and motioned the others to join. "It's so good to have you all back."

Once the hugging and kissing were over, and the kids wiped the old lady slobber from their faces, Nana pushed Colby back by his shoulders and gave him a more penetrating stare. Bellatrix resurfaced, and the old woman's eyes cleared of the normal cataract induced cloudiness.

"Something has changed within you, my boy. What happened in that forsaken place?" Bellatrix gave Shelly a sideways glance and accepted her look that said 'later'.

Colby pulled away and shrugged. "We had our moments." When he felt that was inadequate, he offered to share more once they had eaten. Then he saw Jenkins leaning against the doorway between the kitchen and living area. "Jenkins! What are you doing here?"

* * *

The old man walked up and hugged Colby. "Glad you made it back in one piece, though I knew you would."

"And how exactly did you know that you old fool?" Bellatrix said.

He frowned at her and turned Colby back toward his plate of snacks on the island counter. "Inside information."

"What are you talking about," Colby asked. "Are you referring to that Daphne woman?"

The mention of Daphne brought more than one set of wide-eyed responses. The barrage of questions that followed was mostly from Bellatrix and Betelgeuse. Colby noticed his mother smiled a bit, but offered no help in calming the old couple. He also saw the familiarity the two had with one another by the way they stood and purposely avoided getting too close.

"Yes, she was there and seems the one behind our being tricked into going into the Shiznet in the first place."

"The Shiz-what?" Betelgeuse asked. "Did she ever look different?"

Colby understood where that question was leading. "There were three of her, each nuttier than the other."

Betelgeuse turned to Bellatrix. "That changes things if the three of them are working together."

"Wait you know them?" Colby asked. He turned directly to Jenkins. "And what is your part in all this?"

Without missing a beat Betelgeuse said, "I'm your grandfather."

"What?" Shelly and Colby said together.

* * *

"Yeah, it's true," Bellatrix said. "Though I've done my best to keep him away, he always turns up like a bad rash on my ass."

"Well that's an image I won't soon forget," Shelly said and turned to Betelgeuse. "Where have you been?"

"And why not tell me before when we played Runes in the park?" Colby asked. "Did you plan meeting me there all along? Is your name even Jenkins?"

Betelgeuse raised his hands in mock surrender. "So many questions. All will be answered in due time. For now, I will say my name is actually Betelgeuse, and I will need to talk to Colby alone for a few moments." He looked at Colby and waved him over to join him in another room. "If you would do me the honor."

Colby followed Betelgeuse out onto the front porch and folded his arms across his chest. He leaned back against the railing and waited.

"I will apologize now if the answers I provide are not what you want to hear or seem lacking in substance, but there are some things you are not ready to know."

"Whatever that is supposed to mean, I don't know or care at the moment. What I would like to know is why now? Why are you showing up at this time of my life and not sooner when I could have used a father figure?"

"Well straight for the jugular, there's no doubt where that part of your personality comes from."

"Terse at times and crazy as the day is long she may be, but Nana or Bellatrix, whatever you wish to call her, has been there. You were not."

* * *

"That was not by my choice my boy. You had a little something to do with that."

"How is this my fault?" Colby remained uncharacteristically calm and flat in his tone.

Betelgeuse took the time to think of how to respond. There was more going on than was prudent to divulge to this Colby. "You seem different than the last time we met."

"I've been through some stuff lately. Answer the question."

"I will tell you what I can if you agree to tell me what happened in that realm and how you became so much more powerful than last we met."

Colby nodded his agreement and listened as his grandfather told him where he was during Colby's younger years and why he stayed away.

Betelgeuse found out about Colby a few years after the events that hobbled his magic. A note was delivered to him that gave instruction to observe but not engage with his grandson until new instructions were received. When he was contacted again, it was by an old acquaintance that kept watch over the ancient witch in Uxmal. The man sent him a talking stone, an enchanted crystal used for long distance communication, and instructed him to begin covert observation of Colby and start pushing his talent with runes.

"I couldn't resist showing up in the park and meeting you and perhaps manipulate your interest in the game of course."

"Gary was responsible for that."

"No he really wasn't, I just made him think he was. Anyway, that is beside the point. There is much more I would like to share, but it isn't time for you to know everything."

*  *  *

Colby huffed. "I really wish people would stop thinking I can't handle things." He looked out across the street and waved David Bodine, Jasper's father, around back when he saw the man arrive with food. They shared a knowing smile, and Colby returned his attention to Betelgeuse. "I suppose it was Pace, the man from Uxmal, who sent you the stone? What is his part in all this?"

"I really can't say. As long as I've known the man, I don't really know much about him, nobody does or did…he showed up one day in the ancient kingdom when we were at war with the Shizumu. He offered to help create a place for them to live rather than be destroyed and we accepted. No one ever questioned his origin or agenda. We were just grateful for the assistance."

"And now, what do you think of him?"

"I don't know. The man hasn't been seen in the last several weeks. He disappeared shortly after your return home from the Yucatán."

"Figures," Colby said. "Will you be sticking around?"

Betelgeuse smiled. "If you'll allow it, I would like that."

"Then tell me about this Daphne woman and her two older sisters."

Betelgeuse lost his smile. "They were my charge to watch over and keep them from being let free. They caused a bit of trouble a long time ago and had to be contained."

"Why not destroy them. It seems that would have saved us the trouble we face today."

Betelgeuse shrugged. "It's a bit more complicated than that. Perhaps it is a story best told by your mother."

* * *

"What has she to do with them?"

"Aria created them."

"She created them, how?"

"It's a long story, I think it best we let her tell it. Let's just say she used a few borrow spells from your grandmother including the one Bellatrix used for that messenger she sent to fetch me earlier today. Rigel, I believe he calls himself."

"Rigel? No, he's a Professor at my school, though I would say he's a bit fake sometimes."

Betelgeuse frowned. "I know a skin-walker when I see one. I just wonder where the old bat got the source material. I hope she didn't steal a fresh corpse from the morgue."

Before Colby could argue any further. Shouting from the back of the house distracted their debate. He ran down from the porch and around the house, hearing Mr. Bodine's raised voice along with another. Rigel.

# Chapter 38


## #Death


"What are you doing there Professor," David Bodine said. He found Rigel peering into the kitchen from a side window. When Rigel turned to face him, David saw the red in the professor's eyes. "Get away from there."

When Rigel stepped away from the house, his shirt caught on a rose bush and tore the sleeve away. The skin below showed through and revealed a particular mark. A tattoo with initials A.S.C.

"I know that tattoo. Jarrod had a tattoo done with the initials of his wife and children. Why would you have that same tattoo?" David backed away and dropped the food.

Rigel moved closer, not bothering to cover the evidence. "Oh my, you have stumbled upon something now haven't you David. I really hate to break my promise to give you back to the Shizumu as a host, but I can't have you spoiling my disguise."

Colby and Betelgeuse turned the corner in time to see Rigel moving closer to David with deadly intent in his red glowing eyes. Before Colby could muster a hashtag spell, a bolt of energy flew over his shoulder, coming from Betelgeuse, and knocked Rigel back and on his ass.

* * *

"That should have destroyed him," Betelgeuse said. "This isn't any ordinary skin walker. What has your grandmother been up to."

"Grandpa, I'm telling you that Nana didn't make him. He's just-"

"He's got your father's skin," David shouted.

Colby didn't know what to say, or think, or do. He stood there stunned with inaction.

By now the rest of the household exited the back door and surrounded Rigel who was still close to David.

David Bodine, a man who runs a multi-billion dollar company and withstood years of torment being inhabited by a Shizumu, lost his composure and began babbling.

"He did it to save you, but he had help. Jarrod did not go into this alone and without extra magic. I was there lending what I had left." Mr. Bodine began to weep. "I gave all the remaining magic my dying wife lent me, to see that Jarrod's plan succeeded. I continued his design to this very day keeping Jasper as my son. But then I betrayed my promise to Jarrod and his poor boy is left ill-prepared for what is coming now."

David wiped his eyes before continuing his tail. When Aria fled under the assistance of her split soul, Jarrod's two best friends were there fortifying a spell on the chamber. They were surprised by the escape of the Shizumu, but prepared for anything. They were shrouded in a spell of absence, something that shielded their souls from the enemy. The Shizumu did not sense their presence in its haste for escape. All it focused on was distancing itself from the realm where it had spent unknowable time in desperation. The agony the soul feels when separated from the energy of life.

* * *

The Emassa could supplement the split part of a Nefslama, but it could not sustain. It could not fill the emptiness. It could not ease the ache of separation. It could not fix the mistake of splitting from the bond of body and soul. This was the drive of the Shizumu; to reunite with their lost half. The bond that should never be unnaturally broken.

In the quest for ultimate power over nature and the universe, those first Nefslama broke the one fundamental law set forth by the architect of the universe. They meddled with the power that bound all things and tried to reinvent it. Man, in any manifestation across the universes, was put there to learn and grow, but too late did that first Nefslama learn that she was not meant to attempt superiority over anything no matter how small.

The transgressions of man are vast in the quest to conquer mortality. They conquer the lands and seas. They rise above the beasts and enslave them under domestication and the naive belief the strong rule the weak. When they began enslaving themselves, that is when the creator sent his warnings. Disease, catastrophe, age, and weakness, then death. The senior races across the universe rebelled but none so boldly as the Nefslama. The Nefslama chose to escape their fate by transgressing the boundary of reality and infested another world.

During their transfer between realities, someone discovered how to prevent death and limits in power. That is when they began splitting their souls. Without the connection between their body and soul —the link to the source of everything— they could become immortal.

It was not long before they recognized their folly. The souls wanted back in, but there was no easy way to rejoin a host that refused mortality. The spell that kept them apart soured, and the Shizumu rebelled.

"That is the birth of how we have come to the situation we face today," David said. "The displaced child wants to destroy, regardless of the resulting chaos."

* * *

"That isn't entirely true," Aria said.

"It is not far from the truth daughter," Betelgeuse said. "You must realize that spell you altered came from somewhere and was banned for a reason long before your birth here on Earth."

Aria realized then that the Shizumu were not first created after her spell of cloning herself. They were also already in existence before Daphne began building her army of them.

"All those Shizumu in that realm, they were not all creations of Daphne?"

"No dear," Betelgeuse said. "Very few were her servants, most were there by choice, at least in the beginning."

"Why now?" Bellatrix asked. "We sent them somewhere they could survive. They agreed to wait until we could fix the folly of the first to perform the spells of separation."

"Because you never did," Rigel spat. "You protected the responsible parties including yourself. You then gave up the quest, and they found out." Rigel began to glow red. He turned on Bodine and plunged a conjured dagger into his heart. "I would have preferred to watch you burn by re-infestation with one of my comrades, but this will do." He smiled as the man fell free of the blade and lifeless to the floor. His body glowed red for a moment then vanished.

Rigel looked surprised at the disappearance of the man but was so directed by his vengeance-filled bluster that he dismissed the anomaly and turned on the old woman. "Now then, where were we?"

Jasper was screaming for his father. Only the stronger hands of three Dregg were barely able to hold the boy back from attacking Rigel.

* * *

Rigel made his way toward Nana who he knew to be the recent resurgence of the Bellatrix of ancient times who banished him, to begin with.

"You should have stayed locked away where you couldn't harm anyone ever again," Bellatrix said. "It wasn't enough that you corrupt my daughter, but now you've come back to what, replace her husband and corrupt her children?"

Rigel laughed. "I assure you I have no designs for your precious daughter." He spat in Aria's direction. "That infatuation ended when she gave me what I wanted."

"Mom, what is he talking about?" Shelly asked.

"Yes mommy, why don't you tell everyone how you used forbidden magic for me. How you wanted nothing more than to prove your loyalty and love for me by granting me unknowable power. Tell them how you messed up the spell because of your inadequate talent and doomed me to a fate of walking in other people's skins. Tell them how you betrayed me and then betrayed me again."

Aria wept and turned away. She saw the tattoo on his arm, knowing the skin Rigel wore was that of his brother and her husband, Jarrod.

Rigel looked at the tattoo and laughed. "Too late you find out the fate of your beloved and my brother. You both betrayed me together. But look who has the last laugh Aria. I have his skin now, would you love me better this time if I was him?"

Rigel shifted his appearance to that of Jarrod Stevens. He moved closer to Aria and used Jarrod's voice. "Love, it's alright. Everything is going to be just fine. I'm here."

Aria turned at the soothing sound of her long-lost husband's voice. She began to step toward him until the maniacal laugh escaped the lips that curled and darkened as a more beastly façade washed over the skin walker.

"How easily you are fooled into believing anything. Your blindness to the truth has always been your weakness, something your son seems to have inherited."

Colby stepped forward and pulled his mother away. He then turned back to Rigel and flexed his hands out at his sides. The point of his right index finger began to glow purple.

Rigel laughed. "Are you going to use that to phone home little boy."

Colby laughed back. "No, but I might phone a friend." Without a word, Colby signaled his friends and sister using the bond he maintained with them. He observed Shelly materialize behind Rigel and prepared to attack.

Colby and Shelly reached toward one another and sent energy from their hands toward one another, trapping Rigel between the flow.

"Use that spell," Shelly said.

Colby knew what she was talking about, but didn't know how Shelly was aware of it. Later, they would talk. For now, he needed his friends to join their enchantment.

In a single swift movement, each of Colby's friends surrounded Rigel and extended their arms so that they touched energies with the person to their left and right. A magical barrier strengthened as the power of Emassa flowed between them from Colby.

Rigel started to show his concern and began launching a defense of energy blasts and static charges at the children, but their shield absorbed the magic and neutralized his spells.

Colby raised his hand while maintaining the connection required to power their shield. His memory of the in-between place, the space that connected the void and the earthly realm, played a spell back in his mind on repeat. The spell that his own voice told him to remember. **#BanishToTheVoid**.

Colby wrote the spell and let it hang in the air before him where Rigel could see it. The nervous laugh Rigel made, told Colby he was concerned. This gave Colby more confidence this might work.

As he let go of the spell and drew from his magical core to power it, a unified gasp left the mouths of everyone watching. They all got a glimpse into the extent of Colby's newly acquired reserve of power. He began refilling his magical reserve the moment he let go of the Shizumu that stretched his capacity further than he could imagine possible.

"My heavens, what has happened to you in that place my child," Bellatrix whispered.

Rigel pleaded. "No please, don't send me back there. That place is maddening and the others they don't-"

Colby allowed satisfaction to seep into every word he now spoke. "There are no others there anymore Rigel. There is only the gateway and nothingness. I have destroyed the Shizumu realm. You will be quite alone."

"Daphne!" Rigel shouted. "Don't let them send me back there."

In response to his call, Daphne appeared within the circle next to Rigel. One of them appeared, the oldest looking. She grabbed onto Rigel and attempted to pull him through a vortex and away. Her vortex wouldn't form.

* * *

Daphne looked at Colby and then tasted the air of the spell forming around them. Her face twisted in anger as though she was being violated. "Where did you learn this spell. Nobody knows this except me and my books have been destroyed."

"Well someone knew it well enough to share it with me you crazy bitch. And thank you for joining us. One less bad guy, or girl, to track down and eliminate."

Aria grabbed Colby's shoulder from behind. "No, you mustn't destroy them. We need them both."

Colby shook his head. I can see a need for him if dad wants his skin back, but your looney look-alike has got to go."

Aria stood firm and pushed her hand into the shield. "I said no."

As her arm broke the barrier, the spell fell apart with Colby's concentration. Rigel and Daphne wasted no time and vanished into a portal created by Daphne. They got away.

Rhea ran to Aria and began healing the charred skin of Aria's arm that resulted from disrupting Colby's powerful enchantment.

# Chapter 39

## #TimeTravel

"Why did you do that mother. Are you drunk as usual?" Colby was showing no emotion. "You're lucky that burnt arm is all that happened to you."

"If you kill them, you kill any chance of your father's return."

"I wasn't going to kill them. I was sending them to the void, for safe keeping until I...until later."

Aria shook her head. "If you separate one Daphne from the rest it will cause...complications."

"Care to explain?" Shelly said as she pushed her way through everyone now crowding for information.

"They are connected to me. I made one, the first, a copy. That one went mad and created the other two." Aria moved toward the back door. "I need a drink."

"You don't get off that easy child," Bellatrix said with Betelgeuse's agreement. "Tell them the whole story.

* * *

So she did. Aria explained how she tampered with forbidden magic to impress her mother and Daphne was the result. When her clone created the others and went off the farm, they captured and bound her inside the statues where she no longer resided. But there was more.

Aria was enamored by Rigel a very long time ago. He was just using her for her talents, but Aria was blinded by infatuation. When she tested her spell on him, it split his spirit as he wanted, and he gained magic beyond what would have been normal for someone of his abilities. Aria performed the same spell on herself but Rigel tampered with it, and Daphne was the result.

Rigel wanted a different version of Aria. One that shared his vision of the magical beings of Earth rising up and ruling the human race. When she realized her mistake, Aria went to her mother who in turn sought the wisdom of the Council of Elders.

Though they could not reverse what happened to Aria, they tracked down Rigel and Daphne. Daphne escaped, but Rigel was banished to the realm of the Shizumu who were trapped centuries before during the war with the Nefslama.

At the capture of her lover, Daphne lost all her sense and began a campaign of vengeance. She used Aria's original spell to clone herself again and again. Unfortunately, with copies, they degrade with every reproduction. Each one was slightly different in appearance, ability, and mental stability.

The splitting of her soul and cloning wore heavily on Aria, but a new interest grounded her. The love of a young man who helped to stabilize her spirit and curtail the drain of magic the clones caused, was what allowed Aria to return to a functioning life. Though her magic was partially hobbled by order of the elders, Aria didn't mind because she found true love in this man, Saiph. The problem was, he was the brother of Rigel.

* * *

Though Saiph was not implicated in Rigel's plans or activities, the council forbade Aria and Saiph to continue their courtship. They disobeyed and ran away. Saiph used his exceptional gifts to hide them from the council for over a millennia. By the time they were found the first time, the Council of Elders was disbanded, and there was no one to enforce their forbidden love.

Eventually, the couple settled in Chicago and started a family. Saiph couldn't stay away from magic however and continued to draw attention. The younger, more progressive, generations of Nefslama began to be attracted to Saiph, and they set up the community and schools of magic for their children. Things worked well for a little while until Colby was born.

"See, I have always told you things were your fault little brother."

"Very funny Shelly." Colby looked at his mother then to Nana and Grandpa. "I've heard enough for now. I need to go check on Jasper."

"Just a second young man," Nana said. "Where did you get that spell? I know through Bellatrix's memories that the books containing that and all Daphne's spells were destroyed."

Colby looked back but continued heading for Jasper. "I told it to myself in the flow between the void and home."

Colby sat next to Jasper and hugged him. He didn't care who saw, and neither did Jasper.

Jasper grabbed Colby and pulled him close, all the while he sobbed and shook with grief. "I can't believe he's gone, Colby."

"He's not."

* * *

Jasper pushed himself back from Colby but didn't let go of his arms. "What are you talking about? I saw Rigel kill him."

Colby smiled. "Then he glowed red and disappeared, right?"

"Yeah, so some spell on that blade the bastard used or something."

"No. I might have already made an agreement with a particular Shizumu that I came across in the Shiznet as we left."

Jasper let go of Colby and stood up. "What did you do?"

"I gave that Shizumu permission to seek out her husband. She found him and apparently he accepted her request."

Jasper, as strong as he was, was equally thick in the head. Colby explained that while the others entered the void, Colby couldn't let himself be responsible for the end of all the Shizumu. He took them inside himself and while they traveled back to Earth, Colby made a bargain with them. They could find 'willing hosts'. One of those Shizumu was that of Jasper's mother. She was separated from her host when she could no longer stay inside the cancer-ridden body and joined with his father.

"That's what he meant when he said he gave up what magic my mother left him?"

Colby nodded. Before he could continue, Colby looked up to see David standing behind Jasper.

"She sacrificed herself to save my life," David said.

Jasper spun around and nearly fainted, which was amusing for Colby to witness. Colby watched them embrace for a moment before he decided to interrupt.

* * *

"Mr. Bodine, it's good to see you, but I see you are alone. I'm sorry."

"Don't be Colby. You gave me something more precious than the day your father gave me Jasper. I got my wife back if even for a few brief minutes. Thank you."

Jasper cried. "She's gone? Again?"

"Not completely, but the magic is gone, and I'll never be able to use the Emassa again. But your mother is in my heart, quite literally as it were." David laughed one of those painful and joyous laughs.

"Wait a minute," Jasper said. "What do you mean that Colby's father gave me to you?"

David reached into his wallet and pulled out a wrinkled and aged note. He unfolded it with great care and showed it to Jasper. "Your mother and I could never have children. Jarrod knew this since he was my closest friend. When I returned home from that fateful night," David continued while giving a sorrowful glance to Colby then back to Jasper, "Your ailing mother rushed to me with news of finding you on our doorstep with this note."

Jasper looked at the note. It read: 'Take good care of this special boy. He has a great destiny ahead of him and will be a great friend to my own son. Great joy and love to you and your new family while I must cause pain to my own. Until the day I hope we may meet again, Your best chum, Jarrod Stevens."

Colby pointed to the note. "May I see that?"

David handed it over though he did so as if giving up a great treasure. "I must admit that even to this day I don't understand everything that occurred that night, and this note is a bit out of Jarrod's character, but I had a son, and my wife was happy, so I just accepted it."

* * *

"It's out of character because my father didn't write this." Colby lifted his wrist and sent a hashtag voice command into his watch. **#TheJournal**.

Colby held out his arms as the journal his father left him materialized in front of him and fell. He unlocked it with a touch and opened the tome to the page where his father left a personal message. When he placed the note David gave him next to the handwritten message in the pages; he saw a distinct difference.

"See they don't match. Someone else wrote this and passed it off as a note from my dad."

"That looks like your chicken-scratch Cheese-curd!" Shelly said as she butted in. "Hey, Mr. Bodine, good to see you breathing and everything."

Mr. Bodine snickered and thanked Shelly for her strange greeting. He took the note back from Colby and placed it back in his wallet. After putting his wallet back in his breast pocket, he held it there. "My two greatest treasures next to my heart , you and your mother."

Colby looked at Jasper and stared until his friend felt uncomfortable and slugged him. "Sorry, I think I need to go talk to grandpa. Will you excuse me?"

As Colby began to turn, Jasper grabbed for him but missed, and his hand landed on the journal. A static ripple of energy shot between his and Colby's hands on the cover and down to a lock. The next section of the journal snapped open, and the book fell to the ground.

Colby looked down at the heading of the book and quickly snatched it up and closed it. "I'll be back in a bit. Why don't you all see what can be salvaged of the dropped food and keep Nana from making anything please."

* * *

"Where are you going?" Shelly asked.

"I'll be back." Colby grabbed Gary by the arm and dragged him along as he approached his grandfather. "We need to talk. Now." Colby bumped into his grandfather since one hand held onto Gary and the other his journal. Using his ability to transport, he moved the three of them to his father's study.

Colby slammed the book down and opened it to the newly unlocked pages. "Explain this." Colby pointed to the heading of the first spell in the new pages. "The bonding of Emassa to magical servants?" He didn't bother to read the subheading that read, 'Making a Golem'.

"That's…interesting. I haven't seen a spell of this complexity in-"

"Cut the crap gramps! Why would this open now when Jasper and I were touching the book? Why was that note in my handwriting? And why is my best friend a…a golem."

"Well, that would depend on which best friend you refer too," A new voice in the room added.

Pace walked over from the dark corner of the room and sat in a chair across from the couch. Pace motioned to the empty spaces and told them to have a seat.

"What are you doing here?" Betelgeuse asked.

"Good to see you too, gramps," Pace said. "Please sit."

"Gramps?" Betelgeuse mumbled. "Who is he calling old?"

Colby didn't miss the meaning behind that comment though and shared a momentary look with Pace. The man winked at Colby and smiled. Colby felt dizzy and sat back in the cushy leather sofa.

* * *

"Are you ok Colby?" Gary asked.

"I don't know. I guess I'll live. Isn't that right…me?" Colby looked directly at Pace.

"I was always the quick one. Though you're a bit fatter with magic when I was that age." Pace laughed and then cleared his throat. Before anyone could interrupt, he continued. "I have a bit to say, and then I really must leave since my time is nearly up. So pay attention because there will be a lot for you to figure out on your own."

Colby started to say something but stopped when his self glared at… himself.

"Good. Now, yes Gary is a golem. Yes, Jasper is also. Yes, I wrote the note to David when I left the golem Jasper on his doorstep. Why I created golems? You'll have to figure out using the rest of that journal and a little intelligence. Yes, I knew about Rigel, No I couldn't stop him. Daphne is a new development that Jarrod caused, and I didn't realize until it was too late to change. Time is delicate; I can't tell you more." Pace stood and prepared to leave.

"Really? You just verbally vomit all that up and expect us to connect the dots?" Colby was mad at himself.

"I forgot how petulant I could be." Pace sighed. "Look…me, I wish I could say more, but I have been here since my time-magic nearly ran out millennia ago. You have yet to harness it. You will see younger versions of me along your path as I've seen that destiny was altered a few times already. I have one last time jump left in me, and I really want just to go home and see how this all turned out."

Colby moved to intercept, but Pace pulled away and tittered.

* * *

"No touching…have you learned nothing in your watching of sci-fi and theoretical physics? Two bits of the same matter occupying the same space and all."

"But you touched me in Uxmal?" Colby said.

"I used a protective shield over my skin boy." Pace rolled his eyes. "Gramps, do me a favor and get this kid some real books on Emassa and magic use. There's only so much I can reprogram in his magic app before I've done more than I should."

Pace winked his eye at an empty spot beside the window, then blinked from existence.

Gary stood at the door looking at Colby, waiting to be told what to say or do.

"Look," Colby said. "This changes nothing. You are still my friend regardless of your origin."

"But I betrayed you?"

"If this spell is to be understood correctly, I betrayed myself. You are an extension of me." Colby looked to his grandfather for confirmation.

"You would be correct. They are very advanced golem though, and rightfully their own creatures, but you do exert a connection to them. And I don't think they are the only ones."

Colby sighed and headed to the door. "I really don't want to think about that right now."

# <u>Chapter 40</u>

## #SomethingReturns

Colby, Gary, and Betelgeuse walked wordlessly down the stairs and joined the others in the dining room. Everyone stopped eating to wait for an explanation.

"Later, I'm starving," Colby said.

Colby dug into the plate of food Nana, Bellatrix, set before him.

"Not to worry Fart-blossom, I didn't cook any of this."

"It wouldn't matter if you did. I'm hungry enough to eat a pile of burnt peanut butter and banana french toast right now."

Everyone laughed except Nana. She just frowned before getting up and meeting Shelly who just came down the back steps. "What have you learned?"

"Gary, are you going to eat anything," Colby asked.

"Yeah I guess. I just wanted to check out this device we used to enter the Shiznet."

* * *

Nana turned from her whispered conversation with Shelly. "I thought that thing was gone?" Nana said.

"It came back when the children returned through the vortex beneath the academy." One of the recently transformed Nefsmari offered the information as he made a plate of food. "I forgot all about it."

"It's still active," Gary said as he pulled the crystal from a side compartment. "Oh, Shiz!"

"What's wrong?" Colby got up from the table and ran over to Gary.

"Remember how Hashtag Magic made it into the Shiznet?" Gary asked. "Well, it just made it onto the Internet."

Colby looked from the device to the others. "My Hashtag Magic has just become open source."

Aria doubled over with pain. "Daphne is using Emassa. A lot of it. And you're not going to like where."

###

"That boy's little application for magic is quite handy don't you think?" Daphne asked Rigel as they stood before the ruins of Stonehenge.

"Yes well, it does make things a bit faster to accomplish. Whatever made you think of hacking it?"

"Oh it wasn't my idea, it was hers." Daphne pointed to one of her replicas as the others stepped out to join her."

"Did they have to be here?" Rigel complained. "They aren't exactly stable."

* * *

Daphne laughed. "And you think I am? They are needed if this is to work."

Rigel grunted. "Well, let's get on with it before we are discovered. The boy might have done something to lock us out of the gateways, but that doesn't mean we can't use its magic to release old friends."

Daphne, all three, laughed and raised their arms. Each one released a hashtag spell from their stolen smartphones and Rigel joined them.

**#BringForthTheDruid**.

A static charge built up around the uprights at Stonehenge. An outline began to form from coalescing mist that settled into the places where missing and broken stones were missing from the original gateway structure. Purple magical energy buzzed and cracked as it fought the presence of a robed and hooded figure that appeared beyond the horizon of a opening portal.

From between two uprights, a crack in space and time opened as white light poured from the beyond. A gem-topped staff protruded from the opening and proceeded the emerging figure. As the Druid exited the vortex, he extended a hand to feel the power of the purple energy that attempted to bar the way to Earth. He made a humming sound that instilled an admiration for the power. He snapped his fingers and stepped aside as eleven other hooded figures followed him out the gateway.

The leader acknowledged Rigel and the Daphnes before looking around and then toward the star-filled sky. "When are we returning to this realm?"

Rigel took a tentative step forward. "It is the year 2015 of the common era. That makes it nearly 3000 years since last you walked this realm, my friends."

* * *

The Druid looked back at the henge and again at Rigel. "Friends, we have little use for and never in thy time hast thou been friend to the Druids."

Rigel grew anxious. "Allies then. You see the power that allowed your return?"

The Druid looked back at the energy surrounding the Gateway. "Aye. It be greater than that which we acquired whilst creating the Realm Gateways. Hast the Traveler grown in strength whilst we remain in exile?"

"It is a new Gatekeeper," Daphne said. "A young boy."

The druid touched the gateway again and rubbed his fingers together before lifting them to his lips. The shadow melted back enough to see the moonlit features of the lower half of the Druid's face. He tasted the magic on his fingers. His eyes glowed a pale purple and cast a glow from his sunken eyes.

"This is not another's essence of Emassa. I think this is where it begins."

"Where what begins?" Rigel asked.

The Druid's laugh echoed across the plains and out along the open hills. "The end of all magic."

<u>**Author**</u>

**Hashtag Magic Series**
Blue Screen of Death
Control+ALT+Delete
Web of Trolls
Open Source (Q3 2017)
Selfie Sacrifice (2018)


**Chronicles of Aurderia Trilogy**
The Balance
River of Souls
Queen of Shadow


<u>For more books and information</u>
**Follow the Author:**
Facebook: http://fb.com/Author-JStevenYoung
Twitter: @jstevenyoung
Website: http://www.jstevenyoung.com

www.ingramcontent.com/pod-product-compliance
Lightning Source LLC
Chambersburg PA
CBHW062016190726
48284CB00012B/289